OPPO

ALSO BY TOM ROSENSTIEL

Shining City

The Good Lie

OPPO

A NOVEL

TOM ROSENSTIEL

ecco
An Imprint of HarperCollins*Publishers*

HarperCollins books may be purchased for educational, business, or sales promotional use. For information, please email the Special Markets Department at SPsales@harpercollins.com.

A hardcover edition of this book was published in 2019 by Ecco, an imprint of HarperCollins Publishers.

FIRST ECCO PAPERBACK EDITION PUBLISHED 2021

Designed by Michelle Crowe

Library of Congress Cataloging-in-Publication Data

Names: Rosenstiel, Tom, author.
Title: Oppo : a novel / Tom Rosenstiel.
Description: New York : Ecco, 2019.
Identifiers: LCCN 2019008549 (print) | LCCN 2019009533 (ebook) | ISBN 9780062892621 () | ISBN 9780062892607 | ISBN 9780062944894
Subjects: LCSH: Political fiction. | GSAFD: Suspense fiction.
Classification: LCC PS3618.O8388 (ebook) | LCC PS3618.O8388 O66 2019 (print) | DDC 813/.6—dc23
LC record available at https://lccn.loc.gov/2019008549

ISBN 978-0-06-289261-4 (pbk.)

21 22 23 24 25 LSC 10 9 8 7 6 5 4 3 2 1

For the Ravenswood Gang

Just keep stirring the pot; you never know what will come up.

—Lee Atwater

And the Boss said, "There is always something. . . . Man is conceived in sin and born in corruption and he passeth from the stink of the didie to the stench of the shroud. There is always something." Two miles more, and he said, "And make it stick."

***—All the King's Men,* Robert Penn Warren**

I refuse to accept the view that mankind is so tragically bound to the starless midnight of racism and war that the bright daybreak of peace and brotherhood can never become a reality. . . . I believe that unarmed truth and unconditional love will have the final word.

—Martin Luther King, Jr.

CAST OF CHARACTERS

RENA, BROOKS & ASSOCIATES

Peter Rena, partner

Randi Brooks, partner

Ellen Wiley, head of digital research

Arvid Lupsa, digital researcher

Hallie Jobe, investigator

Walt Smolonsky, investigator

Maureen Conner, former Senate aide

Jonathan Robinson, political communications

Ang Liu, new investigator

Samantha Reese, former army ranger, security consultant

REPUBLICAN CANDIDATES FOR PRESIDENT

Richard Bakke, senator from Kentucky

Curtis Gains, congressman from Florida

Janice Gaylord, cosmetics magnate

Jennifer Lee, governor of Georgia

Jeff Scott, governor of Michigan

Tony Soto, senator from Nevada

DEMOCRATIC CANDIDATES FOR PRESIDENT

Omar Fulwood, congressman from Philadelphia

Jonathan Kaplan, senator from New Jersey

Cole Murphy, congressman from Ohio

Maria Pena, governor of New Mexico

David Traynor, senator from Colorado

OTHER NOTABLE CHARACTERS

Wendy Upton, Republican, Republican senator from Arizona

Gil Sedaka, chief of staff to Senator Upton

Bill McGrath, GOP political consultant, unaffiliated

James Nash, president of the United States

Emily Upton, sister of Senator Upton

Matt Alabama, senior political correspondent, ABN Network

OPPO

PROLOGUE

TOYOTA CENTER ARENA
HOUSTON, TEXAS

Quiet came over the auditorium like a great intake of breath.

The arena, designed for basketball, was a vast, Texas-size gaboon of light, shadow, and sweat. Twenty thousand souls were gathered inside. And just now, as if with a single beating heart, they'd all become silent at the same moment.

The effect was galvanizing. We are one.

Just as it was night after night.

Onstage, warm-up speaker Titus Glover, the likable sidekick from a popular sitcom, paused for the silence to become total. Then, in a voice ragged from so many days on the road, he called out: "WE WILL . . . !" And held the mike toward the crowd to respond.

"BE HEARD!!!" twenty thousand answered back.

They'd been waiting for this moment. It signaled Maria Pena, finally, was about to appear.

Glover called to them again: "WE WILL!"

"BE HEARD!!!!"

Fifteen seconds, Glover knew, was a good length for this kind of call-and-response to last. Long enough for momentum to build but not slip. The monitor facing him at the foot of the stage counted down the time.

At zero, the high-tech curtain behind Glover came to life, revealing that it was also a video screen. The nice effect prompted a murmur of pleased surprise from the crowd. Now people saw images of themselves, shot in the last few minutes, faces full of emotion, expressions of hope, fists raised, voices chanting, close-ups and long shots. The crowd cheered in recognition of itself.

Now the video image switched to a volcanic eruption, the earth bursting forth into fire. The crowd applauded, knowing what came next: the magma would flow onto a prairie, a geologic miracle of computer generation, and the prairie would burst into flames.

It was prairie fire, sweeping across the land, a new movement being born. The images were metaphor. The metaphor is us. We are the prairie fire.

"WE WILL!" the crowd called to itself.

"BE HEARD!!!"

About three-quarters of the way toward the back, a man in a blue ball cap and a black T-shirt with the words BAKKE IS RIGHT printed on it moved in behind a man and woman in their early twenties. Her T-shirt read CLIMB A ROCK. The boyfriend, a tall skinny kid, had on hiking shoes. His T-shirt read HAVE A HAPPY DAY.

"WE WILL!"

"BE HEARD!!!!!!"

The man in the ball cap stared at the couple. They were standing near a portable speaker tower set up for the event. It was ideal.

"Hey, dickhead, don't you want to be heard?" he asked the kid.

"What?"

"Why aren't you chanting? Don't you want to be heard?"

The young man tried to look away.

"I asked you if you want to be heard, asshole."

The woman next to the skinny guy turned toward the man in the ball cap.

Oh, yes, the woman, the man in the cap thought. Isn't that just perfect?

"Hey, man, *you're* being the asshole," she said to him. "What are you doing here anyway if you support Dick Bakke for president? You do know this is a Democratic rally, don't you? Asshole!"

"Oh, you're a pistol, aren't you? I'd like to get a better look at your ass," the man in the ball cap said.

"What did you just say? What did you just say to me?"

The man in the ball cap saw the rage in her eyes and was amused. Now the beanpole boyfriend was facing him, too.

"I said I don't think your asshole buddy here really wants to be heard." He grinned at them. On the face of the scrawny boyfriend, the frozen look began to thaw out into some half-assed manly resolve.

"Hey, dude, we're not looking for trouble," the kid said. He glanced at the BAKKE IS RIGHT T-shirt the man in the ballcap wore and added, "We're here to listen and cheer for Maria Pena. But if you're supporting Bakke, you're welcome to be here. Our country needs to come together. We all want to be heard."

A pause to count to three. Make the kid think he's getting through. Then the man in the ball cap said:

"Well, you look to me like you're too afraid to be heard, you piece of shit. So let me give you the 411: freedom doesn't come free. You have to fight for it. The fact you don't know that means you don't deserve it."

The skinny kid turned away and looked back at the stage, trying to ignore him.

"Don't turn your back on me, you douche bag," he told the kid. "You want to be free but you don't want to do anything to earn it. You want other people to win your freedom for you. You make me sick!"

He gave the kid a push from behind.

"Hey, man, why don't you just fuck off?" the woman said.

And she gave *him* a little push back. Which was just what he wanted.

He grabbed the skinny guy, not the girl, and spun him around so they were facing each other. Then he pushed the kid—hard. But while he did so, he held onto the young man's sleeves to make sure the kid didn't fall. Instinctively, the kid grabbed the man's arms to help keep himself upright. Now, clinging to each other, the two men appeared to be wrestling. The man in the ball cap pulled the skinny kid toward him, harder this time, setting his weight as he did it.

As the two men were about to topple over, the man in the Bakke T-shirt pushed the skinny kid expertly away, with just enough force that the kid landed on his feet. The man who pushed him, however, had propelled himself backward into a crowd of people behind him. They, in turn, toppled into the portable speaker tower. The tower tottered, then fell. And as it went down, the man in the ball cap screamed at the skinny guy and the girl: "What the hell's wrong with you two?"

Then the chaos and the screaming started and the arrests began.

DAY ONE

MONDAY

FEBRUARY 24

ONE

DIRKSEN SENATE OFFICE BUILDING
WASHINGTON, D.C.

The senior senator from Arizona got a droll smile on her face and leveled her eyes at her chief of staff.

"May I ask you a purely tactical question?" Wendy Upton said.

Gil Sedaka knew something was coming. "Sure," he answered. "That's what you pay me for."

"How do you stop middle schoolers from acting like idiots?"

She had that deadpan look even Sedaka had trouble reading.

"You can't," he said. "Or I never could. Charlotte is better at that." Charlotte was his wife.

Upton shook her head. "No, you have daughters, Gil. These are boys. They're dumber than girls and easier to outwit."

"Who are we talking about?" he asked.

She handed him her phone. On it was an email. "John Bosun and Phil Decker," she said.

Bosun was the senior U.S. senator from Wyoming and Decker the junior senator from Alabama.

"Christ, Wendy," Sedaka chided his boss. "Double caffeine this morning?"

She was usually irritated by blasphemy, but she let this one go.

"You see what they snuck into the tax bill?" she asked instead, pointing to the email. "That's what I'm talking about."

Around midnight last night, in a procedural sleight of hand, the honorable gentlemen Bosun and Decker had slipped an amendment about women's health into a tax bill for next year. The amendment invoked two changes: The first, a sop to insurance companies, would remove mandatory health insurance coverage for certain tests needed only by women. The second, aimed at satisfying religious interest groups, would allow employers to remove any medical procedures or tests from their insurance plans if they framed their objection on religious grounds. And there was no review. It gave employers carte blanche to cut medical coverage.

Sedaka made a sour face.

Neither amendment would become law. They both knew that. President James Nash, the Democrat in his last year in office, was already going to veto the bill because of other riders he objected to. But before he did so, Senators Decker and Bosun wanted to force Democrats to be on record voting to raise taxes and deny people religious freedom—in an election year. At least that's how their campaign ads would portray it.

That was governing now in the Senate of the United States. Or at least a large part of it. Engineering meaningless votes designed to create fodder for campaign attack ads.

"It's a middle schooler's trick," Upton was saying. "Like sticking a 'kick me' note on a shy kid's back." The anger in her voice surprised her. There was sadness, too. "It will get a laugh from their friends for ten seconds and then get them in trouble."

But she would stop it. From inside their own party. She shifted in her chair and looked out her window, as if she could see the rest of the country through it.

"All that stupid amendment will do is antagonize Republican women whose votes we need. Just so these boys can please a bunch of people whose votes we already have. And they're doing it at the worst possible time."

It was a presidential election year. After the endless prologue, the Iowa caucuses and New Hampshire primary had finally happened, followed by Nevada and South Carolina. In the next three weeks, seventeen states would hold primaries or caucuses, all but deciding the presidential nominations in both parties.

The Bosun and Decker amendments weren't even going to benefit the special interest groups they were designed to please, Upton thought. They were just symbols. What angered her was their cruelty and misogyny. The amendments might offer the illusion of lowering premiums, reducing government's role in health care, and protecting religious freedom. They came, however, by denying women health services. And the misogyny was strategic. Upton's party, the GOP, increasingly relied on the passion of male voters, not women—particularly in primaries.

"Bosun and Decker are assholes," she heard herself say.

She almost never cursed, which made the remark more striking. She was offended. Angry. Her soft hazel eyes blazed.

"But," she added, "they're also not the sharpest minds in the U.S. Senate." Something quick, even sly, formed around her mouth, there and then gone. Most people other than Sedaka would have missed it. "They've overreached," she said. "And we're going to stop them."

"Draft an alternative amendment," Sedaka said. "And undercut theirs."

"You are correct, sir," she said with a smile. It was an old joke between them, a line from when they both were young. Ed McMahon, the late TV talk show sidekick, used to say it when his boss, Johnny Carson, made a quip and Ed wanted to make sure the audience laughed. He would guffaw and give the joke an amen: *You are correct, sir.* When Upton and Sedaka were young Senate staffers together, they'd learned that as kids they had both loved Ed's subtle, underappreciated role, which they considered vital to Carson's success.

"We need something, Gil, that creates a safe haven so senators don't have to vote for this Decker-Bosun monstrosity. Craft some language that affirms both women's health *and* religious freedom."

Upton could see Sedaka already writing language in his head. Their alternative amendment would be a symbol, too, she knew, but at least it would replace Decker and Bosun's misogynistic ones with something better—something that didn't trap people into stupid positions to please the far right. That helped Bosun and Decker fund-raise. But it did not help women. Or even most Republicans.

"The Common Sense Caucus will be pissed," Sedaka warned. The Common Sense Caucus was the name of the hard-right wing in the Senate.

"We will explain to those colleagues," Upton said, "that these amendments would hurt Republicans running in tight races more than they would hurt their Democratic opponents."

"I'll talk to legislative counsel," Sedaka said. That was the office in the Senate that made sure the language in bills accomplished what was intended. "Will Farley might be good, too," he added. Farley was Senator Llewellyn Burke's best bill writer.

"I want a woman on it," Upton told him. "Elizabeth Jensen will have ideas."

Jensen was chief of staff for Senator Sandra Mims of Maine.

JUST THEN, Sedaka's phone began to do a little shimmy dance across Upton's desk. He'd left it there when he came in that morning and sat down. The phone was lying on his car keys, not flat on the desktop, and as it began to vibrate with a call, it moved and sang in vibration, "vittt, vittt," as if it were celebrating.

"Sedaka," he answered. No need for first names, or even which senator he worked for. Few ordinary citizens ever talked to a U.S.

senator these days—or chief of staff. Not unless they were very well connected or had bundled enough money for the privilege.

"Gil, it's Sterling Moss calling. How you doin'?" Moss talked so loudly, even Upton could recognize his voice.

Sterling Moss was the campaign strategy guru for Senator David Traynor, a guy running for president in the *other* party.

"Stir, what's up?" Sedaka said, using Moss's famous nickname, "Stir," as in "stir the pot."

"I'm busy trying to win the presidency, dude," Moss said. Sedaka held the phone away from his ear so they could both hear.

Why was David Traynor's political strategist calling her chief of staff, Upton wondered? She and Traynor had little in common, other than that they both leaned from different directions toward the political center—to the extent there was a center anymore. During Traynor's two years in the Senate, they'd barely done more together than exchange pleasantries.

Traynor was a technology billionaire who had dreamed up his first company in his college dorm room. But he was better known for owning sports teams and flying around the planet to every event where celebrities might show up. He was profane, blunt, and swaggering, a man who cultivated a frat boy image to hide his intellect. And when he decided three years ago to run for the Senate from Colorado—while continuing to run his businesses and flying around the world—most people in Washington thought it was a joke. Then he won.

Now, after two years as a dilettante senator, he was running for president, and there was a very real possibility he might win the nomination.

"Then why are you wasting time calling me, dude?" Sedaka asked.

Upton shot her chief a chastising look. She hated any version of dude culture locker-room talk, and she chided Sedaka when he fell into it. Sedaka glared back like she was an annoying big sister.

Moss laughed on the other end of the line, a baritone barroom chortle.

"Wanted to run something by you, Gil. Off the record. Just in theory. Unofficial."

Moss was into weird Washington code talk already.

Sedaka now had to resist the urge to put Moss on speaker. The consultant would be able to tell the conversation was being overheard. So Gil came around to Upton's side of the desk and held the phone so they could both hear more easily. He felt a little naughty.

"Sure," he told Moss.

"I want you to listen carefully, Gil," Moss said. "So when you see your boss you can get what I am about to say exactly right. Do I have your attention yet?"

"You have my attention," said Sedaka.

"I'm wondering, just thinking." A pause, as if Stir's wondering and thinking were weighty activities in themselves. "I'm curious, if your boss is amenable to being considered as a possible vice presidential nominee. Just thinking out loud. Unofficially. Is that something she'd consider? And if so, is that something she would consider from across the aisle?"

Upton and Sedaka's eyes met, widening. They'd worked together so long, their reactions to a lot of things had become alike. And they were enjoying the absurdity of the moment.

Moss was making an exploratory call to see if Wendy Upton, a Republican, popular with women, widely considered a wise and steady hand and a fine mind, would run as number two on the presidential ticket of David Traynor, Democrat of Colorado, breaker of rules, shatterer of expectations, bad boy reformer.

Traynor had placed second in the Iowa caucuses three weeks ago to Maria Pena, the progressive governor of New Mexico. Then Traynor had won New Hampshire, making him the front-runner. But he had come in second again to Pena in Nevada, giving her two wins to his one. And then Traynor had tied for first in an improbable three-way dead heat in South Carolina, breaking the race wide open. The other two winners were Omar Fulwood, the African American congressman from Philadelphia, and Cole Murphy, a former cop and Iraq war veteran who was trying, along with Traynor, to move the Democratic Party to the center. In other words, the Democratic race was up for grabs, but Traynor was a serious contender.

All that complicated math meant that exploring the vice presidency with Upton was not some long-shot gesture by a campaign about to slip below the waterline. If Traynor persuaded Upton to join him—on a cross-party ticket, with most of the primaries still ahead—it would be a bold gesture, a signal he really did want to change how politics was played. It was also a massive gamble: choosing Upton might alienate Democrats and end his candidacy. Or it could catapult him to the nomination on the healing wave of a bipartisanship that could carry through November. It might, if you were an optimist, even change the course of the country.

"But we're not having this conversation," Moss said.

"Not having this conversation" meant that Moss could deny he had ever reached out.

Upton knew there was another meaning behind that phrase, too. This call was not an offer. Not even close.

Before a presidential nominee picks someone to run on the ticket as vice president, several things need to happen.

To begin with, the potential vice presidential candidate has to be vetted within an inch of his or her life.

Then the nominee has to know beforehand that the person they want to pick will say yes. No candidate with any sense would make an offer to someone if there were even an iota of risk they'd be turned down. Political Washington was a small town, maybe ten thousand people. Eventually everyone knows everyone's business. Especially if it's embarrassing.

So this phone call, which was "unofficial" and "just a conversation," meant that Traynor had done enough vetting to be interested.

Now he wanted to know—if he did offer her a place on the ticket—whether she would say yes.

If she signaled interest, Traynor's people would do more vetting. Upton would hand over materials, maybe sit down with Traynor's people, all in secret. That way, if something looked amiss, everyone had deniability. Deniability was important—for Upton as much as Traynor. If it were known you had been looked at and rejected due to something in the vetting, that would leave a black mark on *your* record that never disappeared.

All this coursed through Upton's political brain in an instant, and, she assumed, Sedaka's.

Upton tried to read her chief, a man five years her junior. His political instincts were always sharper than hers, but he was also more emotional than she was.

Sedaka said to Moss: "Stir, this isn't something I can speak for her on, obviously. I need to talk to Wendy. But *I will* talk to her. If I can track her down today." A glance at his boss. "It's a rough calendar. I may not even see her till tonight. But I will say this: I'll recommend she seriously consider it. I think it's intriguing as hell."

That meant exactly nothing. But it bought them time.

Upton also thought she read something else in her friend's voice. The idea excited him.

"Good man, Gil. Good man," Moss said. "That's all I can ask. Get back to me. Quickly. I don't need to tell you this is time sensitive. I can't let this hang out there, with my fly unzipped."

His fly unzipped. Men really are idiots, Upton thought.

Then Moss was gone.

TWO

Sedaka placed his cell phone back on Upton's desk next to his car keys, almost ceremonially, eyes on the senator. And exhaled.

"So that was a thing," he said.

"A thing no one's actually done," Upton said, "since . . ." She stopped. "Has anyone ever done it?"

People had come awfully close to cross-party presidential tickets before.

A dozen years earlier, though the story wasn't public, the Democratic nominee tried to persuade a respected maverick Republican senator to run as his vice president against GOP president Jackson Lee. The ticket would have pitted two decorated Vietnam war veterans against a man who'd avoided combat and taken the country into a disastrous war. The Republican senator, a man named John Conner, was tempted but said no at the last minute. The story had never gotten into the press.

Four years later, Conner, now the GOP nominee, tried to woo his best friend in the Senate, a Democrat, to be *his* VP, which would have given his candidacy a needed jolt. When he was turned down, Conner picked a Wyoming governor he barely knew as running mate instead—Pamela Smiley—a decision he would regret the rest of his life.

"I think technically, Andrew Johnson was a National Union Democrat and Abraham Lincoln a Republican," Sedaka said.

"Just . . . 156 years ago," said Upton, doing the math in her head. "A long and rich tradition."

They were bantering, a little stunned by what had just transpired. And a little giddy.

The vice presidency was something people made denigrating jokes about. Especially in this town. "Not worth a bucket of warm spit," FDR's first vice president, John Nance Garner, supposedly said. Until, apparently, someone calls you up and actually discusses offering it to you.

Upton became more serious. "So, Gil, you're my chief adviser. Advise me. What are you thinking?"

"Mostly, well, holy shit."

She tried not to laugh.

Then she gave him the look, one she had perfected long ago when she was both older sibling and mother to her half sister, Emily. Upton's staff had a name for it: "Senator Disappointed." It meant she wasn't satisfied by the answer and you had to do better.

"Terrific, that's done then," she said. "Anything else on the calendar?"

She and Sedaka had been colleagues for fifteen years, since they worked as equals for Senator Furman Morgan. Gil was the only chief of staff she'd ever had—House and Senate. He watched out for her and, politically, often thought ahead of her.

Sedaka's giddiness was wearing off.

"I think the logic for this is different now than it was few years ago," he said. "A bipartisan ticket wouldn't be a stunt. It's more compelling now. The country is such a goddamn mess. Actually, the analogy to 1864 and Lincoln is pretty apt."

For a moment, neither said anything.

"And, Wendy," Sedaka added, "Traynor could win: with you on the ticket, he could win."

She waited a beat before saying, "Lord help us." But neither of them laughed.

She felt restless. "Look, let's get out of here for a few minutes." She wanted to walk a little and think and not be interrupted. They often did their best thinking outside the office.

"Brantley's?"

It was a coffee place that had been set up near the Senate dining room, open all the time, where you could have more privacy and weren't served by waiters in tuxedos.

They sat in a corner where no one could see or hear them, but Gil still lowered his voice. "As your friend, I think you should say no. A national campaign isn't like running for the Senate. It's incredibly vicious. And frankly, Wendy, you're not nasty enough. A VP candidate has to be a bully."

That was the traditional view, at least. VP candidates were supposed to be able say things the top nominee wouldn't, the blunt instrument used to inflame the base. Except these days it seemed there was nothing nominees wouldn't say themselves. If anything, Upton would give Traynor class.

"There's a 'but' coming next, isn't there?" she said.

"Yes, there is," he said slowly. "But another part of me, the guy who believes in you, wonders a little."

Senate chiefs of staff were powers unto themselves on Capitol Hill, and they tended to come in two flavors. There were "policy chiefs" who knew issues and guided their senators in crafting legislation. And there were "political chiefs" who thought mostly about helping their bosses get reelected, analyzing every vote from that perspective, and strategizing how far to allow a senator's conscience stray from party orthodoxy. Sedaka was a hybrid, which suited

Upton fine. She was a policy wonk, and she needed someone who could help her think through the politics. But she could have never abided someone purely political.

"A part of you wonders what, Gil?" she said. "You need to use your words today."

He gave her a look. "A part of me wonders if you helped Traynor win the nomination whether together the two of you might just be able to take the country in a new direction. Help it begin to heal a little."

She gave him a skeptical glance but didn't say anything, and Sedaka pressed his case:

"Maybe Traynor really does want to change the paradigms in politics. I think he's serious about entitlements, and reforming social programs, doing real tax reform, not the ugly thing we do now."

"So he says."

"Don't believe him?"

"Just because he's new to politics doesn't mean he's not full of shit."

Gil laughed.

"Plus, he seems to have no interest in learning how laws are made," Upton said. "He spends more time on his jet than in the office."

"We don't make many laws anymore, remember?" he said. "We do symbols. Weren't we just drafting some?"

He put down his coffee and leaned toward her again. "Look, I think a bipartisan ticket now could be a meaningful statement. Especially coming from Traynor. And you."

There was no disputing Traynor was different. The Colorado senator was so new to politics, he could genuinely claim he was trying to change things. He was an outsider who talked like a Silicon Valley CEO, not a politician, and he had a different kind of politics, too. He called himself a "Libertarian Democrat" who wanted to shrink the federal bureaucracy while protecting people's civil rights.

In stump speeches he declared he wanted "to disrupt government from the bottom up. But to make it work better, not to burn it down." And he would always add, "Burn things down and millions will die in the fire. That's not government reform. It's insurance fraud."

The language about burning things down was an allusion to a loose collection of groups called the Shut It Down movement, which was finding a resonance on both the left and the right. The Shut It Down crowd called for a constitutional convention to rethink the rules governing how Congress was elected and operated.

"His answer to the Shut It Down movement is pretty good, right?"

"The guy can talk, I grant you that," Upton said. But she was frowning.

She took a sip of coffee and then blew on the cup. Steam mushroomed into her face and softened it.

"What do you have against him?" Gil asked.

"Where do I start?"

Traynor was rash, a showman, and seemed to flout every rule.

She, by contrast—an army veteran, an accomplished prosecutor, an orphan who had raised her little sister—believed deeply in the power of rules. They might be the only thing, at the moment, holding the shivering country together.

"Wendy, I'm serious. He's offering something here. Something that might change politics."

The way Gil said it seemed to change the conversation. It felt as if he had laid something on the table, as if he had dug into his pocket and pulled out all their years together, their friendship, their hopes, their frustrations, their shared battles, their encroaching middle age, and had thrown them down like an enormous bet into the pot in a card game.

Upton became serious, too.

"You want to talk about the politics? How's this: He's a Democrat and I'm a Republican. If I crossed party lines, it would be a kind of death. I'd become a political orphan. My own party would disown me. And the Democrats would never fully trust me." She paused. "Any more than I trust them."

That hung in the air a moment between them. "I don't believe that," Sedaka said. "You would be his successor. A heartbeat away from the presidency."

"In theory," Upton said.

But it was not, they both knew, very likely to occur. At least not based on history.

They were as familiar with the statistics as athletes are with the records in their sports. Since 1900, only five vice presidents had ascended to the White House—three by death and a fourth by scandal. The lone exception, the only vice president to be elected to the White House, was George H. W. Bush, who also was the last sitting president to lose reelection four years later.

No one grew up aspiring to be vice president. No one. Not in the history of the world. Not ever. Including Wendy Upton.

"He also just might be better than whoever wins the nomination in our party, Wendy."

That earned a grimace from Upton.

The Republican race was dominated at the moment by the two most conservative and, Upton thought, dangerous candidates in the race: Governor Jeff Scott, a charismatic populist from Michigan, and Richard Bakke, a mean-spirited but undeniably smart senator from Kentucky.

Upton leaned back in her chair. "So your first reaction is 'Holy shit,'" she said. "Your second is I'm not tough enough to do this. And your third is we might just change the country and save democracy."

Sedaka shrugged. "I'm still processing."

The Disappointed Senator face reappeared.

"You know I'm going to turn him down," she said. "I have to. It would end any chance I have to be a serious lawmaker."

"Unless you win."

"You think I should take that risk for David Traynor?" She blew on her coffee again. "You know I'll say no." Then she gave him an inquiring look. "You've got something else up your sleeve. You're trying to draw this out. You don't want me to say no too quickly."

Sedaka blushed. She had him.

"You want to make me take it seriously enough to get Traynor to meet me face-to-face." That would make Traynor's consideration of her more real. "And then you want it to leak, don't you?"

Sedaka lowered his voice. "It wouldn't be the worst thing in the world if people knew he'd considered you. In some ways it's the best possible outcome, being considered for VP, rather than being it."

"Careful, Gil."

But Sedaka was warming to his argument. "That may even be what Moss wants," he tried. "Maybe Traynor's not even serious about this. Maybe he just wants people to know he's considering you. That serves his purposes, too, right? Let it be known he's thinking about crossing the aisle? Show he's a different kind of Democrat?"

Upton considered this as her chief plunged on. "For all we know, *they* intend to leak this."

Upton put her coffee down. "Don't handle me, Gil. I have political consultants for that."

"I'm not handling you, Wendy. All I'm saying is drag your feet. Let me say you're seriously thinking about it and we need more time."

And slowly, almost reluctantly, she let herself smile, a younger smile, almost a teenager's, from a woman who had barely had the chance to be one. On the few occasions it came out, something about that smile broke Sedaka's heart a little.

"You already told him I wasn't around. We haven't talked. You aren't sure when you can find me."

Sedaka smiled back.

She had read somewhere that presidential campaigns are dangerous for the people in them because they're make-believe. You talk as if you were president, imagine you are, and it almost begins to feel like you might be. But you're not.

She worried Gil was already beginning to play make-believe.

"Don't get too cute with Traynor's people," she said. "It's okay for us to consider this. But we both know the answer is going to be no."

Sedaka's expression told her that was all he wanted to hear.

A few months earlier, serious people had asked Upton herself to run for president. She'd said no. She wasn't ruling it out forever, she told them, but she didn't think she knew enough yet and couldn't look voters in the eye and claim she was the best-prepared person in America to lead the country. Not yet. Maybe someday.

Sedaka had told her he felt all the more loyal to her because of that. Who in Washington anymore, he said, or anywhere else if they had a national reputation, seemed to think they needed to wait and learn more about governing before they could run for president?

She looked at him now, his face excited by what they'd agreed to. It wasn't much, simply stalling for time. But she was grateful she had this one person she could trust. That was rare enough. She didn't have many people in her life.

"Okay, then," she said, getting up. "I've got a meeting." Then, turning, she almost added, "But be careful, Gil." But she didn't say it. Just turned and walked away.

THREE

Sedaka sipped his coffee and lost himself in the possibilities.

Then his private cell began to vibrate again, this time no dancing.

"Sedaka."

"Gil, it's Bobby Means. How you doin'?"

"Bobby. I'm great. How's the campaign?"

"Awesome. Grueling. Fantastic."

Sedaka laughed. He liked Bobby Means. Bobby Means was smart and clever and a good old boy from South Carolina, like Sedaka.

Bobby Means was the chief campaign strategist for Dick Bakke.

"Gil, I wanted to broach something with you. 'Cause we've been friends a long time," Bobby Means said.

Means had a mouthful-of-marbles South Carolina accent that came and went as circumstances required. It was thick as warm molasses now.

"I know Dick and Wendy have had their political differences," Means said.

That was an understatement on a massive scale.

"But you got to agree they are two of the smartest people in the Senate."

That much was true, too, far as it went. Bakke had clerked for the Supreme Court—which was even more impressive because he'd gone to a law school that was barely accredited. Upton, an army veteran and former JAG attorney, was widely considered the sharpest member of the Senate Judiciary Committee.

"And bein' smart is a good thing in a political leader, don't you think, Gil?"

"On balance, yes, I'd say much preferred to the alternative."

They shared a staffer's laugh, one fueled by the privilege of seeing United States senators up close and at their most befuddled.

Aside from both being smart, however, the differences between Wendy Upton and Richard Bakke were pretty epic. They represented wings of the Republican Party so far apart the bird could barely fly.

Bakke wanted to pull the GOP further to the right and tear down much of its philosophical orthodoxy. He also thought Upton an insufferable prig, overrated by the liberal press.

For her part, Upton thought Bakke was a dangerous and unscrupulous man who'd destroy the party and put Democrats in ascendance for a generation.

Not that she ever had, or would, say such a thing out loud.

So yeah, they had had their differences.

"Gil, I'm calling, buddy, just to feel you out on something. Just exploring."

What. The. Hell, Sedaka thought. Is this really happening again?

"Okaaaay, Bobby," Sedaka said slowly.

"I want to know how Senator Upton might feel about being considered for the number-two spot on a Bakke ticket."

Sedaka felt a thin band of sweat suddenly appear down his back. Two calls in an hour about being vice president? One from each party? He glanced back to the entrance of the coffee bar, hoping Wendy might still be there lingering. There was no way she was going to believe this.

He paused a second. "I'll talk to her," he said. His voice sounded oddly deep, as if he were a boy trying to sound like a man.

"Glad to hear it, Gil. Now, I'm serious, hear? I think this could be really something. I do. I believe Wendy and Dick would bring out the best in each other—because of their differences, not despite them. They'd make each other better. They might make each other great."

All melted butter and sugar, Bobby Means.

"So talk to her, Gil. I mean soon. Like this morning. And get back to me, hear? We'd looove to announce somethin' 'fore next Tuesday."

Next Tuesday was the first Super Tuesday primary of the campaign—eight states.

"Don't keep me waitin', Gil. Bye-bye."

When he put the phone down, Sedaka's heart felt like a pinball ricocheting off his organs.

A few minutes ago he was trying to figure out how to leak the dalliance with Traynor to benefit Wendy. Now, making that dalliance public seemed a hundred times more dangerous. Especially if Traynor's camp were to leak it. A few minutes ago he was trying to figure out how to stall for more time. Now, time seemed like a ticking bomb. A few minutes ago he was trying to contemplate how to maximize the upside to Traynor's offer. Now he couldn't quite fathom what was upside and what was disaster.

There was an old saying in politics: every crisis is an opportunity. If that were so, then every opportunity also had to be a crisis.

DAY TWO

TUESDAY

FEBRUARY 25

FOUR

THE CAPITOL BUILDING
WASHINGTON, D.C.

Of course it "leaked."

The hint of "overtures" to Wendy Upton was buried in a piece the next day in the *Washington Tribune*. It was one of those stories journalists generously called "think pieces" that were really just a grab bag of rumors and ruminations. The reporter, a national correspondent named Gary Gold, had tossed in a list of names being bandied about as possible VP candidates, but he mercifully hadn't included, or didn't know, any details. "Among those being vetted," he'd written, followed by a small list of names that included Upton's. "So strong is the electoral appeal of the maverick Arizona Republican," Gold had thrown in, "her name comes up in conversations in both parties."

That was it.

By itself the reference had done no harm. Nor had it made much of an impression. There were no calls afterward from curious reporters seeking comment, or from enthused friends offering encouragement. Whatever tip Gold had, in other words, apparently it wasn't something circulating widely around town. For now, the two secret approaches to Upton were still secret.

The night before, Sedaka had also gotten a call at home from Michael Woo, the state archivist back in Phoenix.

"There are people here," Woo had reported, as if he were shocked someone had walked into the state archives at all, "poking into the senator's records."

So she was being vetted. By whom, Sedaka wondered. Traynor's people or Bakke's? Wood hadn't known who they were. They'd registered only their names, no affiliation. Most vetters were lawyers, who don't reveal their clients. But Sedaka hadn't been able to match the names Wood gave him to any law firms.

The next morning and part of the afternoon passed quietly, full of meetings and calls. Upton and Sedaka weren't able to sit down and talk more about the two offers or how to respond. But they had to figure out something. Two offers—from competing parties—meant the chances of more details leaking out about them were doubled. And if more did leak, they would have to manage the messaging about them even more carefully.

They finally had a chance for a serious conversation that afternoon. They found it in her Capitol "hideaway" office, the small space inside the Capitol Building given to each senator where they could have some privacy.

"I think you've been avoiding me," Sedaka said when he wandered in.

"We're stalling for time," she said. "Remember?"

He sat down and didn't say a word. He just gave her a look, half amused, half terrified: So what you gonna do now?

Then the phone rang. Sedaka picked it up—insulation for the boss in case it was someone she wanted to avoid. The surprised voice on the other end, expecting to hear the senator herself, was Jerry Farmer, Upton's campaign finance chairman and their biggest fundraiser.

He must have called Upton's main office, and the switchboard put him through. "She there?" Farmer said. His voice sounded coiled up.

Sedaka handed the phone to Upton, but she picked up the extension instead and pointed for Sedaka to stay on the line.

"Wendy, I'm calling because I just got what I consider a meaningful phone call, and I need to convey a message to you."

First name, Upton thought. This isn't formal. And Farmer sounded truly stressed.

"Hello to you, too, Jerry. A call from whom?"

"A friend, calling on behalf of another friend. But it's the message that's important, Wendy. Not who it came from."

Everything about this registered alarm.

"You can convey the message, Jerry," Upton said. She used the tone she had perfected years ago as an army prosecutor. Cool and a little scary. "But you will need to tell me who the message is from."

"That doesn't matter," Farmer said. "The person who called me was just conveying the message for someone else. Whom, by the way, he didn't name. The man who called me, Wendy, was just a messenger."

Upton looked at Sedaka.

"What was the message, Jerry?"

She swept a legal pad and a pen from her desk and started to take shorthand, a skill she had taught herself in college.

"The message, Senator, was this," Farmer said unsteadily. "If you accept the offer to run as vice president, there are people who know something about you, which they are prepared to use to destroy you. Even drive you from the Senate. And out of public life entirely." Farmer took a breath but it wasn't long enough for Upton to interrupt. "Now, Wendy, I don't know any more than that. But that's what they said."

Upton felt a cold sensation down her neck, like the day her parents died.

"What was the message *exactly*?" she asked.

"*That* was the message," the money bundler said. "Word for word. 'If you accept the offer to run as vice president,'" he repeated, clearly reading now, "'there are people who know something about you, which they are prepared to use to destroy you. Even drive you from the Senate. And out of public life entirely.' I was told to write it down. And the man who called me had written it down, as he had been instructed to do. Then he read it to me and told *me* to write it down. That was the message."

Farmer quickly added: "Are you considering the vice presidency?"

She ignored the question. A glance at Sedaka. "Destroy me with what?"

"I have no idea, Wendy."

"And you didn't ask, Jerry?"

She had always found Farmer a little too eager to please, a little too transparent.

And life on Capitol Hill was dominated now by money in ways that had become grotesque and outsized. She spent countless hours dialing for dollars and attending fund-raisers, as did all her colleagues. Money was also how the leadership kept party members in line. The Senate Majority Leader and the Speaker compiled millions in super PACs and doled it out to members in tough races. Big donors loved to give to the leadership PACs: it meant you only had to convince a few people to bend to your will, not each member.

The system had become, in every sense of the term, pay to play. But it was the payers who controlled it.

"Wendy, the man who called me is a friend. And an admirer of yours. Someone who has given you and the party a lot of money. But he was just a messenger. He didn't know. He didn't ask."

"Is that what he told you?" She made the question sound like an accusation.

"Yes, that's what he said. And I didn't ask any questions. Christ, Wendy, I'm also calling as your friend. As someone who doesn't want to see you harmed. I didn't ask what the threat was. And I frankly don't want to know. I don't want to be any more a part of this than I have to."

"Should I thank you for that, Jerry?"

"What do you want me to say, Wendy? That I interrogated

the man? Well, I didn't." Apparently, the self pity in his voice even sounded unpersuasive to Farmer, for he now began to explain himself. "I didn't ask who the message came from. And he wasn't going to tell me. But the person who called me is a serious man. And he wouldn't have called me unless he had to—unless this was coming from serious people."

There was pause, and then he added, "Wendy, don't blame me for this. For whatever it is."

Farmer made it sound as though Upton had embroiled him in some scandal of *her* making.

"Wow, Jerry, thanks so much for being such a great friend. Just do me one more favor, if it isn't too much of an inconvenience. If he calls again, try asking some follow-up questions. I'd sure appreciate it." She hung up before he could respond.

There are people who know something about you, which they are prepared to use to destroy you.

What did that mean? Who? Destroy her with what? Upton felt everything shift, like a tectonic plate undergoing a change in pressure.

She glanced at Sedaka. Then she looked out the small window at the view of the Mall, the view she so loved. It was a glistening winter day, sunny and crisp, which at the moment seemed to taunt her.

At fifty-three, Wendy Upton could be easily mistaken for someone ten years younger. Her blond hair, the color of straw, fell to her shoulders, but most days in Washington she wore it up, a habit she had adopted in the military so it would fit under a hat. She was very fit; she ran, did triathlons, ate well. And her entire career she strove to be the most prepared person in every room. She hoped that any attention she drew to herself came slowly and was earned by knowledge she had that contributed to solving whatever problem needed to be solved—not by stunts or speeches. She distrusted people who attracted attention to themselves for the sake of the attention; Lord knows there were enough people in her trade already doing that

And every workday she dressed in a suit—jacket and pencil skirt—yellow, blue, or black. Red was a cliché.

She had worked her whole life, come from nothing, an orphan. She had fought for everything she had accomplished, risen higher than she could ever have imagined, and taken pride that it was all earned, never given. And, now, in an instant, it felt as if perhaps none of that mattered.

FIVE

BALTIMORE, MARYLAND

Randi Brooks closed the folder from which she had been reading, glanced at her partner, and frowned at their client.

Fabian Grimaldi was a pear-shaped man with a meticulous silver mane and an expression that suggested he was never wrong. He was wearing a handmade indigo blue suit, and his tie was the trademarked maroon of the football team he owned. From the bottom of his shirtsleeves winked diamond-encrusted cuff links bearing the words SUPER BOWL CHAMPIONS.

Grimaldi didn't look back at Randi Brooks. The owner of the Baltimore Wolverines instead spoke to Brooks's male partner, a lean, cool figure, who had been silent throughout her report.

"Do you agree?" Grimaldi asked Peter Rena.

The quiet man just gazed back at Grimaldi but said nothing.

Randi Brooks answered him. "Fabian, do you think I'd give you a report Peter and I didn't agree on?"

"That's not what I meant, Randi. I just wanted to hear Peter—"

"He raped her, Fabian," she said.

But she was just repeating what she'd told him moments ago, what she'd spent forty minutes telling him, walking meticulously through the details of the evidence she, Rena, and their team had assembled.

Grimaldi, however, was a big-picture guy. He had long ago been able to afford to hire others to master the details. He'd also stopped concentrating during Brooks's presentation fairly early on. And it was obvious to everyone what big-picture question he wanted to answer now. He wanted to ask the two men in the room if they thought, man to man, what his star receiver had done was rape. And whether he could get away with it.

Then again, Grimaldi hadn't become rich enough to own an NFL franchise, a soccer team in Italy, and a venture-capital fund as well as build the second-largest box manufacturing business in the United States by being stupid.

Though he didn't quite admit it to himself, the two investigators also intimidated him. Peter Rena, dark, watchful, an ex–Special Forces military investigator, had an air of melancholy and quiet danger about him. His partner, Randi Brooks, was less subtle but in her own way just as unnerving. She was only about an inch shorter than Rena, who was around six feet. On legal matters, she spoke with a carbon-steel precision that was a hell of a lot different than his pant-wetting business attorneys. And when animated on other subjects, she was given to flights of creative profanity worthy of the best coaches he had ever known.

So after being interrupted by her, he was now silent.

Trent Fowler, the Wolverines' general counsel, tried to rescue his boss. "You make it sound like the legal case is pretty strong against him."

Brooks said: "DNA. Bruises. Eyewitnesses. Contemporaneous accounts from friends of the victim, to whom, by the way, she spoke immediately afterward. They all say the same thing. Frank Verosian followed this young woman into the ladies' room of that bar. They may have been kissing at a table a few minutes earlier. She may have gone into that bathroom with the idea of having sexual intercourse with Verosian. But at some point she changed her mind. He hit her. She screamed. Or maybe she screamed, and he hit her; that is the only point about which there is some confusion. Then he had intercourse with her against her will. She struggled against him. She verbalized her lack of consent. At that point he was committing rape. That lack of consent was overheard by third parties. It's a strong case."

Brooks took a breath. "And Verosian has some history. There was another incident in college. He was nineteen. It was pretty thoroughly covered up. But we found it."

Muscled, charming, and marvelously sure handed, Frank Verosian—"Vero" to millions of fans—was the Wolverines' All-Pro receiver, the team's second-best player, and the man who made their Super Bowl–winning quarterback, Kyle Tucker, great.

"I didn't go into the earlier incident yet, but it is thoroughly described in our report. The details, which a competent attorney should be able to get admitted at trial, are chilling and legally damning in their similarity to the current event."

"What about the girl's background? Did you look at that?" Grimaldi asked.

Peter Rena spoke at last.

"Fabian, you asked us to find out what happened here. We did that. Your player raped this young woman, who is just eighteen. If Verosian's legal team wants to hire investigators to probe the victim's personal history as part of a legal strategy to challenge her, they can do that. We don't work for them. And that is not a task we would contract to undertake. Our job was to find out what happened. And tell you the facts."

Grimaldi stared back at Rena in a way that made his displeasure abundantly clear, though it didn't seem to bother the investigator as much as Grimaldi expected.

"That's right, Fabian," the lawyer Fowler said. "I asked Peter and Randi to look into this so we would know what was coming at us. I didn't want to rely on Frank's lawyers for this. They're his lawyers, not ours."

Grimaldi was seventy-three years old and had owned the Wolverines twenty-five years. But he recognized that America was changing, and it was *that* America to which he had to market his team. So he would change, too. After a moment he muttered, "Goddamn it."

RANDI BROOKS DIDN'T SAY A WORD as the elevators glided down to the parking garage. Grimaldi owned the twenty-four-story office building. And the garage.

She didn't say anything, really, until after slamming the door of her BMW. The exact words were less legally precise than the ones she'd offered in Grimaldi's office: "Fuck him. Fuck his money. Fuck this shit. And fuck you, Peter, for being a man."

Then she turned the car on and added, "You want to say anything about what happened in there?"

"I think you said it all just now," her partner answered, "rather eloquently."

She stared at him. Then she dissolved into an enormous, disgorging, and cleansing laugh. And Rena, swept up in her relief and anger, joined her.

The business cards for Rena, Brooks & Associates said BACKGROUND RESEARCH AND CONSULTING. Translation: people hired them to get to the bottom of things—usually when the consequences of not knowing were extraordinarily high. Either that, or things had already gone so badly wrong, knowing the full truth was the only option left.

The business varied. Companies hired them to vet potential CEOs and sometimes high-profile employees in trouble, including athletes. Given that they were based in Washington, D.C., they also did a fair amount of work for people in politics, though they tried to avoid working directly for campaigns. The current occupant of the White House, James Nash, had hired them twice in the last two years—to vet and confirm a Supreme Court justice and conduct an internal White House investigation of a controversial terrorist incident.

A few years back, a senator who owned an NFL team had hired them to scrub the background of a possible first-round draft pick about whom there were difficult rumors. Since then, more NFL teams, and some NBA, had asked them to look into the backgrounds of controversial high draft picks or incidents involving high-profile players.

Brooks wiped the laughing tears from her eyes and navigated her 5 Series BMW out of the parking garage.

The car emerged into an unseasonably sunny late February day in downtown Baltimore and headed away from the Inner Harbor toward 95 South to D.C. Rena pulled out his phone to see what email and text messages had come while they were in the meeting with Grimaldi and his lawyer.

There were dozens from the two hours he was offline, and more in the secure and encrypted messaging app they used internally at the office. There was an email from Victoria Madison as well. Vic was the plainspoken, wise, and beautiful daughter of the Supreme Court justice they'd helped confirm. She lived in California, and she was running out of patience with Rena for not moving there to be with her, leaving behind the Sodom and Gomorrah of craven cynicism that she believed Washington had become. She was also irritated that Rena thought he couldn't share much of what he worked on, at least when it came to politics. That seemed only to exacerbate his natural tendency toward keeping his feelings to himself. Rena had begun sharing more with Vic about his work than he used to, except when it was absolutely impossible. "An experiment in trust," Vic teasingly called it. "Or treason," Rena suggested. "How's my soldier?" Vic's email read. "Haven't heard from you in a few days." He needed to call her.

Then Rena's phone rang. He glanced down suspiciously—most

calls these days seemed to be criminal scams—but he recognized the number.

"Senator."

"Peter, how are you?"

The voice belonged to Lew Burke, the senior senator from Michigan.

Llewellyn Allen Edmund Burke was Rena's former boss, and a good deal more than that.

A decade earlier, Rena had blown up his military career by refusing to ignore evidence of sexual harassment by a general about to be promoted to head Central Command. Burke, chairman of the Senate Armed Services Committee, had rescued the foolish young army major by hiring Rena as an investigator on Armed Services. That signaled to the army that Rena had done nothing wrong. In the eleven years since, Lew Burke had continued to guide Rena's life. It was Burke who had urged Rena to start his consulting firm with Randi Brooks, though she was a Democrat and Rena a Republican. In the eight years since, it was often Burke, one of the few publicly bipartisan politicians left in Washington, who guided Rena and Brooks's work from a distance. For Burke, friendships were not random accidents. They were bonds and responsibilities. And they defined one's life.

"I'm afraid, Peter, I need to ask a favor."

"Sir."

"How soon could you and Randi be at my house?"

The reassuring voice—flat as a midwestern plane tinged on the odd word by a New England prep school drawl—sounded uncharacteristically tense. "I'm afraid it's rather urgent. And perhaps, on your way, you and Randi can discuss whether she would have any problem doing work for Senator Wendy Upton."

SIX

MCLEAN, VIRGINIA

Llewellyn Burke and his wife, Evangeline, lived in a terra-cotta-roofed estate in McLean, Virginia, perched above the Potomac River. It was a 1920s-era home—Spanish style, tile roof and white plaster walls—a house more at home in the Hollywood Hills than among the faux colonials of Washington. It was also modest compared to its neighbors on the bluff, especially the fifty-room estate of the Saudi prince next door.

Most extraordinary, though, was the setting. Behind the house, down stone steps, past a small swimming pool, lay a secluded patio on a cliff overlooking the river. One heard the water before seeing it. In a canyon two hundred feet below, the Potomac churned deadly white, and it did not calm until it eased under the Chain Bridge and entered Georgetown. There it became wide and deceptively passive as it meandered past the monuments of the federal city, hiding its lethal currents below.

A housekeeper greeted Rena and Brooks at the door. She led them to the rear patio, into the crisp, almost spring-like February day. When they reached the second level and heard the roaring river, they found Senator Burke sitting with Senator Wendy Upton of Arizona and another man, her chief of staff, Gil Sedaka.

The two fixers didn't know Senator Upton well. When they'd guided the nomination of the iconoclastic Rollie Madison to the Supreme Court two years earlier, Wendy Upton had been the first Republican on Judiciary to announce her approval. Others followed.

Eighteen months later, she'd been a needed voice of reason during joint congressional hearings investigating a terrorist attack in North Africa that killed a U.S. general and three other Americans. Rena and Brooks had been hired by President Nash to conduct an internal White House investigation of the incident and keep Nash two steps ahead of the media and Congress.

In both experiences, Upton had been intellectually honest, independent, and someone whose opinion carried weight with other senators. Rena and Brooks considered her sharp, modest, and impeccably prepared. And behind the scenes, where it mattered most but was recognized least, she could be shrewd and strategic. At one critical point in the Africa hearings she had undercut their nemesis, Richard Bakke, from making a cynical grandstand that might have done them in.

She reminded Rena of a prodigiously gifted musician whose dedication to practice created the illusion of effortlessness.

Her appearance was also deceiving. She had a round face, hazel eyes, and a porcelain complexion, which combined to make her look delicate, even vulnerable. But her soft features, Rena thought, tended to mask her intelligence and her will. Anyone who doubted her grit also probably didn't know her story. Upton's parents had been killed in a car accident when she was sixteen. She had taken the GED, sued the state to become an emancipated minor, then raised her ten-year-old half sister so the two could stay a family. She ran her parents' business until her sister was old enough that Upton could finally attend college. It was the first step in what would become a life of fiercely independent actions.

Burke rose to greet them, made gracious introductions—ever the well-bred scion of a Michigan auto dynasty—and invited everyone to sit. In his early sixties, with dark hair graying at the temples, Llewellyn Burke had a gracious and listening manner that people instinctively trusted. His sea-blue eyes were welcoming and optimistic, just as Rena's nearly black ones seemed brooding and sad. But today Rena noticed age lines on his friend he hadn't seen before, small rivulets, like new creek beds of stress, stretching from his eyes toward his temples.

Burke looked gravely at Rena, then at Brooks. "You know how much is at stake in this election," he began.

The election—the brutal chase for the presidency—had begun in earnest. The first Super Tuesday primary—eight states—was a week away; another "super" contest, six more states, followed the week after.

"Something ugly happened today," Burke said. "Something we need your help with. A phone call." Burke's halting speech was unlike him. "Wendy, perhaps you should explain."

Upton looked at her chief of staff, Sedaka, who shook his head. She had to say this herself, he was telling her. She did, with a calm that would have been beyond most people.

Over the last two days, she explained, she and Sedaka had received four phone calls about the vice presidency. She walked through each one: the first from the Traynor campaign, the second from Bakke's, and the third last night from the state archivist.

Then a call this morning from her finance chairman in Tucson passing along the threat, conveyed through a major donor: if Upton agreed to the vice presidential spot, someone knew something so terrible about her that it could end her career. She recalled the words from memory, though Rena could see she had written them down on paper in what looked like shorthand: "If you accept the offer to run as vice president, there are people who know something about you, which they are prepared to use to destroy you. Even drive you from the Senate. And out of public life entirely."

Driving here, Rena and Brooks figured they were being pulled into something political. Maybe a background check on Upton—a quick vetting she could give suitors who might offer her a VP slot. Maybe, they thought, there was something difficult in her background, and she wanted a read on how damaging it might be.

They hadn't expected this. This would mean reverse engineering someone else's vetting of Upton—to find out who was threatening her and with what.

And they'd have only days to do it.

For while the primary campaign for president seemed endless, in reality its fulcrum point was brief, usually just a few weeks. The parties had arranged the schedule to avoid drawn-out fights, which meant, ironically, that the nastiest skirmishes occurred early and quickly, before most states had voted or most voters were paying attention. They were at that fulcrum point now.

If Upton wanted to accept either offer to run as vice president, she would have to answer in a matter of days or the offer would vanish.

The race, meanwhile, had already become ugly. After eight years of tactical moderation by James Nash, as he tried to manage the country's fissures, the populist edges of both parties had grown impatient and increasingly angry, though Nash had accomplished more than people realized. The Democrats, for their part, were engulfed in a brutal internal war. Progressives wanted to pull the party to the left around "economic justice." Moderates wanted to create a more diverse coalition of ideas to welcome former Republicans alienated by the right. To Rena, Democrats had been wandering without ideological focus for forty years—ever since the noble but failed experiments of the Great Society foundered in the unpaid debts and ideological scars of Vietnam.

The GOP, meanwhile, had now fallen into a war for its own soul. The Reagan Revolution was spent, depending on one's view, either having succeeded too well or worsening the problems it claimed it would solve. Wherever one stood, mistakes abroad and economic fears at home had swept up the GOP in a rising tide of conservative populism. Just as Democrats no longer could define what their party stood for, Republicans could no longer decide what conservatism meant. Should it be small government, balanced budgets, and a libertarian tradition of leaving people alone? Or did conservatism mean drawing inward, toward economic nationalism, tax cuts, anti-immigration policies, and enshrining evangelical morality into political law?

Rena, an avid reader of history, believed the world teetered at a pivot point between two epochs. On one side was the industrialization of the nineteenth and twentieth centuries. On the other was globalism, world migration, and digital and algorithmic revolution. No one seemed to understand the political implications of this new world—even the corporations that controlled the technology running it. But the past no longer seemed to offer a path to the future. The unfinished dialogues of the Founders over the meaning of the Constitution and the Bill of Rights—and the intentions behind words like "created equal" and "justice for all"—had broken out into new and ugly arguments about old feuds, like festering wounds that had never healed.

The one shared emotion was fear—that the political system was failing and American power was waning. The number-one book on the *New York Times* nonfiction list was Evelyn Bock's *Dusk in America*.

Rena was watching Upton, doing what Randi Brooks called his "reading" of people, sensing their hidden feelings and motivations from the way they moved, their body language, and the timbre of their voices.

There were two obvious questions they needed to ask her: Did she know what secret could be used against her? And did she suspect who might want her destroyed?

Brooks moved, just slightly, toward Upton, squaring her body to face the other woman's. "Did these offers to run as vice president come out of the blue?"

The question implied more than it might appear: Brooks was

trying to find out who else might know of the offers—and so be a suspect.

"Out of the blue," Upton repeated. She knit her fingers together. "I don't know David Traynor very well. I know he likes to surprise people. He hinted once, as a joke, that we should run together. But we are not close and hadn't discussed this." She took a breath. "About all we have in common is we're both called mavericks."

"Had you ever discussed joining the ticket with Bakke's people?"

Upton suppressed a smile. "Politics makes strange bedfellows," she said. "Obviously, Dick and I have little in common other than party." A glance at Sedaka. "An alliance would be a classic maneuver: I broaden his appeal as he tries to block Jeff Scott or Jennifer Lee."

Jeff Scott was the governor of Michigan who had surged unexpectedly to front-runner status in the GOP primaries. Jennifer Lee, niece of a former president, was the best-financed candidate in the race but so far had failed to catch fire.

Some in the GOP, Rena and Brooks also knew, had wanted Upton herself to run, a move Rena thought would be powerful. His partner, a liberal Democrat, had always believed the first female president would be a Republican; a Republican woman would pull from all voter groups, something that would be harder for a female Democrat.

Rena noticed Sedaka, the chief of staff, shifting in his seat, a sign something had been left unsaid. He asked Upton: "What in your past could destroy you?"

"I have no idea." She said it quickly and a little defiantly.

"And *who* do you think might threaten you?"

"I don't know that, either."

She was strong, frightened, angry, and she wasn't helping them.

"No idea at all?"

"Maybe I should focus on my enemies more and my friends less."

That seemed to get a reaction from Llewellyn Burke. "Maybe we all need to do more of that these days."

The remark was uncharacteristically dark for Burke, and Rena thought he saw something in his friend's face he hadn't fully grasped before: how much this campaign posed a threat to Burke, too. Especially the unexpected success of Jeff Scott, the first-term governor from Burke's home state.

Llewellyn Burke was a man who believed in the institutions of American government, and even more in the subtle norms that underlay them—in compromise, collaboration, and respecting the validity of the other side's right to disagree with you. Burke's true power in Washington lay largely behind the scenes. He was part of the hidden city, a network of people who comprised what remained of a bipartisan political center, a place, however diminished, where compromise and solutions could still be found. And Burke was one of the last figures in the city trusted by people on all sides.

The race for the presidency, however, was threatening to further dim whatever light was cast by the political center. Two of the three leading contenders for the Democratic nomination dismissed what one of them called the "incoherence of political compromise." The leading contenders for the GOP ticket were also radicals—ultraconservatives who despised the idea of a political center even more than the Democrats.

Those two men were Richard Bakke, the senator who'd made the offer to Upton, and Jeff Scott.

Bakke, the leader of the GOP radicals in the Senate, had also been Rena and Brooks's antagonist during the investigation into the African incident last year. He had no love for Lew Burke.

Yet Scott represented the bigger threat to Rena's mentor. Not only was he taking over control of the party in their home state, he also represented a new and more polished radical Republicanism than Bakke's. Both men espoused anti-immigration policies, wanted to tear down institutional barriers to change, called for remaking the courts, and touted economic nationalism. But while Bakke was a harsh personality, Scott was a quiet midwesterner, handsome, charismatic, a decorated war veteran, and a full generation younger than most leaders in his party.

In purely political terms, however, Scott was probably even more extreme than his rival. He threw around talk about "a national emergency of values and institutions" and the country "at the abyss." He embraced the language of other populists globally, terms like *deep state, fake news,* and *failing media.* He also added science and the academy into the mix, talking about "left-wing professors" and "radical science." He often described his opponents as "enemies of the people" and talked about "patriots and anti-patriots" and "American and un-American."

But he seemed to do it all with a wink, casually, almost jokingly. Perhaps he didn't mean it.

But he did mean it, Rena thought. In Michigan, Scott had already begun dismantling much of the state's institutional and political establishment to amass unprecedented power and weaken his critics.

Yet somehow Scott made it seem as if he were being pulled into action almost against his will, at the last minute, as things fell into chaos—*please, Jeff, we need you to save the town, the state, the whole country*—like a reluctant but iconic American movie hero, played by Clint Eastwood or Gary Cooper. The truth was that Scott's people often quietly hastened the predicament that needed solving.

And in the last three weeks, against all predictions, he had emerged as the leading Republican contender for president.

Free elections are like MRIs into the body politic, a quadrennial moment when we tour the country, sending messages of hope and anger, and see how people state by state respond. The census every decade may count how many people live in the country. Our long, relentless campaigns tell us what is in their hearts.

Watching Burke, Rena saw something he'd never seen before in his friend: fear of what the campaign was revealing. Fear of the American people.

Rena was watching his friend, listening to Upton, and to the river, and though he didn't know it, what he saw was wounding him, too.

Brooks, meanwhile, was losing patience with Upton. "You don't know who is coming after you? Or what they might have?"

Upton shook her head, and Brooks turned to Sedaka: "Who do *you* think is threatening Wendy?"

"I have my theories, but I'm not ready to offer them yet," Sedaka said.

The man didn't appear enthused about the two fixers being here. Or maybe it was Upton putting herself under Burke's protection he didn't like. Whatever it was, Rena and Brooks would have to speak to him away from the senator.

Rena's partner was way ahead of him.

"Well, you're both going to have to do a helluva lot better than this if you want our help," she said, her voice rising over the sound of the river. "And I will tell you this now. If you want to find out who's doing this to you, we will have to turn your life inside out. You're gonna have to trust us more than you trust your closest friends. And you're going to have to tell us more than you may have ever told anyone else about your life."

She made herself look larger and turned to Sedaka. "And you have to get comfortable with this or get out of the way."

She turned back to Upton.

"Senator, we barely know each other. But if you want this, you cannot have any secrets from us. And we will have to do this very quickly. A couple of days. So you have to decide right now."

She put a sympathetic hand over Upton's across the patio table. "Do you want our help?"

Upton took a deep breath. And for the first time in front of them revealed something about herself:

"I came from nothing. My sister and I didn't even have parents after I was sixteen. I built my life myself. I won't be intimidated or bullied, especially for something that never happened. I couldn't live with myself if I did. It would mean I am not the person I believe myself to be. That other people rely on me to be."

Then she gave Brooks a piercing look and said: "What would you do?"

Randi smiled. She liked this woman.

And Upton said: "So how do we get started?"

SEVEN

TUCSON
1983

Why couldn't Emily concentrate?

They were sitting at the kitchen table in the apartment above the tavern and the small grocery store their parents owned, and Wendy was helping her sister, Emily, with her math. Emily was barely trying. She would get the numbers mixed up in her mind. She never seemed to pay attention for very long. She was so easily distracted. She even mixed up her letters when she read sometimes, getting them in the wrong order.

Emily was ten already and in the fifth grade. That meant they were learning fractions. Fractions, decimals, and percentages. Which you had to do constantly to make change downstairs in Mom and Dad's store. So Emily should have been good at fractions long ago. She still struggled with her multiplication tables, too, which she should have mastered last year, in fourth grade. It seemed like Emily wasn't trying.

Emily wasn't dumb. Wendy knew that. She just didn't concentrate. She got distracted; she didn't seem to try.

"I'm tired and I'm bored," Emily said, her voice slithering into a full whine when she got to the second half of the sentence.

"You think I'm not?" Wendy shot back. "You think I'm excited to be doing *your* fifth-grade math when I have my own homework to do?"

Wendy wanted it to sound harsh. And a little mean. She wanted to shock Emily, and shame her. But she recognized her mistake the moment the words had come out. They had the opposite effect from what she wanted. Then she felt badly for hurting Emily's feelings. It was easy to hurt her little sister with words, even though Emily pretended not to care.

Now Emily was mad.

"Well, *I'm* not making you do my homework with me," Emily said.

No, Mom and Dad are, Wendy thought. "You're good with school and especially math. Better than me," her mom would say. Better than I, Wendy would think.

But Wendy worked with Emily on a lot more than math. Their parents owned the bar and restaurant downstairs with its little half-assed grocery store on the side. Together they were Shiny's Tavern and Grocery.

With the words BAR, FOOD, GROCERIES in neon light, in that order, on the sign just below the name.

Mom ran the grocery, Dad the tavern, with Mom doing the books for both. The two girls, Emily and Wendy, worked the shop on the weekends and often more than that. Wendy was sixteen, old enough to waitress in the bar, as long as she didn't serve liquor. But she learned to talk—to anyone and everyone. She also learned to watch and listen—as men complained and told their stories and revealed even more of themselves in their lies. She learned about people from the stories in that bar, about their hopes and dreams and what drove them and disappointed them. She could hear the story of Arizona, too, she thought, in the families who came to eat. And sometimes, when the men in the bar went to the bathroom, she would see what a Jack and Coke tasted like, or a Canadian and Seven, or an old-fashioned. Just a sip, and no one seemed to notice.

When she got to be fourteen, two years ago, her stepfather, Wade, had taught her how to make pretty much every drink there was. Or at least any drink the hard-cores in downtown Tucson might want in a place called Shiny's in 1981.

Emilio, the cook, had taught her how to do short order. Her mother had taught her how to run the grocery. That's why you are so good at math, her mom would say. You've already been using it for near on a decade. I'll teach you how to keep the books soon.

There was a knock on the door. And three men came in without waiting for an answer. That would always be part of Wendy's memory. Bob, the substitute barman, just came right in, having coming up with the others from downstairs, three sets of heavy shoes on the steps. People were always coming up from downstairs, into the two-bedroom kitchenette apartment. Usually they knocked lightly. Tonight, it had been a hard knock, and they hadn't waited for an answer before they entered.

Behind Bob, Wendy saw two policemen. A tall one who was white and was getting fat and who reminded Wendy of the former U of A football player who was a regular at the bar downstairs, who liked the barstool nearest the bathroom and told old stories about his varsity days. Behind the big cop there was a younger one, a Mexican American whose hair was almost completely shaved and whose tiny mustache was so faint it looked like a dirt smudge. They wore grim expressions, and Bob walked into the room with pain so deep in his eyes, Wendy knew everything at once.

"Girls, I have to tell you something," he said. Now his whole face was in pain. "Come to me." He put his thick hands around their backs and pulled them into his arms. He smelled of cigarette smoke and stale liquor. "Something has happened. Something terrible."

EIGHT

DALLAS, TEXAS

Before he got out of the rental car and headed into the glossy swagger of Texas pride and ambition awaiting him inside, Matt Alabama took a moment.

He hadn't seen the footage of the fight last night between supporters of Maria Pena and the man in the Dick Bakke T-shirt. Before ambling into Biernat's steak house to interview Richard Bakke, he wanted to see what had happened.

The senior national correspondent for the ABN television network, Alabama had covered seven previous presidential campaigns; this would be his last. For his valedictory moment, ABN had asked him to go on the road, visit each major candidate's campaign, and place them in some historical perspective. Or at least a TV version of historical perspective.

Alabama kept the rented Ford running so the heat stayed on. He plucked his iPad from his bag on the passenger seat next to him and began searching for the video. The longest piece was from the BNS cable network, narrated by a pretty young brunette anchor. Most of BNS's female anchors were brunette, while the conservative cable networks' were blondes. When had hair color become ideological?

"The incident occurred in Houston at a rally for New Mexico

governor Maria Pena," the brunette read. The best footage of the fight itself came from a cell phone, shot by a bystander. A man in a black T-shirt with BAKKE IS RIGHT written on it was shouting at a man and a woman. The woman pushed the man in the T-shirt. Then the two guys appeared to grab each other, and the man in the Bakke T-shirt seemed to be flung to the ground. Then the image began to shake and the footage ended.

"The Bakke supporter," the anchor narrated, "told police he was pushed into a tower that held up a bank of loudspeakers. The loudspeaker tower toppled over. Four people were hospitalized. Three people involved in the altercation were arrested."

The few seconds of actual fighting were replayed again, the image magnified and blurrier from being shown in slow motion. There were shorter bits of video shot from other angles and apparently other cell phones. There were some still images.

"The three people taken into custody are expected to be released on their own recognizance," the anchor woman said. "This is one of the stories we'll be following for you."

Alabama watched two more TV packages and read a few newspaper pieces. In his experience, violence and arrests weren't unheard of at political events. They were rare, however. And something this time felt different to Alabama. There was something going on out there in the campaign, something he hadn't seen or felt before in all the races he had covered. Something ugly.

Candidates usually talked about uniting people. Except for the fringe guys, the ones who never rose above a primary base of 30 percent. Not anymore. Division had become the animating principle in American politics—not just for protest candidates but for almost everyone. Us vs. them. It was there in the call-and-response chants featured at virtually every event.

At Pena rallies they chanted, "We are the ninety-nine percent," a reference to the idea that the establishment in both parties catered to the most affluent 1 percent that financed their campaigns.

At Bakke's events they chanted, "Take back America." Take it back from whom? People of color? Jews? Immigrants? The real menace, Alabama thought, was that the threat was so obvious to the audience it needn't be named.

At rallies for Jeff Scott, the new rising GOP star, Alabama had heard shouts of "Shut it down." That was the mantra of the fringe group that wanted to suspend Congress and hold a new constitutional convention to reconfigure the government. They were showing up at rallies and getting coverage from major news media outlets, a tactic designed to propel their marginal ideas into the mainstream. And his gullible press colleagues, Alabama thought, were falling for it.

He tossed his bag into the trunk, checked his jacket for a notebook and pen, and headed into Biernat's. The place, which was named for the owner and pronounced béarnaise, like the sauce, was one of the power lunch and dinner spots in Dallas. Like Rick in *Casablanca,* Al Biernat was apolitical. Yellow dog liberals, blue dog moderates, and red meat conservatives converged here with equal enthusiasm. And the most desired locations were to be at one of the famous "Dallas Nine," the nine leather booths that flanked the big-windowed southern wall.

Richard Bakke was in booth five, sitting with Texas senator Aggie Tucker. The two men were best friends in the Senate, which was especially important this week. The Texas primary was next Tuesday, and "Craggy Aggie" was the most popular collector of votes anyone had seen in a generation in the giant, over-confident, solipsistic Lone Star nation-state of Texas.

"The media has arrived at last," Bakke drawled. "Now we can finally order a T-bone, and lunch will be on ABN. A matter of the network's high ethics."

Alabama tried to match Bakke's reptile smile as he slid in next to Senator Tucker. He wanted to face Bakke. They were just talking on background, off camera. Alabama had learned over the years it was essential to see these people offstage as much as possible. It was the only way to really fathom the characters they played onstage.

"Don't be sarcastic about ethics, Senator," Alabama said. "If you become president, you'll be glad we have them."

"I'd be glad if you had 'em covering me in the Senate," Bakke said.

"I'm gagging on the bullshit already, Dick. Can we bring the volume down?"

A sly smile from Bakke and then a nod.

"Ah, my children," Tucker purred. "I'm pleased you're finally getting along."

OUTSIDE, a kid with a backpack approached Biernat's on foot. By the windows, he had been told. They would be by the windows on the south wall. His phone had a compass, and it told him which side of the restaurant was south. He could see the windows now. Tall things, floor to ceiling, with fancy ironwork in them. They were beautiful, he had to say. All he had to do was see which was the one where the bald head of Dick Bakke was sitting.

ALABAMA WAS TRYING to lighten the mood. "You ready to be bipartisan tomorrow night?"

That was why they were all here. Tomorrow evening Bakke and seven other candidates would participate in what was being called "The Bipartisan Debate." Multiple Democrats and Republicans would share the stage, though still running in separate primaries. The idea, dreamed up by the host cable channel and the cohosting digital platform company, was to help bring the country together. That's what they said at least.

"I'm always ready to be bipartisan," Bakke declared. "I just don't find the radical liberal Democrats want to meet me halfway."

"I'm not taking notes, Senator. So relax. If the Democrats have gotten more liberal, it's because the Republicans got a lot more conservative first. Or do you want to debate that, too?"

Bakke eyed Alabama. The reptile smile was replaced by a more thoughtful frown. "And I thank God we did," Bakke said. "I have spent my life trying to pull my party back to its roots. Trying to expunge the accommodationists who blurred the distinctions between liberals and conservatives. The so-called responsible center. Look, I get that the solution to one crisis usually creates the problems that become the next. But our country has been in trouble for sixty years. The liberal hegemony from Roosevelt to Johnson nearly ruined us. It's just that people are only now seeing it. History has a way of creeping up on you."

It was a variation of the speech Bakke would be giving in a couple of hours, and the message he had been refining for the last decade and a half.

But if this campaign had a new meanness to it, Bakke's rise in the GOP didn't just reflect it; he'd helped create it.

Bakke had a derisive edge, a gaudy, nasty quality, like a gangster's shiny suit. He was clearly brilliant, a poor kid who had risen to become a Supreme Court clerk and a U.S. senator. But something about him resented where his accomplishments had taken him, and he reveled in being angry about it. He was openly disliked by most of his Senate colleagues, who thought him selfish and disloyal.

But those same qualities seemed to make him wildly popular with many people in the country—and not just the ones liberals might guess. Bakke's cutting edge delighted supporters across a spectrum of American conservatives. He was the proud, rough-boy champion of outsiderness—of chain restaurants, gas-guzzling cars, guns, country music, cheesy Americana culture, and mean in-your-face tweets that mocked Democrats as stupid and clueless. Liberals hated Bakke more than any other Republican. He made fun of their urbanity, their snobby food, their multiculturalism, the elite colleges they strove to get their kids into, their concern for refugees suffering in countries far away, and their lack of compassion for those suffering here at home. Richard Bakke thought liberals fools, deluded, overprivileged dupes who imagined they wanted to make the world better but were just feathering their own establishment nest—and didn't even recognize they were frauds.

His critique had won over a good deal of the intellectual right, if not his fellow senators. "He is the rare politician who does not pander," a conservative legal scholar Cary Holden had written in *The Week Ahead* magazine. "He has a vision of how America should change and how government should be dramatically rolled back. And while that vision has an underlying element of anger to it, it is distinctly honest, one not masked by glossy pictures of a false future. He frightens liberals because he is telling the truth."

Yet Dick Bakke had been caught off guard in the last six months by the rise of Jeff Scott. The boy hero governor of Michigan had genuine charisma Bakke lacked, and a smile that no amount of work by the California cosmetic surgeon who had fixed the flagging skin under Bakke's chin could do anything to match. Scott did not possess anything like Dick Bakke's legal mind or his grasp of policy. But Scott had channeled Bakke's vision and added something Bakke could not: charm.

Scott could never have risen, Alabama thought, had Bakke not come first. But he might take Bakkeism higher than its author ever could.

Alabama had no inkling of the offer Bakke had made the day before to Wendy Upton. But the fear Alabama sensed Bakke might be feeling was exactly why Bakke had reached out to her. If she could be persuaded to join him, Bakke hoped it might just be enough to help him keep the nomination from Scott. Though he had doubts about whether he could trust her.

They sat, and Aggie Tucker told stories about Biernat's and the chaotic scenes of celebrities angling for tables—rap artists and their arm-candy girlfriends at one booth, a famous televangelist and his wife and children at the next, two booths over from the Dallas quarterback sitting with Jon Bon Jovi. They ordered, and Bakke nodded to Alabama.

THE KID WAS IN FRONT of the window now. He could see Bakke. He just needed to get a little closer. He pulled his pack off his back and felt inside for the weight. There it was. Okay, keep walking.

"What needs to happen for you tomorrow night, Senator?" Alabama asked.

"In the debate?" Bakke said. He glanced at Tucker. "You can't win a debate with eight people in it."

"You can lose one," Alabama said.

Bakke cackled a little too loudly.

He was nervous, Alabama thought. That was rare. The man was usually all sly bluster.

"I want to ask you something serious," Alabama said. "Off the record. Okay? Something I don't understand."

Bakke hesitated. He didn't like to enter uncharted territory with reporters—territory that might include serious questions and possibly honest answers.

"That fight last night at the Pena rally. Why would anyone who supports you go pick a fight wearing one of your T-shirts?"

Bakke, bald since he was twenty-five and now fifty-two, had aged into his looks. He raised his eyebrows above his hawk nose and looked at his friend Tucker.

"Aggie and I were just wondering the same thing," he said.

"Maybe the man really loves you and is dumber than a rock," Alabama said.

"Or maybe," Tucker interrupted, "someone is screwing with us."

That was what Alabama was wondering, too: whether something

more complicated, more nefarious was going on. The campaign was ugly enough already. But he didn't want to let Bakke know he wondering about that. Not yet.

"You know, Senator, you campaign mean," Alabama said. "Your rhetoric. It's angry. It's divisive. And maybe you reap what you sow."

Bakke smiled dryly and shook his head. "The country is angry. It's feeling mean. For a reason. I didn't start this."

Then the window shattered, Bakke ducked in fear, and a brick flew over them and landed on the table.

NINE

OFFICES OF RENA, BROOKS & ASSOCIATES
WASHINGTON, D.C.

Rena made two calls from the car outside Senator Burke's house. One was to the office. "Assemble everyone," he told Ellen Wiley. "All hands on deck."

The other was to an army friend named Samantha Reese, who now did occasional security work but lived in Colorado. "How soon could you get to Washington? I may need you."

Then he and Brooks drove back over the Chain Bridge, onto Canal Road, and cut through the backstreets of Georgetown to get to the office near Dupont Circle. When they arrived, the full investigative team of the consulting and security firm of Rena, Brooks & Associates was gathered in the attic conference room on the fourth floor of their town house offices at 1820 Jefferson Place.

The attic had a dark wood floor that had sloped with age, and the ceilings were lower than current code would allow. But Rena loved the old townhouse, partly because Teddy Roosevelt had once lived there. And for all its age and limitations, the attic had been modernized with state-of-the-art electronic insulation and various other security additions. Anyone, government or private, attempting to eavesdrop from an adjoining building, or even a drone, would find their signals jammed. It was, in the parlance only a few thousand

Americans needed to ever think about, "a hard-target environment with high-surveillance integrity."

The seven investigators assembled around the conference table had not so much applied for their jobs as they had been collected over the years by Peter and Randi, first as friends and then as colleagues. When each was finally asked to join the small band, their coming seemed inevitable. There was Hallie Jobe, the quietly disciplined daughter of a black Baptist minister from Alabama, whom Rena had befriended in the army. Jobe later joined the FBI and earned a law degree at night before joining her old mentor Rena here. There was Walt Smolonsky, the lumbering, bearlike former D.C. and Capitol cop, whom Rena had befriended when Smolo moved from police officer to Senate investigator. There was Maureen Conner, the meticulous former prosecutor and chief of staff to Senator Fred Blaylish of Vermont, for whom Brooks had been a Senate investigator. There was Jonathan Robinson, the young, aggressive former political consultant who specialized in crisis communications.

The firm was particularly well known for its digital skills. That department was handled by just two people. One was Arvid Lupsa, the Romanian immigrant in his twenties who looked like a 1960s beatnik. The other was Lupsa's boss and Randi Brooks's great friend, Ellen Wiley, the grandmotherly woman who had once been chief librarian at the *New York Times* Washington bureau. With her reading glasses dangling from a gold chain around her neck and dressed in craft show outfits inspired by the aesthetics of the 1970s, Wiley was one of the most cunning experts in using the Web anywhere in the world. Though over sixty, she was a master hacker and a legend among computer forensics experts a third her age.

There was also a new person in the attic now, a young Chinese American woman named Ang Liu, whom Brooks had taken under her wing after meeting her at a conference in Palo Alto last year. Liu, a computer science and law school graduate of Stanford, had become disillusioned by what she saw as the insistent utopian naïveté and male-dominated arrogance of Silicon Valley in general and the digital platform company where she worked in particular. Money had become a kind of poison, Liu had told Brooks one evening during the conference. "This is the dangerous delusion of the valley, that if I get rich by selling a company or idea, I'm making the world better. Sometimes breaking shit just means you've broken something."

"You need to work for me," Brooks told her. And now she was here.

In the year and a half since the last midterm elections, the final interval of the Nash presidency, much had changed in Washington, a festering anger that the presidential campaign was now revealing like an untended infection. Washington had been swept up by accusations of a cover-up over the terrorist incident in Africa that resulted in the death of four Americans. Senator Richard Bakke, now running for president, had been a leading member of the congressional committee set up to investigate the incident.

Bakke's aggressiveness on the Oosay committee had backfired.

But he had recouped by leading a revolt against Senate Majority Leader Susan Stroud that cast her out of her leadership role.

In the House, the conservative Common Sense faction had risen up as well. The Speaker of the House had recently announced he would retire in November.

All that only increased the pressure on anyone willing to risk bipartisan compromise, people like Burke and Upton. And there was even more pressure from the Shut It Down movement, the seemingly leaderless push, born in social media, for a constitutional convention to rethink how government was organized and elected.

Brooks glanced at the faces in the room, then began. She explained the calls Sedaka and Upton had received—the two "feelers" about the vice presidency and then the threat delivered thirdhand from a donor to Upton's Arizona office.

"Our assignment is to find out who is blackmailing Upton and with what," she said. "And we have almost no time to do it. Two or three days."

Maureen Conner made a grim face.

Rena rose. "There are really two investigations," he said. He moved in the direction of two easels he had asked be set up with flip charts.

"One is to discover the blackmailer: Who hates Upton and wants to stop her? They could be a political enemy, not a personal one, someone with a grudge, a policy disagreement, someone from another wing of the party."

He wrote "Possible Blackmailers" on the top of the first flip chart.

"The second inquiry is to find what in Upton's life could be used to destroy her."

He wrote "Blackmail Event" on the second easel.

Rena examined the faces in the room. "The two things may be entirely separate. The blackmailer may have nothing to do with the incident they are trying to blackmail her with. They may have just stumbled over it, looking for anything to use against her."

He and Brooks had worked this out on the drive back from Burke's.

He stood by the first easel with the words "Possible Blackmailers" written on it and flipped over the page. On the next sheet he drew four columns down and then labeled them at the top. Each one listed the kinds of enemies he and Brooks thought Upton might have. The first column was labeled "Rival Candidates," the second "Political Organizations," the third "Donors," and the fourth "Other Enemies."

"This is an initial list of who might have motive to stop Upton becoming vice president," Rena said. "It could be a campaign that doesn't want her joining with Traynor or Bakke. It could be one of their PACs, or some rich donor acting on his or her own. Or it could be some other enemy who has heard about these offers."

Walt Smolonsky said, "Hell, that could be anybody except Traynor or Bakke."

Jon Robinson said, "It could even be one of them, if they heard about the other one."

"The second investigation," Rena said, focusing them again, "is what she is being blackmailed about."

He moved to the second easel, labeled "Blackmail Event." Rena flipped the page and wrote at the top "Key Moments in Wendy Upton's Life."

"We need to try to isolate what Wendy Upton might have done that could be used against her."

Rena looked at his partner. And she took the cue to keep the group on task: "Here is how we will work," she said. "We'll start with a flash biography."

A "flash biography" meant they would write, probably overnight, as thorough a client history as they could produce in a few hours. To do so, Rena and Brooks would break up their staff into two-person teams and assign each team to research and write a different chapter of the target's life.

Then they would reassemble—probably early tomorrow morning—to discuss what they'd found and plot their path ahead. Rena and Brooks believed the first hours of an investigation were the most valuable. You assembled information more quickly at the beginning and with a more open mind than you would have later. You saw the pieces of the puzzle come together into patterns, the picture forming quickly, and you also saw the gaps. Later, when you had been staring at the puzzle longer, you often saw less of the big picture because you were looking too closely. So it was critical in these first hours, they believed, to catalog in writing any questions, suspicions, and important holes they noticed.

Rena added: "Tonight, we look for both the blackmailer and blackmail event. As you go through Upton's life, look for moments where she was susceptible to some temptation or mistake, where she might have made choices that could be used against her. At the same time, also look for moments where she might have made an enemy."

Rena waited for expressions of understanding.

"The blackmailer is likely a person with power and money. They may not know Upton. They could be purchasing the story to use against her. It could be from someone peddling it. More likely, they've hired private investigators who have dug it out, probably through interviews. If it existed in public documents, it would be known already."

"You think she's lying when she says she has no idea what it could be?" asked Smolonsky.

"I don't know," Rena answered coolly. "She is hard to read."

"She has to have a book on herself," Robinson said. "We getting our hands on that?"

A "book" was the compilation of opposition research, or "oppo," that Upton's own people would have put together about her for past campaigns. That was the first rule of opposition research. You do it initially on yourself, not on your opponent.

Once a politician today reached a certain level, say statewide or certainly federal, they would hire someone to compile a book on themselves.

Usually the book you did on yourself was produced internally, often by a consultant or a law firm paid by the campaign directly. Often the first oppo book was produced by young lawyers based entirely on public documents. The book identified anything vulnerable about you that could be depicted in a bad light. You would use the book, as your campaign progressed, to develop rapid responses to the attacks you anticipated would be coming at you.

Rena, Brooks & Associates had written many "books." But they had never done so for a political campaign, holding to a vow Rena and Brooks had made to each other when they joined together—he the Republican and she the Democrat—not to do campaign work.

But they had assembled books on prospective CEOs, draft choices, judges, university presidents, even a Supreme Court nominee. This new assignment pushed the limits of that vow. But they had told themselves in the car that they were protecting someone from blackmail, someone they both liked. Whatever their private thoughts, neither had raised an objection to taking the job that Rena's mentor, Llewellyn Burke, had asked them to.

The second step in any campaign was to develop the book on your opponent. Often, those oppo books would be written by outside consultants or law firms. Upton had run twice for Senate and twice for the House. Certainly during her Senate campaigns, in a state as big as Arizona, her opponents, at least her Democratic opponents, would have produced opposition books on her. Could Rena and Brooks get their hands on one of these? That might be difficult, but not impossible.

"We've asked for the book her campaign has produced about her," Brooks said. "Hopefully we'll get that this afternoon."

"Who was her consultant?"

"Jones & Hurd."

They were regional consultants and ad makers in the Southwest. They knew Arizona, New Mexico, and Texas. They hadn't done national races. Only a few consultants had. Their books, in other words, might be less thorough than a firm that had gone through the cauldron of a presidential campaign.

"Who ran against her?" Robinson asked. He didn't mean what candidate. He was asking what political consulting firm had run the campaign against her.

"Foley-Thomas," Brooks said. "We're on that, too."

Ang Liu raised her hand as if she were in school. The lawyer from Silicon Valley was new to politics.

"Is this sort of thing common? This blackmail and opposition research. What do you call it, oppo?"

Brooks looked at Maureen Conner. "What do you think?"

Maureen Conner had worked in politics for more than thirty years.

"When I started," she said, "all this oppo—threatening someone with opposition research into their private life—was rare. You checked someone's record, of course. But hiring private investigators or worn-out journalists to dig into their opponents' backgrounds? That happened only occasionally—usually only if you had a tip." She paused to see if Liu understood. "And oppo like that had risks back then," she continued. "If you were discovered, it could really backfire on you. People were shocked. It was considered dirty politics. And, frankly, it was too expensive—unless you knew there was something specific you were looking for. You had to hire people. It could take months. It happened. But it wasn't the norm."

"What changed?" Liu asked.

"The Internet happened," Ellen Wiley, the computer sleuth, chimed in. "Oppo became easier and cheaper to do. There was a lot more information you could get, and it didn't cost much to get it."

"Culture changed, too," Maureen Conner said. "Voters stopped being offended when an opponent dug into someone's life. The Clinton years made a difference. Tolerance for this has just gone up from there."

"And then there's the money," said Robinson. "There's a hell of a lot more of it to spend digging up dirt on your opponent."

"Why?" asked Liu.

"Because campaign finance reform backfired, like it always does," Robinson said. "People found new loopholes. And then the Supreme Court opened the floodgates with decisions that allowed independent groups to spend any amount they wanted—decisions that equated money and speech."

Brooks, the good lawyer, apparently felt a need to summarize. "So the Web made oppo easier. The culture got meaner. And the courts opened the money gates. There's no stopping now." That seemed to take the air from the room.

"In 1990," Brooks added, "there were maybe a dozen firms doing opposition research in the whole country. By 2000, there were about fifty. Today, there are hundreds—probably 150 in D.C. alone."

That was enough school for now, Brooks thought. She broke them up into their teams—one for Upton's early life through college, law school, and the military. A second on her move into politics and her policy positions as a congressperson and senator, looking for enemies. A third would look at her campaigns for the House and then the Senate, looking for clues of enemies there.

It was a little after three in the afternoon. They would work all night. Those who needed to would make arrangements at home.

"We'll reconvene at nine tomorrow morning," Brooks said. "Grab whatever sleep you need to put in a very long day tomorrow. And the next few days, too."

As people filed out, Rena and Brooks stayed behind.

"You okay with this?" he asked. He meant helping a Republican.

"Hell, yeah," she said. Something about Upton's story energized her. "Upton wants to fight back against this kind of blackmailing crap? We need to make these fuckers pay." It was a game effort. Her smile faded quickly. Something about Upton's story also depressed her. "You?"

Rena had complicated feelings about doing political work that steered too close to campaigns. Those feelings were made more complicated by his relationship with Vic Madison in California, who found politics ugly and degrading. Rena didn't love politics the way Brooks did. He worked in it ambivalently, and he disliked the term *fixer.* But the more Vic pushed him, the more Rena realized he was drawn by the work they did for public officials, the work Vic wanted him to stop doing. Vic's pressure was having the opposite effect than she wanted, and Brooks wondered if now this assignment would draw Rena further into politics and perhaps pull Rena and Vic further apart, even break them up. Rena had never wanted to be a consultant or a fixer. He had wanted to be a soldier, married to Katie Cochran, the sister of his West Point roommate. He wanted to have a family and to command soldiers and defend his country. He was forty-two and very little in his life had turned out as he had planned. He was confused by that, and by people admiring and praising his skills for something he wasn't sure was a job at all—cleaning up the messes of powerful people in a dirty town. "Sweeping up after the circus," he sometimes called it.

"I'm okay," he said. "If Upton wants to fight, let's fight for her."

That earned him a Brooks smile.

"You know she's a Republican," he teased.

"These days? Barely."

"And if we find something that disqualifies her?"

"What disqualifies someone for public office these days?" she said.

Rena raised a bottle of water. "To the wisdom of the public."

"We toasting it?"

He shook his head. "Just betting the future of the country on it."

TEN

GEORGETOWN

Bill McGrath's office in Georgetown was hard to find and inconvenient to get to.

Georgetown offered the best views in the city. But a half century earlier, residents here had refused the subway, and now traffic was so thick, it was usually faster to walk here than drive. Most Washingtonians kept their distance, leaving the neighborhood to tourists, commuters, and residents. Having your offices in the maze of colonial alleys and limited parking was a signal you didn't need to be easy to find; clients would get to you anyway. Georgetown was an attitude.

The offices of McGrath, Garrity, Cashen, and Dunne offered only initials on the door: MGCD. There was no expensive art on the walls to impress visitors, nor pictures in the lobby of the presidents, senators, governors, and foreign dictators who'd been clients. There was only the bustle of people, mostly young and attractive, hurrying from one apparently urgent meeting to another.

A head-turning young blonde with Ivy League poise greeted them from behind a teak reception desk. A first job out of Yale or Brown, Rena thought, the child of someone with connections.

They were there to see Bill McGrath, Brooks said. The young woman spoke into a headset.

A few minutes later another blonde, a little older but just as striking, met them in the lobby, introduced herself as McGrath's personal assistant, and led them to a corner office down the hall. The view was breathtaking, the Kennedy Center and Watergate through one window, the knot of high-rises in Rosslyn, Virginia, through the other.

A big man in an open dress shirt and cowboy boots rose from behind a messy desk. "Peter Rena! Randi Brooks!"

The bellowing voice was exhausted and hoarse.

A political consultant in season, working nonstop and sleeping little.

Brooks extended an uneasy hand in greeting: she and McGrath were not friends but old antagonists, back when she helped Democrats get their appointees Senate confirmed and McGrath tried to block them.

He was an ad-making political consultant, which was different from a general campaign strategist, a pollster, or a get-out-the-vote technician. Ad makers specialized in "messaging," distilling ideas and arguments into simple language that could be delivered in fifteen or thirty seconds and, more important, might convey subtextual messages that went much deeper and had the power to persuade. Properly shot, a soldier or a salute or a flag could be a trigger for long-held political feelings in a voter's mind that lingered long after the ad was over. It was a scandalously profitable game, usually a 15 percent commission on top of "the buy," the amount a campaign spent placing a given TV "spot." The system encouraged candidates to buy far more TV spots than anyone wanted to see.

McGrath's real gift, however, was his knowledge of the American voter. A blue-collar kid from California, he'd worked on local campaigns since high school. He was nearly finished with his Ph.D. in political science from Michigan when he decided he knew swing voters better than any scholar he'd ever met. He'd grown up with them in San Jose, pored over the data about them in his campaign work, talked to them in focus groups, sat in their kitchens, messaged them in ads, and then watched their reaction show up in the numbers. They were as familiar to him as family.

"We appreciate your seeing us," Rena said. "We know how busy you must be."

McGrath waved his hand as if it were nothing. "You said I would regret it if I didn't. What could I do?" A mischievous grin. "You're a manipulative bastard, Peter."

He pointed them to visitors' chairs in front of his desk, not one of his couches—a sign the meeting would be brief—and moved back behind his desk.

Now in his late fifties—no longer the boy genius of the GOP—McGrath wore a graying goatee and his blond hair, thinning, long in back; he was loud and brash and charming and always moving—hands fiddling, eyes dancing. It was hard to take your eyes off him.

Rena waited until McGrath had sat down and begun to fidget again before saying anything:

"Bill, will you promise that nothing we talk about leaves this room, including our ever being here?"

That earned a sly smile from McGrath, followed by a shrug.

"I want a verbal commitment," Rena said. "Because we need your brain to help us stop something terrible from happening. Something that could distort who becomes the next president."

McGrath leaned back and folded his arms. No more smile.

Rena had just set a trap. McGrath could tell them to leave, but that would mean he wouldn't learn their tantalizing secret. Or he could keep listening, which would mean he had tacitly agreed to Rena's condition of confidentiality.

McGrath's eyes held Rena's. "I heard you were the most dangerous fucking interrogator in the army in your day."

"I'll take that as partial consent," Rena said. "Do you have any commitments in the presidential race that prohibit you from helping us?"

For consultants, presidential campaigns were aggravating and messy. There were too many advisers in every meeting; almost every campaign ended in failure; afterward blame got sprayed around like Agent Orange. A young consultant could help make his or her reputation in a presidential campaign, but veterans like McGrath tried to avoid them.

"Not for money," McGrath said. "Just offering free advice, if anyone asks."

"Then if we pay you, do we have your counsel in confidence?"

McGrath leaned forward. "Tell you what. I'll give you the lay of the land. And you have my word whatever you tell me remains in confidence. Just because I'm intrigued and amused."

"I need to pay you or we're leaving," Rena said. "We're not here for your amusement."

"I don't really do anything anymore unless it amuses me."

"You should worry about that," Rena said. Then he took a notebook from his pocket, wrote something on it, tore out the page and handed it to McGrath.

It read: "I, Peter Rena, hereby hire Bill McGrath to help me with an assignment that neither he nor I can ever discuss. I will pay him X for these services. If either of us violates this contract, the violator will pay the other ten million dollars." The X had a space next to it where McGrath could write in an amount.

Rena had signed it.

"Do you have ten million dollars?" McGrath asked.

"You do."

Another impish smile. "I'll charge you a dollar for my services," McGrath said. "More than they're worth." And he signed his name.

Rena leaned forward and asked: "Who would want to destroy Wendy Upton?"

ELEVEN

McGrath smiled like a leprechaun.

"So Upton's being courted to be vice president," he guessed. "And someone has threatened her. Already."

He looked down at his hands as if he just discovered he had stopped fidgeting. "That means whoever's threatening Wendy is afraid she could help someone win the nomination."

It had taken McGrath only about fifteen seconds to intuit from Rena's question what was going on.

Always having been on the other side, against him, Brooks had never seen McGrath behind the scenes like this. She was impressed.

"Jesus, she's a person who commands real respect, isn't she?" McGrath said. "Even fear."

He was puzzling out the implications. "That's such a rarity. Genuine respect in politics, it's like uranium. It can be used for power or destruction." McGrath turned to Brooks. "She's hired you to find out who's threatening her?"

Rena ignored the question and repeated: "Who would want to destroy Wendy Upton?"

McGrath popped out of his chair and walked over to a wall of opaque glass that doubled as a whiteboard. On it, he drew two lines in the shape of an L, the axis lines of a graph. Inside the L he drew five circles.

"This is the modern Republican Party," he said.

Rena made a skeptical face.

"Vertical line is where people are on social issues. The higher you go, the more liberal folks are. Lower, more conservative."

He pointed to the horizontal line he had drawn at the bottom of his rough graph. "This is where folks are on government regulation vs. free markets. Further right, the more distrust of government. Closer in, the more tolerant they are of it."

He had drawn circles in every part of the graph.

"So you can see, Randi, the GOP is a lot more diverse than you liberals think. We're not all white, or working class or racist."

"How does this help us, Bill?" Rena asked.

"This graph will help you find your blackmailer."

"How?" Brooks asked.

"No one of these circles is big enough to win the nomination by itself."

The biggest group McGrath had drawn he'd labeled "Die Hard Conservatives" and written "30%" inside.

"To win the nomination, a candidate must win their base, vanquishing their natural rival for that group, and also win big chunks of other people's groups. That's the trick of the primaries. Win your circle, and enough of other people's, to make a coalition."

"How is this helping us?" Rena asked again impatiently.

"If we walk through which campaign is fighting for which circle, you will have your suspects and your motive," McGrath said.

"The blackmailer may not be a campaign," Brooks said. "It might be a PAC, or even some donor who hates Upton."

"Oh, I'm almost certain it isn't a campaign," McGrath said. "Not directly. It might be some crazy asshole inside a campaign going rogue. Or inside a PAC. It might be some insane donor." He paused and looked at his whiteboard. "But these circles, these voter groups, will give us a motive."

"We need names, Bill," Rena said. "Not theory."

"We'll get there," McGrath said.

He moved toward his five circles. "Dick Bakke and Jeff Scott are fighting to win this group." He pointed to the bottom right, the circle labeled "Die Hard Conservatives." "They're the core of the GOP, small government and socially conservative. The religious right is in here."

A glance at Rena. "Scott and Bakke are splitting this group. So they both need to pick up big chunks of other circles. Wendy Upton could help either one of them do that. And then the other one would be highly motivated to stop her."

That meant, Rena and Brooks both knew, that Michigan governor Jeff Scott, or someone backing him, would be a prime suspect. But so might Bakke if he heard about Traynor.

McGrath's eyes twinkled. "But Wendy can help other people, too."

He pointed to the circle at the top right, which meant socially liberal but also wary of government, and wrote "Free Market/Libertarians."

"This is what's left of the old liberal northeastern Republican party. Small government, fiscally conservative, but pretty tolerant on social issues. They're not gone, but they're geographically dispersed, so people think they've vanished. They're about 25 percent of the party."

McGrath said: "Jennifer Lee is fighting with Tony Soto for this group."

Lee, the governor of Georgia, was the niece of former president Jackson Lee and the new great hope of the old GOP.

Soto was the young Latino governor of Nevada, who, if he could win the nomination, some Republicans hoped might woo Hispanics to the GOP and give the party a new direction.

McGrath said: "If Upton joined with either Bakke or Scott, then Lee and Soto would both be threatened by it. Because Wendy has real appeal with these libertarians. Or if she signed with Soto, let's say, then Lee would be threatened. And vice versa if she aligned with Lee."

"You think Jenn Lee would go that far? Blackmail Upton?" Brooks asked.

"Not her. She wouldn't have the stomach for it. But there are a lot people who've given her a lot of money, and they'd pay even more to stop Scott and Bakke. These folks, a lot of them on Wall Street and even some Silicon Valley folks, worry their party is being hijacked by populists. They hate Bakke. And they fear Scott."

"That include Steve Unruh?" Brooks asked.

Steve Unruh was the political guru who had built the Lee dynasty and now financed Jenn Lee through his super PAC. He'd raised a lot of money, but he wasn't getting much for it.

"Maybe," McGrath said.

He turned back to his graph. At the top, which meant socially liberal but to the far left, indicating tolerant of government, he had written "Angry Anti-Elites."

"These folks here are pretty liberal socially and don't hate government. They just think it doesn't work for them anymore. They're not rich like the free-market libertarians. They're suffering. They believe the system is rigged against them, and they hate the modern Democratic Party because it abandoned them." He stared at Brooks. "They're middle class. They're my parents."

McGrath took a breath. "Scott and Bakke are fighting over this group, same way they're fighting over die-hard conservatives. They're the angry candidates, and these are the angry voters. But Wendy has real appeal among these voters, too, because of her renegade biography. So if she aligned with anyone—Scott, Bakke, Soto, even Lee—she would be a threat to all the others."

That gave Soto and Lee as much reason to fear Upton as it did Scott, thought Rena.

In the circle at the bottom left McGrath had written "Nativists/ Preservationists."

"These folks down here are pissed, too, but they blame immigrants and the global economy for taking away their jobs rather than the government. They're angry about political correctness and feel like people of color get too much of a break. They're close to what liberals think of as the white working-class stereotype, but hey, these people used to be Democrats. They live everywhere, and they make up about 20 percent of the GOP vote. When liberals say the GOP is racist, this is who you elitists have in mind. But it's a crutch for liberals. *You disagree with me. You must be a racist and a misogynist.*"

McGrath was looking at Brooks. "Scott appeals to this group. So does Bakke. They channel that anger. But Upton is popular with these folks, too, because she fought the government when she was a teenager and won, and she's ex-military. And her magic is she doesn't play angry."

McGrath stopped.

"Here's the thing about your girl, Wendy. She pulls from every one of these damn circles. She's the common denominator—a missing piece of the puzzle for each candidate. Truth is, she'd help a candidate in either party. If I graphed the Democrats for you, you'd see something similar."

Rena and Brooks stared blankly back at McGrath. They'd not mentioned Upton being approached by David Traynor. And they had no intention of doing so.

There was a small circle near the middle called "Alienated/ Disengaged."

"The 10 percent who are just pissed off in general. But they vote. And they swing—usually against whatever party has the White House. So this time I figure they'll go GOP."

McGrath stepped away from the glass wall.

"I thought you were going to name our blackmailer for us," Rena said. He was losing patience with McGrath's circles and graphs.

"Weren't you listening, Peter? I just did." McGrath grinned. "Dick Bakke, Jeff Scott, Jennifer Lee, and Tony Soto are your top suspects. Probably not them personally, though you never know. But maybe some crazy cabal, or some rich asshole, who supports them."

McGrath started pacing. "And add Janice Gaylord to that list, since she doesn't want Upton joining anyone's ticket. She wants to be vice president herself. And she's mean as an angry mule."

Janice Gaylord, a billionaire Texas cosmetics magnate, was the other woman in the GOP primaries besides Jennifer Lee. She was deeply religious and was trying to inspire women voters, just like Lee. But she wasn't getting much traction. Which meant she was basically running now in the hope of being picked for the second spot on someone else's ticket. That made Upton a threat to her. And she was reputed to be mean enough and rich enough and ambitious enough to blackmail Upton all by herself.

"You just named the top five Republicans in the race," Rena grumbled. "That doesn't narrow things much."

"Yeah, well, hey now. When you look at this," McGrath said, "you two need to understand something about campaigns today. They're different than even ten years ago, when you were directly involved, Randi. Some of these candidates are just vessels. The parties are weaker than ever. The real power today is money—not the parties, or voters, or even any one candidate. It's the PACs. And the donors behind them. And the biggest money is dark. No one knows entirely where it's coming from. A lot of these PACs are 501(c)(4) organizations, your so-called donor-advised funds. They don't have to report where their money comes from. But you know this."

McGrath's leprechaun whimsy had vanished.

"You know, when I worked in the former Soviet Union in the early 1990s, after the fall, this Russian oligarch told me, 'You're not really rich unless you own your own army and have your own political party.' I thought the guy was kind of ludicrous and disgusting."

McGrath grimaced.

"Well, in the United States today, the rich spend as much money on private security as we do as a nation on police. And there are about fifteen billionaires who are basically trying to buy the parties and control who becomes president. The amount of money they've put into super PACs and campaigns dwarfs all other funding sources. That's the game now—big donors and dark money. Outside contributions approached $1.7 billion in the last presidential campaign—half again what it was four years before. And it's in both parties, don't kid yourself."

McGrath's face was flushed. "The owner of the Chicago fucking Cubs dropped twenty million dollars in a final month on ads in the last cycle to try to stop Jim Nash. More than Reagan spent total his first time out. These people aren't kingmakers. They want to make the rules, too, and make sure the king they have bought plays by them."

McGrath glanced at his drawing on the wall. "Right now, they're split. Some are betting on Bakke, like the Grantland brothers. Some on Soto. Trotter Cardoff and the Fund for Freedom are behind him. They think Tony can win and would be obedient. A lot of money is on Jennifer Lee. Jeff Scott has got some heavy people behind him. And Janice Gaylord used to pay dark money. Now she's financing her own campaign."

McGrath had begun sweating. "Would any of them threaten Upton?" he asked.

The question, however, was rhetorical. McGrath's answer clearly was yes.

He was bouncing on his toes now in front of his graph of the conservative landscape in America. The exhaustion in his voice gone, he was full of energy.

"And don't forget the people who run PACs, too. Not the billionaires, but the ones who bundle their money, the political operatives who run these PACs, are under enormous pressure to deliver. If you've raised three hundred million dollars and promised to elect a president in return, you're pretty much dead if you can't make good. Those guys could easily go crazy."

McGrath sat down behind his desk, beads of sweat on his forehead. "So I'd say your suspect list is anyone backing any of those five campaigns. Bakke, Scott, Lee, Soto, or Gaylord. Look at the money. And the bundlers in the PACs who've made promises to get it."

Only those candidates with no chance of winning were missing from McGrath's list, which at this point was three marginal candidates, Senator Homer Stiles, a friendless man from Montana, Governor Stan Drinkard of Louisiana, and Curtis Gains, a Florida congressman.

"You guys have taken on a pretty bad job," McGrath joked.

Brooks wasn't laughing. "What about Democrats?" she asked.

"What about them? You imagine one of them is thinking that far ahead to be worrying about Upton?"

If a Democrat knew David Traynor was considering joining forces with her they might, Rena thought. They also might want to threaten Upton if they thought she would join a ticket with Dick Bakke. But they weren't telling McGrath who had made offers to Upton.

"*I* would be thinking about her," Brooks said.

"In my humble experience, most Democrats aren't as smart as you, Randi," McGrath said. "But if you want my take on them, we'll have to do it in another meeting. I'm late."

On the sidewalk outside, Brooks asked, "Do you trust him, Peter? Or did we just let the whole effing world know what the hell we're doing?"

"I think I do," Rena said. "But I'm not sure it matters." His voice was strange. "We may not be able to find out who's doing this and keep it a secret."

"If it gets out, haven't we failed?"

The question seemed to stop Rena.

"At least we got the most expensive political consultant in the country to work for us for a dollar."

TWELVE

WEST END

Rena wanted to go home, even for an hour or two—for a run and a shower. Then he'd join the others exhuming Wendy Upton's life.

The truth was that he felt an unexpected wave of sadness washing over him. The prospect of the campaign becoming this vicious depressed him. He wasn't fascinated by the mechanics of politics.

Not the way his partner was.

Even if she did tell him again and again he was a natural at the game.

The country seemed to Rena locked in a repeating argument that kept looping back on itself. Each new public event triggered the same accusations of ill motives and ignorance about the other side. And each new cycle eroded the previous version, the debate getting nastier and smaller.

Conservatives despised liberals for their softness, their political correctness, for apologizing for America, for their addiction to government and their demands for economic and social redistribution. Liberals despised conservatives because they imagined their economic attitudes were short-sighted and social and moral beliefs were intolerant, racist, or ignorant. In America, Rena thought, we no longer respected the validity of each other's positions or even our right to have them. Angry and afraid, people were seeking solace in tribal identities that only made problems worse.

Rather than offering to fix this repeating loop of distrust, it seemed most of the people running for president were trying to exploit it.

With the threat to Upton, someone was also trying to use blackmail to bend the race even more.

Rena wanted to go for a run and clear his head.

He found himself in his den, however, looking at old books. He picked out a time-worn copy of journalist Theodore White's *The Making of the President 1960,* the book that first pulled back the curtain of presidential campaigns and created the "behind the scenes" style of journalism that dominated the way we now looked at politics—and helped make it look like cynical theater.

In the beginning, however, White had marveled at the miracle of American elections, not seen them as manipulative.

"The general vote is an expression of national will, the only substitute for violence and blood. Its verdict is to be defended as one defends civilization itself," read one passage Rena had underlined years ago.

If that were true, wasn't the process to be defended "as one defends civilization"? So the verdict has integrity? What place was there for the kind of threats being leveled against Upton?

"Only one other major nation in modern history has ever tried to elect its leader directly by mass, free, popular vote," White wrote seventy years ago. "This was the Weimer Republic of Germany, which modeled its unitary vote for national leader on American practice. Out of its experiment with the system it got Hitler. Americans have had Lincoln, Wilson and two Roosevelts."

Were we the same country now? Or were we so worried our glory was behind us, like Germany or Italy, that we would grasp for its return by abandoning the democratic principles that made us Americans in the first place? He had always assumed Jim Nash would be succeeded by someone in the other party. That now looked like it would be Bakke or Scott.

Then Rena ran—a fierce and urgent six miles. Halfway along, his mind drifted back to the names on McGrath's board. Each had motive to destroy Upton. Who on the list also had the stomach for it? Rena tried to think through them one by one.

Bakke certainly was not above threatening people. Yet why would the man who yesterday asked Upton to join him today threaten her to stay out of the race? If Bakke's scrubbers found something damaging about Upton, it made more sense to withdraw the offer and keep the secret for later—in case she ran with someone else.

How likely to threaten Upton were McGrath's other suspects? Jeff Scott, the Michigan governor, whose campaign was surging, had plenty of arrogance to match his charisma. But Rena doubted he was this reckless. Scott was winning. This involved more risk than he needed to take.

Jennifer Lee, the Georgia governor, seemed even less the type. Yet Rena agreed with McGrath that some of the powerful people behind her might be capable of anything.

He had no doubt about the other woman on McGrath's list, Janice Gaylord. The conservative business magnate had no chance of winning the White House. But she did hope for a spot on the GOP ticket as vice president. And Upton potentially stood in her way.

What about Tony Soto, the senator from Nevada, whose image was softer and more compassionate than some of the others? Rena wasn't sure. It was hard to know if Soto was sincere about anything.

McGrath had ignored the Democrats. But Rena could think of at least three camps that would want to block Upton. Progressives Maria Pena and Omar Fulwood argued Democrats had to be much tougher on the GOP and move further left. That meant they were both motivated to want a hard-line GOP ticket to run against. They'd want to block a Bakke-Upton ticket. And the other centrist in the race—the ex-cop and ex-soldier Cole Murphy—despised David

Traynor. If he had found out about Traynor's overture to Upton, that would be a motive.

As Rena was getting out of the shower after his run, the phone rang. His friend the reporter Matt Alabama.

A decade earlier Alabama seemed to have adopted Rena as a kind of younger brother, after Rena had been pushed out of the military and become a Senate aide. He saw in Rena, Alabama had once said, a younger version of himself. What did that mean? "Underneath all the Special Forces machismo and cop savvy, you're a romantic idealist." You mean I foolishly expect the world to be a better place than it really is, Rena said. Yes, Alabama had told him. And there aren't enough of us.

Alabama liked to call at the end of the day to chat, something Rena now did with only one other person, Vic Madison in California.

"Hear what happened today with Dick Bakke?"

Rena hadn't seen any news today. He froze at the thought the Bakke offer to Upton had leaked somehow. "No."

"Someone threw a brick at him. And I was having lunch with the honorable gentleman at the time. Nearly killed me instead of him."

"The day after the arrests at the Pena rally last night?" Rena asked. He was thinking like a cop.

"Peter, something's going on out there," Alabama said. "Something ugly. And different than anything I've seen before."

Rena knew Alabama had covered presidential races for close to thirty years.

"This campaign is about fear," Alabama said. "Not about making the country better. And that is new."

"Fear about what?"

He could hear Alabama sigh.

"It think it's fear there's not enough in the country to go around. That the country doesn't work anymore. Not like it did. And that it can't be fixed."

Rena heard something in Alabama's voice. Was it a hint that

maybe he thought the fears were justified? That Alabama was afraid, too?

"This kind of anger used to be the message of protest campaigns," Alabama was saying. "Now it's everyone. And it's working."

Rena said nothing.

"Pena and Fulwood say the system is rigged for the rich. Scott, Bakke, and Gaylord say it's rigged to help the poor who don't deserve it. But they're all arguing someone is stealing what isn't theirs."

Two questions began to form in Rena's mind.

One was the same Alabama had asked Bakke right before the brick had been thrown: If you were a Bakke supporter and wanted to start a fight at a Maria Pena rally, would you really show up wearing a Bakke T-shirt?

The other was: Who would then throw a brick at Richard Bakke? If he could answer those, he might know who was threatening Wendy Upton.

* * *

Outside, at the end of Rena's block, two men sat in the front seat of a Malibu sedan. They were both wearing headphones, and a computer screen perched on the console between them gave off a soft glow that half lit the bottom of their faces. One man wore a baseball cap without a logo, the other a gray knit cap. When Rena hung up the phone, the man in the knit cap took off his headphones.

"How long do we stay?"

"You gotta go somewhere?" the man in the baseball cap chirped back. "Until the fucker leaves his house. Then we follow him. So settle in."

DAY THREE

WEDNESDAY

FEBRUARY 26

THIRTEEN

RENA, BROOKS & ASSOCIATES
WASHINGTON, D.C.

The next morning it fell to Ellen Wiley, the chief digital sleuth, to begin outlining the tragic and redemptive story of Wendy Upton's lost childhood.

The team was gathered in the attic after a long night inside Upton's life.

"We have two tasks now," Randi Brooks had told them before Wiley began. "Identify those moments when Wendy might have made a choice or a mistake someone could use against her. And look for people who might see her as an enemy—even someone she might barely know."

They had spent all night on the flash bio, every investigator in the firm taking a different part of Upton's life and sending their parts to Wiley. She had woven them into a profile that went beyond facts, that touched on character and motive. People within the firm called these profiles "Wileys."

Sometime around midnight they had been aided by the arrival of "the book." That was the biography Upton's own team of opposition researchers had put together as part of her last Senate race, a year and a half ago. Flipping through it in the middle of the night, Rena and Brooks had quickly identified it as a "first pass" effort, something put together from public records, probably by young associates at a law firm hired by her political consultant. It was a "paper trail" book, done quickly, and if it came up clean, you might do nothing more, depending on your budget, your opponent's, and how tight your race was. The key to any oppo book was that it had to be at least as good as the one your opponent had on you.

Upton had never faced any serious challenge in her races. So no one had ever gone much past what was available online. Going deeper would have required hiring private investigators to rattle around in her life, talking to people and looking for trouble. But that, apparently, was exactly what someone had done now.

Whoever was threatening Upton.

Rena had one comfort as he listened. Walt Smolonsky from their team had flown to Arizona last night. This morning, he could start looking not only at Upton's life. He also could start looking to see who else might be in Arizona doing the same thing. And if they were lucky, maybe he could find out who they worked for.

"THE WENDY UPTON STORY really begins with the death of her parents," Ellen Wiley began, glancing at notes she had made.

It was the legend that had launched Upton's political career, Wiley said. The story of the heroic orphan who forged her life out of hardscrabble tragedy.

Upton was born in 1967. Her parents divorced when she was four, and her mother remarried a schoolteacher, a man named Wade Upton, who adopted Wendy. A few years later, Wade lost his job in a wave of school cutbacks, and the Uptons took over running a little tavern and convenience store Wade had inherited from his parents.

"Wade and Beverly had another child, Emily, six years younger than Wendy. The family lived upstairs from the bar. They mostly just got by."

Wiley looked up from her computer over her reading glasses: "Then there were deaths."

In 1980, when Upton was thirteen, her biological father died of cancer. Three years later Upton's mother, Beverly, and stepfather, Wade, died in a car crash. Upton was sixteen. Her sister was ten. They were orphans without any other family.

"The state wanted to put the kids into the system. The girls were both minors. There was no living family nearby. Wendy refused to let it happen. It was 1983, the summer after her sophomore year in high school. Wendy took the GED and passed, which gave her a high school diploma. Then she sued the state to treat her as an emancipated minor who could be responsible for her sister."

"Jesus," Smolonsky said from his hotel room in Tucson.

"There's more," said Wiley. "The state still wanted to put the little sister in the system, even after granting legal adulthood to Wendy. It argued that taking care of a ten-year-old sister while trying to run a business was too much for a sixteen-year-old to handle. Wendy rallied the folks in the neighborhood and the patrons at the tavern-restaurant to support her, including some regular who was a lawyer. The community got all its ducks in a row behind her. She got a lot of publicity. She sued the state a second time and won custody of her sister."

"How rich is the documentation?" Brooks asked.

"Mostly sealed," Wiley said. "But from age sixteen, Upton spent the next four years being a parent and local business owner."

"How does a kid own a bar?" asked Jonathan Robinson.

"Someone held the liquor license for her so Upton could run the place until she was twenty-one."

When Upton turned twenty, Wiley explained, her sister was finally ready for high school. Wendy enrolled at the University of Arizona in Tucson. She commuted to school during the day, ran the business in the evening, and raised her sister at the same time.

"And she graduated college in two years," Wiley said.

"Girl in a hurry to catch up," said Robinson.

"Right," said Wiley. "About to turn twenty-three, she was a full-time parent and tavern owner and a new college graduate."

"At age twenty-three I was knee-deep in . . ." Smolonsky began.

"Uh-huh," Hallie Jobe cut him off. The minister's daughter didn't want to hear about the rest of Smolo's extracurricular education. She nodded to Wiley to continue.

"Upton joined ROTC in college, on top of everything else. When she graduated, her sister was halfway through high school. Upton enrolled in law school at the University of Arizona on the army's dime."

"She was in law school, running the tavern business, and raising her kid sister in high school? What could go wrong?" said Arvid Lupsa, one of the two computer detectives.

Brooks said to Smolonsky: "Walt, you're going to look at the early years in Tucson—running the family business as a kid, then college and law school, even though chances are she's being targeted for something she did later."

"On it," said Smolonsky.

"Two years after sister Emily graduated high school," Wiley continued, "Wendy graduated law school. She was twenty-six. Basically, she had caught up. It was 1992."

Rena noticed the faces in the room were swept up in the story now. This was important to keep them going for what would likely be days without rest.

"She owed the army time as an attorney," Wiley said. "She went to work in the judge advocate general's office. The younger sister, Emily, now twenty, took over managing the family business, the bar and the store."

"Wow," Jonathan Robinson said, shaking his head.

Hallie Jobe took over the narrative now: the military years.

"Upton was a JAG attorney for the next six years, 1992 to 1998. A good one, apparently. Made her name prosecuting sexual harassment cases."

"Might have made enemies doing that," Robinson suggested.

That earned a stare from Jobe. Although she had reasons to be suspicious of American institutions—she was a black woman—she who also was a proud former marine and staunch defender of the military.

"A lot of people in the military care about reform, too," she said testily. "More than you'd get from the media." She paused. Jobe didn't like to show emotion, but she was tired. It had been a long night. "And it looks like Upton was a careful reformer. Her literature says 'she worked within the system for responsible changes to the rules for handling sexual misconduct cases in the military.'"

"Responsible changes? What does that mean?" Brooks asked.

"It means she's got a lot of military and ex-military voters in Arizona," Conner said.

Jobe was becoming more irritated by the liberals in the room. She thought Conner and Brooks didn't understand how the military operated and the range of people inside it.

Rena tried to keep them on track: "Check out if she made enemies from her sexual harassment work. Maybe some case she prosecuted turned someone to revenge."

Jobe nodded she understood.

And Maureen Conner took up the description of the congressional years:

"She did a rotation as military liaison to the U.S. Senate. It's a yearlong gig. Upton was thirty-three years old. It was 1999. There she caught the eye of Furman Morgan, who at the end of her rotation encouraged her to leave the military and take a job on his staff."

There was a pregnant silence. Senator Furman Morgan, the now-retired senator from South Carolina, had been a legendary "ladies' man" in his youth, as he would have been described back then.

"This was an older Furman Morgan," Conner said in response to the sardonic looks.

In his dotage, which went on a good while, Morgan eased into becoming an even more effective senator, a champion of minority rights, a bipartisan colleague, and even a gifted recruiter of talented staff, particularly strong women. Yes, they were usually attractive. But Morgan had mellowed in his old age and become a revered figure. He had retired just last year at age eighty-eight, seemingly in full command of his faculties.

"Then 9/11 happened," Conner said. "Upton had been a staffer for a little over a year. Morgan persuaded his new star aide to go back to Arizona and run for office herself. He told her the country needed more elected officials who understood the military. She then served two terms in the House before running for the Senate in 2006 and won her first time out. She's in her third term now."

"Look at her committee work," Rena said. "Where she might have come down hard on somebody, a special interest or an industry."

"Ang and I have it," Conner said, referring to the newest staff member, Ang Liu.

"What are her Senate committees?" Brooks asked.

"She sits on four," Conner said. "Judiciary, Finance, Armed Services, and Energy and Natural Resources."

"Heavy list," Brooks said. Some senators had three committee assignments.

"She's young and vigorous."

"And she chairs the subcommittee of Finance on taxes."

"Jeezus," said Smolonsky from Tucson. "That's a lot of chances to make enemies."

Jonathan Robinson, the former political consultant, said, "Well, she's tough on corporations hiding profits overseas, and on exotic tax maneuvers. So she has antagonized some on Wall Street. She bucks the party on women's health and climate change, though she's quiet about it. She's a big champion of small business over large corporations. And she believes in using the tax code to motivate behavior—not regulation. That puts her at odds with the antitax crowd in the party and the Democrats who want regulation because they can't get Republicans to vote to do anything but cut taxes. Hell, who does that leave out as potential enemies?"

Rena wanted to keep spirits up: "Maureen and Ang, don't skip over those two years before she actually ran for office—when she was a Senate aide. I think it's a porous moment."

"A porous moment?" Liu asked.

"A time in someone's life when they might have relaxed and opened themselves to others—shared secrets," Brooks said. "Usually a moment of transition, making new friends. Congressional staffers gossip with each other, and there are a lot of them. You meet a lot of people all day. You have a lot of friends who in turn have a lot of friends. And Upton was still pretty young. Thirty-four, thirty-five"

Jobe said: "And she wasn't as responsible for her sister anymore. She had left the military, too. If she was going to let loose, try things, or let her hair down with people, she might have done it there."

"Porous moments," Liu repeated.

"You look for change in a life, a wrinkle, a bump, a vibration, an acceleration," Rena explained. "People have patterns, though they may not know it. Look for a moment where the pattern involves slowing down or speeding up, or some break in the pattern itself."

Brooks added one more piece of counsel: "We look for adjacency to bad people, too, people in their lives who went on to become notorious. Were there ever any of those near the subject? That's what we mean when we say we are looking for sources who might be selling bad stories about someone."

They were teaching Liu the methodology of suspicion, techniques for uncovering secrets that Rena, Brooks & Associates had developed over a decade. Liu looked intrigued.

"It's not as predatory as it sounds," Rena said. "These are often the moments when people are at their best."

Brooks tried to wrap it up: "I know everyone was up most of the night. So take a couple hours if you need them. Get some sleep. When you come back, look for anything that sticks out in the areas you've been assigned. Any bumpy stones. Turn them over. And put everything into the Grid," Brooks added. "I've opened up a new version for this case."

The Grid was a digital system Lupsa had built to track their work. It broke down all the key elements of any investigation into categories that could be easily sorted and compared, and put everything the team learned into one document. The Grid helped them share information faster, spotted contradictions between conflicting accounts, and protected them against falling in love with a single theory while ignoring dissonant facts later.

"We have two Grid documents at the moment," Brooks said. She touched her computer and the screen on the wall popped to life.

On it she showed the two easels they had looked at yesterday, now in a trackable digital form. The first document was called "Possible Blackmail Incidents/Upton BIO."

"This one breaks her life into periods when there might have been some incident that could be used against her. But again, I think the later years will be more likely."

On the screen was a series of tabs, electronic file folders, each one labeled with a time in Upton's life:

Tavern Years, age 16–20
College and Law School, age 20–26
Military-JAG, age 27–32
Senate Staff Years, age 33–36
House Member, age 36–39
Senator, age 40–53

"As you go through, fill in anything you think might be a possible incident or period of vulnerability."

The next document was named "Possible Blackmailers."

Most of the tabs contained the names of each of the people campaigning for president. Underneath those, in subtabs, were the names of key players in the campaigns, PACs, major donors, consultants, and other kingmakers.

"These folks working for or supporting each of the candidates are people who themselves might be suspects," Brooks reminded the team. "When we're looking at the potential blackmailers, the question is who benefits from hurting Upton and why?"

After meeting with McGrath yesterday, Rena and Brooks considered the candidates themselves unlikely blackmailers.

"It may be campaigns. It may be someone who is not directly tied to these campaigns. And our list may be wrong. We may have knocked people off it who should be on it."

And there was room for more tabs. The Grid could be unlimited.

For now, Rena thought, what was projected on the screen mostly documented how little they knew.

"Ellen will curate," Brooks said, meaning that Wiley would be checking to see what everyone posted in the Grid, both about possible blackmail incidents and possible blackmailers.

AS PEOPLE FILED OUT, Rena asked Smolonsky to stay on the line. "Walt, keep your head up out there. See who else is in town."

This was the other way to track who might be after Upton: find who was nosing around Tucson, if there were any private investigators or lawyers asking questions lately, and see who had hired them in the past—in effect, reverse engineering someone else's oppo. They might find investigators working for Traynor and Bakke. But they might just catch the blackmailer by finding the people the blackmailer had hired.

National investigative firms out of Washington and other major cities kept former law enforcement people around the country on retainer. You want to know something about people on the ground? Tap your local contact in whatever city. These local folks usually know everyone in town who could get you an answer.

So what local ex-cops or new rent-a-cops were poking around Tucson and Phoenix, looking to end the bright and rising career of Wendy Upton?

"On it," Smolo said.

"And go see that goddamn worm of a finance chair who passed on the threat," Brooks said.

FOURTEEN

TUCSON, ARIZONA

Jerry Farmer bore the unhealthy look of a man who got too much of his nourishment and hydration at political fund-raisers.

The finance chairman for Wendy Upton's last Senate campaign had a pallid, precancerous complexion and a quick smile. At the moment, Farmer's smile made it quite clear he had no interest in talking to Walt Smolonsky.

Smolo had shown up at Farmer's office without an appointment and with a message, for Farmer's secretary, that he was here from Washington on behalf of Senator Wendy Upton. When Farmer emerged from his inner office, it didn't help his mood that Smolonsky was six five and about 240 pounds.

"Come inside," the fund-raiser said, adding a glower for his secretary.

He closed the door: "I told the senator's people I didn't know anything."

Smolonsky took a chair that wasn't offered.

Farmer, who'd apparently intended to stand, moved around his desk reluctantly and sat down.

"Yeah, that was a strong move," Smolo said, "calling the senator, dropping the bomb, and saying don't call me back."

Farmer was in commercial real estate, and from the look of the office he was good at it.

"What do you want to know?" Farmer asked. He was pouty. As if Smolo's presence hurt his feelings.

For reasons Smolonsky never fully understood, people often imagined large men to be stupid. And sometimes, to get what he needed, it could be helpful to make them think they were right.

But the better play with Farmer right now was to employ every inch and pound Smolo had in straight-on belligerence.

"I want to know who the hell called you. And who called them."

Farmer laughed.

"I don't know who called them. But I made a promise not to betray the confidence of the person who called me."

"Really? You made a promise? You're making this about loyalty?"

Farmer tried to look offended. He said:

"Who do you think you are, coming in here like this?"

Smolonsky got bigger in his chair.

"You have my card there. I'm a guy who finds things out that people try to hide. You don't have anything to hide, do you, Jerry?"

Farmer frowned and said, "You can tell Wendy I don't appreciate being muscled."

"I bet she's pretty interested in what you appreciate."

At this, and perhaps the recognition that United States senators were still feudal lords in their own states, Farmer changed his tack. He glanced at the card to make sure he had Smolo's name right.

"Look, Walt. See this from more than one perspective. I don't know where this is coming from. The guy who called me is a donor. Someone who gives money. And a lot of it. And persuades other people to give money, too. That's an important relationship. For me and for Wendy."

Smolo said nothing. Farmer kept talking.

"The guy who called me isn't the one making the threat. He's passing the warning along, passing it to me to pass to Wendy. He thinks he's doing her a favor. And the guy who called him was just passing it along. You understand? This was handled. Insulated. So the people behind it were protected."

Smolonsky sighed. "If he really wants to do Wendy a favor, your friend should call the senator himself and tell her everything he knows and everything he suspects. Like you should, right now."

Farmer looked exasperated.

"You guys in Washington really don't live in the real world, do you? This is my state. My city. And Wendy isn't the only person we raise money for. And to be blunt, these relationships back here, they keep going—even after Wendy has moved on. People in politics come and go. The money in a state, that goes on for generations. Everyone has their role to play."

"Even you," Smolo said.

"And you," said Farmer. But the look underneath it was worried. "Call Wendy. Tell her I wish I could help her. But I don't know anything."

"You can count on it."

BROOKS WAS GONE from the office when Smolo called, but Rena was there.

"The guy is terrified," he said.

He tried to explain. "Look, Upton might seem politically invincible to people in Washington, having won all her Senate campaigns easily. But I saw something else in this guy's body language. He tried to look tough. But he couldn't hide it."

That morning, as they walked through Upton's life, Wiley had told them that the hard-right Arizona Common Sense Coalition had mounted a primary challenge in Upton's last campaign. Her opponent, a local radio talk show host named Cal Carter, had campaigned on Upton being a "Rino"—Republican in name only—soft on abortion and "in the pocket of the vaccine industry." Upton had beaten him by thirty points.

But the visit to Farmer told Smolo the ground in Arizona was shifting more quickly and acutely than you could see from back in D.C.

"Something's scaring this guy," he said. "And not just because some rich donor passed along a threat. Something's going on out here. I've got a bad feeling, Peter."

Smolo was a superb investigator, Rena thought, but his friend was also emotional, and his emotions could sometimes slow him down.

"Then we don't have a minute to waste, Walt. Go hard."

FIFTEEN

DALLAS, TEXAS

Matt Alabama liked to stand in the crowd at political events he covered, not in the pen with the traveling press corps. Standing on the floor of the auditorium, he could view the rally from the perspective of the average person in the audience. He liked to move around, too, so he could see up close how different people reacted to certain moments.

Congressman Omar Fulwood bowed his head, closed his eyes, and paused for a moment.

This was the correspondent's favorite part of Fulwood's stump speech—the anecdote in which the young Philadelphia congressman recalled his grandmother teaching him how to respond to cruelty and prejudice when he was a boy.

"She would get down on the floor with me, but she wouldn't take me in her arms and comfort me. No, she wouldn't do that. Instead, she would gently take me by my shoulders and stand me up straight." Fulwood would take his imagined self by the shoulders. "And she'd say to me, in her stern, loving way, 'Always remember this, Omar: You belong. Just as much as anyone else. It's your school, too.'" Fulwood would release the imagined boy and look back at the crowd.

"Later, when I was older and I was complaining about something, she'd give me that same look and say: 'Remember, O. It's your country, too. You don't need permission or special favors."

Fulwood didn't always use the story or tell it the same way. He would shift the emphasis depending on the crowd, adding or omitting different facts, though the basic story remained the same. But he talked about his strict, loving grandmother whenever he thought his followers needed a little tough love—some admonishment for expecting the government to give them too much.

It was a pleasure, Alabama thought, to see a candidate lead audiences rather than just pander to them. It was one of the many things he was beginning to like about Omar Fulwood.

The congressman was a tall, physically imposing light-skinned black man with a faint spatter of freckles on his cheeks. He was more handsome in person than on camera and not as soft looking. People who met him were surprised to see he was large enough to have played tight end in college.

He had made his mark in Congress quickly by finding issues where he and a handful of rising young Republicans shared common ground. Prison reform. Welfare reform. Fulwood had bonded with three young religious conservatives over their deep Baptist roots and their love of music. The Philly native had done a *Desert Island Discs*–style podcast with Rep. Elwood Cochran of South Carolina. They had to choose ten songs they could agree on if they had to live the rest of their lives together stranded on an island. When they were asked which among those ten they would choose if each could have only one, Fulwood had chosen "A Change Is Gonna Come" by Sam Cooke. Cochran, a white former army chaplain, had chosen "The Dock of the Bay" by Otis Redding. Not so far apart.

Fulwood probably wasn't ready to be president, Alabama thought. House members rarely make the jump directly—James Garfield was the last to have done it. And young Omar's candidacy was hanging precariously. He'd shifted pretty hard to the left to run, a calculation to excite primary voters. He was more moderate a congressman than he was a candidate. But it hadn't entirely worked. After coming in fourth in Iowa and New Hampshire, he'd managed third in Nevada and tied for first in South Carolina. Fulwood needed "a clean win somewhere and fast," the *Wall Street Journal* had declared, probably next Tuesday, when eight states were up, including California, Texas, Massachusetts, and Virginia.

Two candidates stood in his way. Maria Pena had the progressive momentum. Billionaire Senator David Traynor of Colorado was leading Cole Murphy in the battle for the party's center.

"You belong, too," Fulwood was telling the crowd—quietly, almost intimately. "We belong together." He let the phrase hang. "Our nation is its greatest, we are only truly strong, when we recognize those values that bind and unite, not divide us. That means the most fortunate among us need to recognize we are stronger when we all rise. Yes, they will need to pay more. History is clear that when the gaps are too great, we all suffer together."

This was the meat of Fulwood's message: He wove a picture of a place where even people who disagreed felt comfortable. Then he explained how to get there together. It was a message of racial unity mixed with economic redistribution. But it was not as angry as Pena's message, or as vengeful.

"What are those shared values that bind and unite us? You know them. We all do. They are enshrined in our holy Declaration of Independence, in our Constitution and our laws." He offered a careful, clever list:

"The right to pray as we want, believe as we want, speak as we want. The right to be equal under the law, and to protect ourselves from government interference. The right to have the chance to become whoever we are capable of being, regardless of the color of our skin or the size of our bank account. This is the gift our founders gave us. Who among us would say no?"

This year, when politicians were peddling anger, tribalism, and revenge, Fulwood was trying to argue for economic justice but make it sound like self-interest properly understood.

It was especially powerful coming from an African American, Alabama thought. For Fulwood represented something rare at the top of American politics, though few recognized it. While black politicians had risen to the top before, often they had atypical African American stories. They were people of mixed race or privilege or both. Not Fulwood. He was a great-great-great-grandson of slaves, raised middle class by a postal worker father and bookkeeper mother. His ancestors had come here in chains, not by choice, and epitomized the great dark stain of the America myth—the fact that "these truths we hold as self-evident," including equality under the law and equality of opportunity, were lies. If Fulwood were successful, if he made it to the presidency with his message of belonging, he would touch that lie, wash it away a little, in a way no other American political figure ever had, including no black American president. If the descendant of slaves could rise and become the Jeffersonian ideal of the American intellectual statesman, then maybe the country really did work as it was supposed to.

He was arguing, in much the same way author James Baldwin had two generations ago, that the only way for America to move ahead was through one Americanism.

The message was probably too subtle, and it had not sparked the same momentum as Maria Pena's more explicitly racial calls for economic justice or David Traynor's promised fantasy that the billionaire entrepreneur was going to "fix" what was broken and create new alliances. But it was Fulwood's message, Alabama thought, that connected the ancient chords of American memory to the current moment.

Fulwood's events featured troupes of young volunteers who called themselves the We Team. These young people, aged fifteen to twenty-five, were recruited and organized through social media and chat apps managed by Fulwood's campaign. At rallies they stood together wearing distinctive blue T-shirts with WE TEAM emblazoned in red and white. The teams were usually situated on one side of the auditorium where they could be easily seen by the crowd and the cameras. And they were a distinct visual element of Fulwood's rallies, a hundred or more fresh faces of all races and creeds standing together. And whenever possible, the We Team was majority white.

Matt Alabama didn't see the skirmish start or the first punches thrown. Being on the floor with the crowd, he didn't have the panoramic view of the journalists in the pen. He first heard someone near him call out, "Oh, no." Then he saw someone pointing. People shooting videos of Fulwood's speech on their phones began to aim their cameras at the growing melee.

A few were close enough to pick up some audio. Police later would distinctly make out the words, "Get the fuck off me, whitey," but were unable to find any visual footage to establish who exactly had uttered them. The video images were striking because of how many people in the We Team seemed to be engulfed in the chaos. There appeared, tragically, to be a racial dynamic to the violence. White We Team members were fighting with black. Fulwood's attempts from the podium to quell the violence proved useless. He sounded weak and a little pathetic, frankly, repeating the word "please" over and over, a point that critics taunted him for in the coming days.

It took security and police to finally restore any semblance of order to the rally, which by then was a shambles. The news media never settled on just a single term to describe what had occurred. But national talk radio host Dash Zimbalist called it a race riot, picking up the phrase from the conservative conspiracy website True Flag, and that characterization got wide circulation. Footage of those five minutes would come to define the short-lived campaign that winter of Omar Fulwood.

Police would make arrests, the second campaign event in three days to feature them. Pena's event two days ago, the brick thrown at Bakke yesterday. There would be the debate tonight. This was not just some change in tenor. It was not easy to penetrate a campaign rally. There were security and metal detectors and guards. This took planning. This, Alabama, thought, was something else.

SIXTEEN

CAPITOL HILL
WASHINGTON, D.C.

Washington was a funnel, and the higher you went the more secrets you knew. Rena and his political communications expert Jonathan Robinson were trying to jump to the top of the funnel.

They were sitting in a small conference room in the offices of Senator Llewellyn Burke. At the table with them was Phil Hurd, the consultant who'd run Upton's last campaign and contracted to produce the oppo book to protect Upton during that race.

Next to Hurd sat the former Senate majority leader Susan Stroud, the woman who, until last fall, had held one of the highest parts of the funnel of power and money in her hands.

Stroud had risen from the Biloxi city council to the U.S. House of Representatives and then the U.S. Senate. There, aided by an intense focus on detail, the patience of the saints, and a superior understanding of the male psyche, she rose to become the first female Senate majority leader in American history. She held the job for ten years.

Late last October, however, the changing nature of the Republican Party caught up to her. To protect a valuable national security secret, Stroud had limited the reach of congressional hearings probing a terrorist attack in Africa. Some conservatives on her right had hoped to use the hearings to weaken President Nash and thus, in theory, help the GOP in the next election. After Stroud did what she thought best for national security rather than politics, the party retaliated. The right wing in her conference mounted a coup, led by Dick Bakke, threatening to block all other legislation if Stroud remained leader. To almost everyone's surprise, she lacked the votes to stop them. She announced she would remain in the Senate until she retired at the end of her term, a little less than two years away. In her place, the GOP picked Travis Carter of Idaho, a coy and reticent man whose underlying ruthlessness—and true role in Stroud's demise—only began to fully reveal itself after he had come to power.

"Thank you, Susan, for this," Burke said as they began.

Stroud's presence was Rena's idea. He'd called Burke that morning and asked if he could get the former majority leader to do a favor for Wendy Upton. They wanted her to help them decode the dark money flooding the parties.

Robinson had prepared a slide deck that would help, illuminated now on a large monitor on the wall behind them. The first slide detailed the money traceable from big donors during the previous presidential campaign, three and half years ago.

Nineteen different people had each spent at least twenty million dollars in public "contributions"—more than a half-billion dollars. But that was only a fraction of the total money billionaires had spent trying to buy the last election. In all, the PACs and super PACs had amassed a war chest of $1.7 billion in 2016—the vast majority hidden in the dark 501(c)(4) "donor-advised funds." Some givers even created what the *Washington Tribune* called "ghost corporations," dummy organizations that bundled money on their own and in turn gave that to the PACs, which hid the donors even more.

There were few clear patterns in the list. There were two megadonors from Nevada, the Grantland family of Reno, who ran the biggest natural resources firm in the United States, and Trotter Cardoff of Las Vegas, the biggest casino chain owner in the world.

Stuart Sherman ran a hedge fund in San Francisco and gave to Democrats. Phil and Gwen Aiken of Illinois owned a packaging company. Wilson Gerard was a major Silicon Valley venture capitalist and owned a hedge fund whose trading strategy was completely algorithmic.

There was a diet store chain owner, an electronic stock trading company founder, real estate and entertainment magnates, and more hedge fund bosses.

Half the people on the list backed Republicans, half Democrats.

The only common denominator was that everyone on the list was a self-made billionaire.

There weren't as many people, Rena noticed, from the new digital economy. That group tended to be younger, and for some reason they weren't trying to personally influence the political system—not this way, though their firms now had huge lobbying efforts.

Robinson's second slide listed the PACs and super PACs—not the individual donors. It was a longer list, more money, almost all dark. Traditional PACs were bound by federal limits on how much of it someone could contribute, and donors had to be named.

But super PACs had no limits on the donations they collected and didn't have to list their donors. Technically, super PACs couldn't give money directly to a party or candidate, but that distinction had been rendered all but meaningless. The 2010 Supreme Court decision in *Citizens United* said money was equal to speech and began allowing these super PACs to do virtually anything they wanted. The ruling transformed politics in the United States almost overnight, turning super PACs and the billionaires behind them into the new true political power. The so-called experts were only beginning to try to trace the effects. Behind most of the super PACs was a major political consultant or professional strategist.

"There's more dark money on the Republican side," said Robinson, himself a Democrat, "because the GOP super PACs are better funded. But the Democrats are catching up."

Robinson touched a key on his computer. The next slide included three columns—the super PACs, the candidates to whom they gave, and, to the extent he and Ellen Wiley had been able to identify them, the donors associated with each PAC.

The people in the room knew the basics of how the system worked.

But seeing the figures in black and white—and how much money was really involved—was startling.

Rena asked: "Anyone on this list give money to stop Upton in her last primary?"

"There wasn't huge money against her," said Hurd, Upton's consultant from that race. "A group of right wingers called the Arizona Freedom Caucus worked against her. They got this talk radio guy, Cal Carter, to run. But it was pretty clear Wendy was going to win. So the big donors stayed away."

Burke turned to Stroud.

She had played this money game in spades as Senate majority leader. Stroud raised money for her own PAC and even more for an "affiliated" super PAC she controlled. That was part of the leader's job now—raising and bundling dark money and distributing it to loyal members of the party.

And it was the means by which congressional leadership imposed party discipline: hand out money to senators in tight races to help them keep their jobs. They, in turn, would be loyal to the leader.

Stroud had lost the job because she'd antagonized some of the billionaires who fueled the PACs.

"This is where we need your help, Susan," Burke said. He'd already shared the secret overtures to Upton about the vice presidency and the threat that had followed. Upton was a Stroud protégée.

"We need to know who on these lists—either the billionaires or the PACs—might hate Upton enough to threaten her," Burke said.

Stroud looked back at him uneasily.

"I know we're asking a big favor," Burke added in that plain, sympathetic voice people found so convincing. "Some of these people are friends and have been backers for years."

He gave her a look.

Burke and Stroud were people who made their living persuading even richer and more powerful people to help them. Now they were negotiating with each other.

"But we're trying to help a good person. A great senator. And you probably know better than anyone else who might have a feud with Wendy. I'm just hoping you might feel freer to help now."

Freer to help, Rena thought, because Stroud had been deposed. She no longer had to play the supplicant to these billionaires to maintain her power. She could now simply be a senator. A citizen.

And she was free to be candid, if she were willing to be, about secrets to which almost no one outside of the Senate majority leader, the Speaker of the House, and a handful of others were fully privy.

It was one of the paradoxes of Washington. Powerful figures rarely shared what they'd learned until after they were out of power. And even then, only a few did so. Their wisdom might have been put to use to help reform the system. The reason that so rarely happened was simple—and disheartening. Half of all former senators—and a third of House members—now became lobbyists after they left office. It was a legal scandal, a form of bribery, Rena thought. It should be outlawed. And it was equally split across parties.

It hadn't always been that way. In the 1970s, Rena had just learned, only 5 percent of former senators and Congress members became lobbyists. The revolving door from lawmaker to lobbyist, in other words, had increased by 1,000 percent in Rena's lifetime. No wonder people thought the system was rigged.

"I can only speculate," Stroud said.

It was a hint, Rena thought, that she would help them, but only to a point.

"I don't know of any true blood feud," she said.

Rena watched to see if Burke might stretch her willingness over the next few minutes. Stroud looked at the list of PACs and donors on Robinson's slide.

The most famous name belonged to the Grantlands, the first billionaires to play this game of trying to reshape politics in their own image on a grand scale. The family owned paper mills, chemical plants, and nearly anything else that involved turning natural resources into money. They were backing Bakke, but maybe, Rena thought, they had a grudge against Upton and had heard through their connections into Bakke's campaign that he was reaching out to her. Maybe they wanted to put an end to that.

"The Grantland family?" Rena asked. "Wendy sits on Energy."

"They're awfully public now about their agenda, even if most of their contributions are hidden," Stroud said. "It'd be a huge risk."

"Has she taken them on?"

"There are three Grantlands, and they don't see eye to eye on everything. The family cares mostly about fighting environmental restrictions and reducing government. But they're actually a little unpredictable after that. Different members of the family have different agendas. One of the three Grantlands would have to be going rogue, which would antagonize another sibling."

Stroud drummed her painted fingernails on the table. "And there are newer players who are becoming more aggressive," she said.

"Who?" said Rena.

"Trotter Cardoff, for one," she said.

Cardoff, largest owner of casinos in the world, was a major backer of Nevada governor Tony Soto's campaign, through a PAC called the Fund for American Freedom. But the PAC had contributions from scores of ghost corporations as well as individual donors.

Soto was threatened by Upton, according to McGrath's theory, because, like Soto himself, she appealed to moderates. But Upton would be a lot less malleable than Soto, which might be a motive for Cardoff to want her kept out.

"I'd watch out for Alliance for Liberty, too," Stroud said.

Alliance for Liberty was a super PAC set up by the hedge fund and Silicon Valley libertarian Wilson Gerard. It was backing Jeff Scott. So were the packaging company founders out of Illinois, Phil and Gwen Aikens, and another billionaire, Lewis Trice from Arizona.

The list of Jennifer Lee's backers was even longer. It had the richest of the PACs behind it, the American Future Fund. Her funders included six of the twenty biggest donors in the country, including the diet company magnate David Reynolds and Karl Sabanoff, whose sports stadium and entertainment complex development company was remaking the downtowns of cities across the country, though almost no one in the general public knew his name.

Cosmetics magnate Janice Gaylord had set up her own PAC with her own money, and then gotten friends and ghost corporations to contribute more. Seymour Millstein was among them. Millstein was the founder of d-trade, the online stock trading company.

And it wasn't just individuals. Scores of other powerful people and corporations were hidden inside the super PACs named on Robinson's slide. Some of these super PACs had amassed so much money, in one case nearly half a billion dollars, they were more important than the parties. That made some of the people who ran the super PACS powers unto themselves, as powerful as the billionaires. The super PAC behind the Lee family, the American Future Fund, was run by Steve Unruh, the political brains behind Jackson Lee's presidency. Would Unruh stoop to tactics like threatening Upton?

The billionaire Wilson Gerard had hired Rebecca Schultz to run his political operations. That made her a power, too. And at least one super PAC, the Club for Freedom, bundled several others into one mega PAC to multiply their influence even further.

Who among all these individuals and groups had Upton antagonized—if anyone? She sat on the committees on Judiciary, Finance, Armed Services, and Energy and Natural Resources as well as subcommittees on taxes and on international trade. That meant she influenced the federal bench, defense contracts, tax policy, and environmental regulation. Potentially, she could be in conflict—or, for enough money, in harmony—with almost everyone on Robinson's slide.

"You're going about this wrong," Stroud said. "If someone has a feud with Wendy, I don't know about it. Look at where she wields the most power."

"The Finance Committee," Burke said.

"Right," said Stroud. "Wendy's chair of the subcommittee on taxes. A subcommittee chair makes a huge difference. They can single-handedly alter policy."

"She ever tangle in subcommittee with anyone on this list?" Robinson asked.

The look on Stroud's face told Robinson his question was silly.

"You know the complexity of a modern tax bill? How many things get put in and taken out? If she made a blood enemy with something in a tax bill, she might not even know. But that's where I'd look first."

"Sue, let's look at this from another standpoint," Burke said. "Who on that list is aggressive enough to conduct oppo research and to make a threat? If Peter starts there, his team can try to match that person with something in subcommittee Wendy has done."

A pause, and Stroud turned and stared at Robinson's slide. She began slowly but started to talk more rapidly as her thoughts deepened. "Everyone talks about the Grantland family. I find them intelligent and reasonable. I'd look at Trotter Cardoff, Wilson Gerard, and Karl Sabanoff. Those three men, frankly, terrify me."

Burke nodded.

"I'd like to think about that more," she said.

Then, to no one in particular, she added:

"When I got to Washington, it was well after the so-called Watergate reforms, after they got rid of the seniority system and the old ways. But there were plenty of people still around from those times, so I heard the stories—about suitcases of money, about the power of the unions and the old lobbies. Back when most business was conducted in closed hearings, a lot of bad things happened. But you could also lie to a lobbyist, tell them you tried to get what they wanted and couldn't—when in fact you knew what they wanted was horrible and you'd never even try."

Stroud looked to see if her audience understood the setup. "Now that nearly all hearings are open, you play for the cameras, and every lobbyist and donor is watching to make sure they get what they paid for. And you're punished for compromising with the other party."

Stroud shook her head. "Every reform has its unintended consequences."

They were a quiet for a moment. Stroud went on.

"My first campaign, my average donation was fifty dollars. Now you raise tens of millions. As leader I raised hundreds of millions. And there are twenty lobbyists for every member of Congress."

"Money flows," Burke said, as if saying an amen, "to where it can have influence."

Stroud added: "And you know why it flows now? Because business knows it can make more money by changing the rules of the game in Congress than it can by competing in the marketplace. They can eliminate risk, get tax breaks, or consolidate so they can't possibly lose. And we've let them. Both parties have."

"What stopped them before?" Burke asked.

Stroud thought for only a moment. "Committee chairs," she declared. "They were powers unto themselves. And for all some of those old southern boys stopped progress—especially on civil rights—they were also a check against other powerful interests."

"I've heard stories," Burke said.

Stroud leaned toward him as if she were going to share a secret. "You know, Furman Morgan told me when he first got elected to the Senate in the 1960s, Sullivan Beauchamp, the Budget chair from Louisiana, kept his tombstone in his office, already carved, so everyone would know all he'd done."

Burke put his hand over his face to cover how hard he was laughing.

"The date of his death was still blank. And there was a little room at the bottom for what he still intended to do. You believe that?"

Burke was wiping tears from his eyes.

"Sitting in his office. He'd show it to you."

"Remember Sam Wainwright?" Burke asked. "Chairman of Armed Services before me?"

She nodded.

"He kept a plaque on his desk that said, 'The Lord Giveth and the Lord Taketh Away. And I am the Chairman. I am the Lord.'"

"Yes, he did." Stroud clapped her hands. "I saw it!"

Stroud's laughter seemed to restore her slightly.

Rena looked back at the half dozen major PACs and the names of the billionaires next to them on Robinson's slide. It included no committee chairs or elected officials, or even the chairpersons of the two national parties. In a list of the powerful institutions that would decide the presidency, they were now absent entirely.

SEVENTEEN

TUCSON, ARIZONA

Walt Smolonsky parked his rented Hyundai in front of Shiny's Tavern and Country Store, the bar and small grocery Wendy and Emily Upton had run as teenage proprietors.

Emily Upton still ran it. Smolo hoped he would find her inside.

He'd spent most of the day getting more frustrated. Since seeing Jerry Farmer, the unhelpful money bundler, this morning, he'd talked to the two county party chairs and other supposed friends of Upton's—always telling them he was vetting Upton for VP. All of them claimed to love Wendy. None of them knew anything bad about her. All of them seemed unnerved when talking about the state of the GOP in Arizona. All of them seemed unhappy. All of them wanted Smolo gone as quickly as possible.

He'd also met with a local private investigator in town named Phil Dixon. Backgrounding firms like Rena, Brooks & Associates usually had relationships with local PIs in different cities. The local talent, generally former law enforcement, could be another pair of investigative hands. They also could work fast. They were either answering questions they already knew answers to or asking old friends for help. Dixon, a former sheriff's deputy, might also be able pick up a sense of whether there were other investigators in town looking into Upton and maybe what they had looked into. If he were really lucky, Dixon might even pick up who those PIs were working for. But so far Dixon hadn't picked up traces of much of anything.

Shiny's looked like a saloon from a western movie. There was a railing outside where you could tie up a horse—if you had one. The exterior was made of tan adobe mud. And the neon sign that spelled out SHINY'S in red letters had a cowboy hat on top.

It was a few blocks past the tony edge of downtown that people now called Snob Hollow. Technically, Shiny's was closer to the Miracle Mile, the red-light district.

It was a little early for drinking, just after 2 P.M., but five men sat at the bar, and a silent boozy couple held down a booth. The place was mostly dark wood, preserved under years of varnish. And under the varnish, years of initials, names, and cryptic messages carved into the wood.

"Looking for Emily," Smolo told a bartender who had more visible tattoos than years likely finished in school.

"Who?"

"Emily Upton. The owner."

"No, pops, who are you?"

Pops? Christ, Smolo, thought. *I'm forty-five.*

"I'm from Washington, D.C. I work for her sister, the senator."

The man stopped drying glasses and gave one of the patrons a look, as if Smolo had arrived from some outer galaxy. "Hang right there, Mr. Washington."

A minute later an attractive but tired-looking woman appeared from the back. She had dark hair and a wary expression. She wore a short skirt, cowboy boots, and a dark blue Mexican blouse. She stayed behind the bar and said she was Emily Upton.

Smolonsky introduced himself and added, "I like your music." Emily was a local singer and guitar player. Smolo had found videos on YouTube.

"Came all the way from Washington for my sister and looked

me up online so you could say something nice?" she said. "Who are you really?"

With a sheepish smile that wasn't working, he went through it all again, including a business card. "My company does background and investigative work. Your sister hired us." He leaned toward her and whispered. "And she's in trouble. Is there someplace we can talk?"

After a few seconds to think it over, she nodded toward an empty booth and came out from around the bar to join him.

She was forty-seven, he knew from the file, six years younger than her half sister, but she looked older. Up close she had a more innocent cast to her face than Wendy. But she did things, like the dark eyeliner around the eyes, to make herself look tough.

"Your sister has been threatened. And I've come to Tucson to try to figure out what it's about."

Emily didn't look surprised, but Smolo couldn't tell if that suggested she knew something or that nothing much surprised her.

"And you think I can help?"

"You're her sister."

"Half."

"You aren't close? You don't talk?"

"Talk? Every Sunday, same time. She's like a clock, my sister. She's nothing," she paused, "if not scheduled."

"Who'd want to hurt her? Maybe someone here in Tucson. From long ago."

To avoid answering, Emily Upton called out to the bartender: "Brett, a club soda." She looked at Smolonsky. "You want anything?"

"Club soda sounds great."

"Two," she called.

"Tell me who might want to hurt her," Smolo pressed.

Emily gave him a long look. "She's a stubborn girl, my sister. Always gets her way. I'd start with the people she beat in life. From the government in town to the people she ran against. Look at the losers in Wendy's life."

Why, Smolonsky wondered, did no one want to help Wendy Upton? Even her sister?

Two club sodas appeared, but they didn't come from Brett the bartender. A girl, about eight, with a mop head of brown curls, carried the two glasses perched on a black circular bar tray. Her eyes poked out over the tray at about the height of the booth table.

"Hey, thank you," Smolo said to the two eyes. "Who are you?"

There was no answer for a second, and then the eyes blinked and a voice from underneath the tray said, "Harry. Short for Harriet. And these are on the house, because you're with the proprietor."

"Oh, am I?"

Emily watched the girl who called herself Harry. "That okay, Mom?" the girl said. "Or you want this gentleman to pay?"

Emily looked seriously at the girl before a smile began to appear. Smolo liked the smile, and began to like Emily a little more.

"I think that is okay," she said to the girl. "This is my daughter, Harriet. Harriet, this man works for Aunt Wendy."

"How do you do?"

"I do okay," Smolo said. "How about you?"

"I do okay, too," said Harriet.

Smolo laughed. "I bet better than okay most of the time."

The girl put the two club sodas on the table and scurried back to behind the bar.

"You grow up in a bar, you learn to talk to grown-ups. You get good at banter. You can talk to anybody."

"That true of you and Wendy?"

"In different ways," she said. She was softening a little.

"So talk to me, Emily. Help me. Someone is threatening your sister, and I feel like no one here back home wants to help."

Emily Upton looked at Smolonsky longer this time and seemed to nod her head slightly.

"Mr. Smolenzky?"

"Smolonsky. Walt. Or just Smolo."

"Okay, Mr. Walt Smolo. If you work for my sister and do investigative background work in Washington, then you already know about her political enemies. What do you really want? You have five minutes."

So Smolo finally asked the question he had come to ask.

"Has Wendy ever done anything in her life that someone could use to hurt her with? She ever crossed a line? Maybe way back."

Emily seemed to harden again. "My sister and I are very different. But I wouldn't hurt her. We're the only family either of us has."

Surprised, Smolonsky said, "I didn't mean you were threatening her. Is that what you thought?"

She stared back at him, wavering, Smolo sensed, about how much to help versus not getting involved. He wondered why.

"Has someone else been here?" he asked. "Trying to find things out about your sister?"

She shook her head. "No. No one has been here." And with a sigh she said, "Look, Wendy and I have different lives. I just want to stay out of hers."

"I need your help," he tried one last time. "No one claims to know anything. And I don't have a lot of time."

Emily held his gaze but didn't offer much more. "My sister was a child hero around here. She took on the government and won, raised her orphan sister, put herself through college and law school, and then slew dragons in the army. Everyone in Tucson loves her. Even Democrats."

"Not everyone," Smolo said.

"Well, I can't help you. And your time's up."

Upton finished her soda water with one long gulp, slid out of the booth, and headed toward the bar without a look back.

AS HE SAT IN HIS RENTED HYUNDAI, the day swam around in Smolo's mind—Emily, the finance guy Farmer, and the others he had seen—

an old law school classmate, the county Democratic and Republican Party chairs, and a college friend. He made another call to the local PI, Dixon, who didn't answer.

He called Rena and walked through his frustration.

"Tell me more about the sister," Rena said.

"She thought I suspected *her* of threatening Wendy. And seemed to want to have as little to do with her sister as possible."

"Why would that be?" Rena said.

"It's a weird vibe out here, Peter. The money guy, Farmer, is terrified. The sister is surly. The party people love Wendy because she wins and hate her because she's hard to control. They're all in politics and they all seem to hate that, too. The kingdom of Wendy Upton back here in Arizona is an unhappy place. I feel like she is barely known to the people she is supposedly close to. She's powerful, admired, brave, and extraordinary. She might even be president one day. But it feels like she doesn't have a lot of friends. Not real ones. At least not here in Arizona."

Rena was quiet on the other end of the line, thinking. He thought of the woman he had met by the river the day before, of her toughness and resolve, and the woman who had bucked her party to help the president last year. And felt a sense of loneliness.

EIGHTEEN

Rena didn't dwell on the feeling. He didn't have time. He and Hallie Jobe had someone else from Upton's past to see.

They were meeting with Henry Nelson, Wendy's mentor in the Judge Advocate General's Corps, JAG.

Though she didn't champion it much in her campaign biography, Upton had become a reformer in the military over treatment of sexual harassment cases. And according to what Jobe had learned, she had pulled Colonel Nelson along with her.

"Guy's got quite a story of his own," Jobe said as they drove across town to see him. "He was chief prosecutor of the army. Huge job. And he blew it up."

Rena, who had blown up his own army career and knew Nelson a little, gave Jobe a look asking for more. "Apparently," Jobe explained, "Wendy really opened his eyes about how the military dealt with these cases. Nelson became even more of a crusader than she was."

Some of the details were coming back to Rena. "But he pushed too hard," he said.

"To put it mildly," Jobe said. "After he didn't get the reforms he wanted from the commander of JAG and the joint chiefs, Nelson went over their heads to the secretary of defense. Total breach of the chain of command." Jobe, an ex-marine, was shaking her head in disbelief. "That pretty much ended his military career. About seven years ago. Guy was on track to become head of JAG himself."

"What do we expect to learn from him, Hallie?"

"I want to find out who in the military might hate Wendy Upton enough to help destroy her," she answered. "Or, maybe, whether Nelson himself might be holding a grudge."

"Why would he do that?"

"He blew up his career," Jobe said. "Maybe he blames her."

"He going to tell us that?"

"No, Peter," Jobe said. "You are going to do your mystical thing and see it in his face with your X-ray intuition. Then we can wrap this up. I have plans this weekend."

NELSON WORKED FOR A NONPROFIT NOW that provided legal counsel to victims of sexual harassment in the military. His office was in Southwest D.C., across the street from JAG headquarters. In effect, he now spent his time fighting the institution he had devoted his life to.

Jobe opened hard. "Who would want to destroy Wendy Upton?"

All they'd told him ahead of time was they were working for her and needed to talk to him urgently. Rena watched his reaction.

"You think I know something that could hurt Wendy?" Nelson asked.

"That's what we're here to learn. Do you?" Rena said.

Nelson was tall and lanky and had grown a goatee since leaving the service. But the ramrod-straight military bearing remained. And his eyes burned, a window into a roiling heart. He was looking back at them, already angry. Who was he furious at?

Rena and Nelson also had history, a couple cases Rena had investigated in the army and Nelson had declined to prosecute. Another he had lost. And they had different styles. Nelson, famous for not suffering fools lightly, rarely held fire. Rena tended to share his thinking only when he believed it served a purpose. It was not a good chemical bond.

"Do I know something that could hurt Wendy Upton? Absolutely not. And if there were anything, I would never share it."

Rena held Nelson's gaze. Then Jobe came between them. She asked Nelson to tell them about his work with Upton and how she had come to change his views of the military and sexual harassment.

"You know how JAG attorneys work, right?" Nelson said. "That they work both sides of the street?"

Jobe's question already had focused him on something other than his dislike for Rena.

They nodded.

In military court, unlike civilian, an attorney might represent a defendant in one case and serve as prosecutor the next. Everyone wore a uniform, and the goal was the integrity of the military.

"Well, Wendy was a superb lawyer, diligent, prepared, aggressive. For both sides. And early on she defended a lot of male officers accused of sexual misconduct. But at a certain point she decided she could only prosecute those cases."

"Why?" Jobe asked.

"Because she concluded the women bringing these accusations, the victims, were almost always telling the truth."

"And why'd she think that?"

"Because they *are* almost always telling the truth." Nelson's voice rose.

"Look, it's absurd to think many women cry rape and pursue false allegations against men out of revenge, or some feeling of regret, or to enhance their own self-esteem. In real life, bringing a charge of sexual misconduct is a horrific process. That's why most assaults are never reported."

Jobe was listening. Rena could see she wasn't sure what to make of Nelson.

"But that presumption, that women will accuse men unjustly, is embedded in military law—even more than civilian. Accusers can be ordered to give repeated pretrial interviews and depositions to the defense. And unlike in civilian court, defendants at trial can call friends to provide 'good character' evidence, which, by itself, if done well, can raise reasonable doubt for acquittal."

Nelson spoke with precision and authority. It was easy to imagine him a fierce courtroom advocate.

"When Wendy came to say she no longer wanted to defend sexual harassment cases, only prosecute, you found a way for that to happen?" Jobe asked.

"And that," Nelson said, "was when she went from being a good lawyer to being a great one."

"You didn't recognize these problems in the system before?" Rena asked.

Nelson gave him a hard look back. "Wendy saw injustice I should have recognized years earlier. Decades before. That is one of the things Wendy does. She notices things other people miss, and she makes you notice them, too."

Jobe glanced at her notes. "But she didn't just stop defending cases, did she? She also began to advocate for changes."

Nelson was nodding. "You have to understand how tilted the system was. Accusers in these cases had no counsel of their own. The commanding officers on base not only convene all court-martials, but as the convening authority they can overturn sentences, too. And too many commanders can't believe, or maybe don't want it known, that there are sexual predators in their command. So some of them may try to hide those cases, not prosecute them, or push for lighter sentences."

"When Wendy began to push to change that," Jobe said, "that didn't make her enemies?"

A smile of remembrance crossed Nelson's face. "Wendy has a way of making arguments that pull people with her. Of advocating in a respectful way and doing it through channels. And of only asking for changes she thought the military would make."

Rena, watching Nelson, said: "But you became impatient. Especially after Wendy left the military."

Nelson took a deep breath. "Maybe because I'd done more cases, or felt more guilt, or had less time left in my career. But yeah, I thought it wasn't enough." He was shaking his head now. "You know that 59 percent of women who report sexual harassment in the military also report being punished for doing so? I was part of that system. I had a duty to change it. You get medals in combat for giving up your life for your fellow soldiers. This, to me, is the same thing."

Nelson had changed things, and it had cost him his career. His outspokenness had helped make reforming military justice a major public issue. And in no small part thanks to his pushing, there were competing pieces of legislation in Congress to change the rules and impose restrictions on commanders' control over the outcome of cases.

"Did Wendy encourage you to become the radical she never was?" Rena asked.

"Still think I'm holding a grudge, Peter? No, just the opposite. She *discouraged* me. Told me I was committing professional suicide." He folded his hands. Rena thought he was, literally, trying to get hold of himself. "She was right, but I have no regrets. I would have regretted not acting."

"There's something you're not telling us," Jobe said.

Nelson scowled back. "What are you suggesting?"

"Your marriage ended, too. You blew up your career *and* your marriage. Did Wendy Upton have anything to do with that?"

The lawyer leaned back in his chair and gave out a deep breath. "You've heard that rumor."

"Yes," Jobe said.

"It's not what you think."

"You didn't have an affair with Wendy that ended your marriage?" Jobe asked.

Nelson was shaking his head. "You have it wrong."

Rena leaned toward Nelson and said in a soft voice, "We're trying to save her career, Henry. And we're just about out of time. We need to know everything. The truth."

"We never had an affair," Nelson said. "No matter what you heard." He was looking down, avoiding eye contact.

"But you loved her," Rena said.

Nelson's head stayed down. Then it slowly began to nod.

"Yes," he said quietly. "I was *in love* with her."

He looked up. "But I never told her. Or even touched her." He took in a deep breath and it seemed to make him shudder. "I know it sounds pathetic. But what I felt for Wendy—what I came to feel—made me realize what I didn't feel for my wife."

Then he exhaled for a long time. "I know how it sounds. To have those feelings and never . . . All this in my own head. An old man."

"Did she know?"

"I never asked," Nelson said. "I guess other people guessed."

Rena imagined Nelson, fifth-generation military, a man tightly bound to duty, finding someone in midlife whom he admired so much he changed everything—for a love unrequited. Or only imagined.

"I know," Nelson said. "A man blows up his career and his marriage because he's in love with a younger woman and never even tells her. But it's not like that. It's not sad." He took another deep breath. "Because I'm living my own life now, not someone else's. My life."

He went on. "Wendy has that effect on people, Peter. She looks more deeply at things than the rest of us. She saw what was wrong with what we were doing. And made me realize how little I saw. She really is extraordinary. I loved her for it." His voice cracked. "But it wasn't that kind of love, and eventually I realized that. I know it sounds pathetic, but it's not. And there's no scandal here. I will attest to that."

Rena said very quietly, "Not pathetic in any way, Henry."

Jobe wasn't so moved. "You still haven't told us who in the military might want to hurt her," she said. "We're still looking for enemies."

Nelson seemed to laugh to himself. "I can name my enemies in the service. And it's a long list. By comparison, I don't know that she has any. Maybe not a single one."

AFTERWARD, as she drove them to the office, down Independence, past Capitol Hill and the monuments, Jobe kept glancing at Rena. "You think he's holding something back?" she said.

Rena, lost in thought, said nothing.

"By the way, I'm getting married tomorrow," Jobe said. "To a goat."

"I always knew," Rena said. "But I don't judge."

"Just wondered if you were listening."

Rena stared out the window and said, "I think he's hiding nothing. I think he stopped trying to hide things years ago. After hiding them for years."

BROOKS WAS WAITING for them at the office.

They had a lot to catch up on.

Jobe described the meeting with Nelson. Rena recounted his morning with Susan Stroud—walking through the maze of billionaires and PACs.

"Our list of suspects keeps getting longer," he said.

"I think I can help a little," Brooks told them. She had spent the morning working the Democratic side, she said, meeting with election lawyers connected with three of the major Democratic campaigns, Maria Pena's, Omar Fulwood's, and Cole Murphy's.

"I was trying to find out if any of them had paid money to scrub Upton." Most opposition research was hidden in payments to law firms, which in turn would hire opposition research and private detectives on behalf of their campaign clients.

"No lawyer would ever confirm hiring someone to do that," said Jobe.

"Ahh, but they might confirm if they hadn't," Brooks said.

"And someone did," Rena guessed.

Brooks winked. "Give that man a prize." She was amped up—from exhaustion and a small victory. "I think we can strike Cole Murphy's campaign off our list of suspects. My friend Raney Levin's firm is doing all their campaign legal work, including funneling the payments for the oppo stuff. She wouldn't confirm anything they'd done, but she was willing to get her guys off the hook for this. She promised they hadn't looked at Upton."

"And you believe her?" said Jobe, who tended to be suspicious of everyone.

Brooks gave her a confident look.

"But no one else?" Rena said.

"And not for any goddamn lack of trying. I drank so much coffee today, I felt like I was studying for the bar exam all over again. I even ate pie with one of them, which I needed like a brain tumor."

"And?" Rena asked.

"And my friend working for Omar Fulwood said she honestly didn't know but might call me back if she has anything to share. I doubt she will. But my friend working for Maria Pena, well, he wouldn't tell me a goddamn thing. Guy's an asshole. A good lawyer; I'd hire him in minute. But he wouldn't tell me whether Pena had done opposition research on Upton or anyone else. Got all high and mighty. Prick. The ethics of being a campaign lawyer? Fuck me!"

Rena waited a beat for Brooks to calm down. "But you think Pena's people might be good for this?"

"If they got wind of Traynor's offer, I wouldn't put anything past them."

One of Pena's key arguments was that the left lacked a killer instinct. She had raised enough money in Hollywood and Silicon Valley to already be doing oppo research on every possible vice presidential candidate in both parties.

"So Pena stays on the list," Rena said.

Brooks nodded and said, "You ready for tonight?"

"What's tonight?" asked Jobe. "You're watching the debate?"

It was the night of the so-called bipartisan primary debate, which promised to be a chaotic and possibly ugly display, four candidates from each party onstage together.

"No," Brooks said, "we're sitting down with Upton. Time for a little intervention."

That was her term for getting in a client's face and scaring them into finally admitting the secrets they hadn't told you before. Tonight they would let Upton know what absolute hell she was really in.

Jobe smiled wanly at Rena. "Who doesn't like a little intervention?"

NINETEEN

NASHVILLE, TENNESSEE

It was the brainchild of the people at Y'all Post, the social media company, and BNS, the cable news channel.

Put people from both parties onstage together. Get them discussing the same questions. And maybe, just maybe, they reasoned, we can find our way back to some common ground.

Matt Alabama feared the bipartisan presidential primary debate might have the opposite effect. Candidates across parties might hurl even worse insults at each other than they would at opponents in their own party. But he tried to resist the journalists' instinct for expecting the worst.

People would watch—of that he had no doubt. The format was novel, and viewers would be curious how far the candidates would go. What was democracy, the organizers argued, if not a gathering of people in the public square?

The event was being held at Belmont University in Nashville. Alabama was upstairs walking past the classrooms in Struhman Hall that had been converted for the evening into "greenrooms" where each candidate could rest and prepare.

He paused outside the one with a handwritten sign on the door that read TONY SOTO. The room was assigned for the evening to the

Nevada governor. Below the sign with Soto's name was a piece of paper with a note: PSYCHOLOGY CLUB MOVED TO 204 TURNER. The door was closed. Alabama knew the young governor liked to do push-ups before debates to burn off pent-up energy.

Two doors down, a thick man stood guard outside the room where Michigan governor Jeff Scott waited. Scott preferred to sip red wine before a debate, something he had read Ronald Reagan was fond of. Closed doors and greenroom bouncers were common at these encounters. People running for president tended to prefer privacy before debates. And they usually despised running into one another.

There were more greenrooms one floor below, where Maria Pena, Jennifer Lee, and Janice Gaylord waited. It was the only floor in the building with women's bathrooms.

Alabama made his way downstairs, past the theater where the debate would occur, and walked into the large reception room next door. Inside, dozens of long portable tables were set up in rows, with names of publications and media outlets written on white placards. Spaced every ten feet or so apart on the tables sat television monitors. This was the temporary press room from which more than a hundred journalists and bloggers would watch the debate. As soon as it ended, no matter what had transpired in the theater next door, the candidates and their aides would rush here to claim victory. Over the years, that spectacle of absurd and grandiose claims had given these makeshift press rooms the name *spin rooms*.

To Alabama, *spin* was another word for lying. It was a polite word for it, which made it a dangerous one, and that was the problem. Somewhere along the line some clever political operative had used the euphemism *spin* to describe the lies that consultants told about their clients who had just puked on their shoes in debates. *My guy didn't really confuse Bosnia with Italy. And, if you skip that one part, he really kicked ass tonight.* And somewhere along the line, reporters had become so inured to the dishonesty, or dazzled by its sheer gall, they started putting the whoppers these consultants told in their stories—and putting the liars live on the air. And then somewhere along the line, someone on television had started using the word *spin* to mean something good. It wasn't lying anymore. It was the art of exaggeration. And little by little, lying was no longer something we decried. It became something we admired.

But language mattered, Alabama thought, and so did its abuse. Someone had to care what words meant, or they didn't mean anything.

He hoped he wasn't getting old and grumpy.

A few campaign operatives were already in the spin room, and reporters gathered around them like moths. The aides were trying to set "predebate expectations" for their candidates. "What we want to do tonight . . ." And "Watch for Maria to draw sharp distinctions between her and Omar Fulwood on . . ." And "All governor Scott needs to accomplish tonight is to mark once again . . ."

In the calculus of primary campaigns, it's hard to win a debate with more than two candidates onstage. It'd be harder, still, in this "bipartisan" configuration, where people running in two different primaries would be onstage with each other. But candidates can get their shots in against a targeted rival. And if their team sets reporters' expectations low and narrow enough, their operatives could always claim their side had done what it had come to do.

Alabama saw Steve Unruh, the former history professor who had helped Jackson Lee become president twelve years ago, standing alone watching the room. Unruh, now in his sixties, ran the biggest super PAC in the country, the American Future Fund, which was backing Lee's niece, Jennifer.

He wore a familiar scowl of concentration, as if he were seeing things others could not perceive. Alabama wondered if the famous frown tonight masked something less than a Zen master's grand plan.

Unruh was under immense pressure. He had raised an extraordinary sum to back Jennifer Lee, more than four hundred million dollars for the primaries alone, a war chest so large it was supposed to make the Jenn Lee nomination inevitable.

Yet the money was quickly disappearing in a haze of third-place finishes. If Unruh couldn't make good on his bet, his donors would abandon him. Worse, his life's vision of a Republican national majority for a generation, something to rival the Democrats' legacy from 1932 to 1968, might be doomed. Unruh dreamed of a GOP that was fiscally restrained, militarily muscular, and socially and racially tolerant. But voters were proving too angry, lobbyists too strong, and the government too dysfunctional to be reformed. Elections kept swapping power between the parties every four or eight years, oscillating the country's politics back and forth, the force of the pendulum swing growing more intense with each election as people grew more disappointed with each outcome. It felt like something was going to break.

Alabama headed into the theater and found his reserved seat. He preferred to see the event from the hall—unlike most reporters, who watched on television in the spin room—so he could observe the body language of the candidates off camera, and watch the reactions of their staff and families.

Not everyone was seated yet.

In a corner, he saw Bobby Means, the political strategist for Dick Bakke, talking animatedly on a cell phone. Alabama could not hear what Means was saying. Had he been able to, he would have heard Means berating Gil Sedaka, Wendy Upton's chief of staff.

"Stop giving me shit and calling it chocolate, Gil. Clock's ticking. So tell her we need a goddamn answer. By tomorrow."

"Give me another day," Sedaka was saying from back in Washington.

"Fuck you," Means said.

"You don't want to rush this, Bobby" Sedaka pushed back. "Nor do we. If it's a good marriage, it's worth another day to think about. Or two."

"I gotta go," Means said. "But if I don't hear from you tomorrow, this goes away. I'm not shitting you, Gil."

"Give me two days," Sedaka said.

Means hung up.

Alabama heard nothing, but he was intrigued by the angry pantomime.

THEN BNS ANCHORMAN JACK ANTHEM and Timbala Kuamba, director of community engagement at Y'all Post, were walking out onstage, asking the crowd to take their seats.

Alabama could see the candidates gathered in the wings offstage, standing in an uneasy line, in the order of their podiums.

A large red light pointing outward at the audience went on at the base of the stage, a signal that the broadcast had begun—online and on cable—and that the audience should be quiet.

"Welcome tonight to the first-ever bipartisan presidential primary debate," Anthem said. "I'm Jack Anthem of BNS, and tonight we make history."

There were eight debaters. The top-four vote getters in the first Republican contests: Jeff Scott, Dick Bakke, Jenn Lee, and Tony Soto. And the top-four vote getters in the Democratic: Maria Pena, David Traynor, Omar Fulwood, and Cole Murphy.

Fifteen minutes in, Kuamba asked the candidates to react to a particularly divisive issue, one that had started among activists on the GOP's far right but had gained unlikely sympathy on the far left of the Democratic Party, as well.

"What do you say to people who are part of the so-called Shut It Down movement, who argue Congress has become so dysfunctional we should have a new constitutional convention to reorganize the House and Senate and rethink our elections?"

Kuamba checked her notes. "Governor Soto, this question is directed first to you."

"Timbala, I appreciate the frustration people feel. I feel it, too."

Soto was always suave and pleasant. He had the look of the most handsome smart kid in high school.

"But I think it's a mistake to give in to fear and anger. I believe America's best days are ahead of us. My father came to this country from Cuba, my mother from Mexico, and they dreamed of a life in America in the 1970s when many people said, oh, that dream is over. Well, they kept dreaming. And their dreams came true. I share their dreams—and those of millions of American parents and children. If we can free people from taxes and bad regulations, modernize our immigration laws, we can do more than continue that American dream. We can expand it for the twenty-first century."

Alabama recognized the words and the music. They were Ronald Reagan's, remixed.

And Soto, graceful, appealing, and handsome, performed them with real emotion and a catch in his throat.

But they seemed out of time, Alabama thought, a pop tune from forty years ago. The audience knew the lines. But, even to those who had once sung along, they felt dated, like streaming a once-beloved movie that, seeing it now, you stopped watching before it was over.

"Governor Scott, what do you think of the Shut It Down movement?" Kuamba asked.

The governor of Michigan had always been careful before in his answers about this group, which had hints, at least on the edges, of armed insurrection. He smiled, almost shyly, but what a smile. "Well, the people behind this movement are right, Timbala," Scott said. "Congress *isn't* working. And, apologies to my opponents who work in Washington, but you are part of the problem. You've proven you're not the solution. I think a constitutional convention is worth thinking about. As Thomas Jefferson, said, 'a little rebellion now and then is a good thing.'"

The man was pandering to a scary fringe, Alabama thought. The Shut It Down movement was insane and dangerous. But its supporters all were likely to vote in the primaries. And Scott was pushing his support for them further than he had before.

Some Scott supporters in the audience were cheering, despite instructions for silence.

"Senator Bakke?" Kuamba said.

Dick Bakke seemed taken aback by Scott's answer. The Michigan governor had never endorsed a constitutional convention before. Doing so opened a new Pandora's box and pushed Bakke further than he might want to go. Alabama thought he could sense the gears turning, recalibrating, in Bakke's mind. Then: "We do need to listen, Timbala. More than that, we need to hear." Bakke was trying to appropriate Scott's answer in his own, one of the catechisms of debate tactics: if you are going to piss on someone's answer, first make sure you endorse it just enough that you don't alienate the audience that liked it. "And yes, I'm in Washington. So I know why Congress doesn't work. No one's made that case in the Senate more strongly than I have. I'm proud of the sentiments that animate the Shut It Down movement. I believe those sentiments exist in part because of criticisms I and a few others have raised about how things need to change."

Then a hard stare at Scott and a pivot. "But to the young governor of Michigan, I say, be careful what you wish for, young man. There is a huge difference between reform and insurrection. Some members of this group have suggested violence. That cannot be encouraged."

There were limits apparently on how far Bakke, a sitting senator and former Supreme Court clerk, would go.

"You quoted Jefferson, Mr. Scott; you might not know that President Lincoln was also an admirer of Jefferson. Lincoln had this to say about a similar time of unrest in U.S. history: 'Don't interfere with anything in the Constitution. That must be maintained, for it is the only safeguard of our liberties.'"

Bakke supporters stamped their feet and whistled. Then Bakke, encouraged, went too far. "I'm just going to say it, and say it plain. Governor Scott, you are a dangerous man. You lack the temperament and the experience to lead this country. You are a despot in the making! A vote for you would undermine our democracy."

"How dare you!" Scott said.

Jack Anthem was banging a gavel. "Gentlemen, please!"

"You're a damn coward, little Dickie!" Scott could be heard saying over the din.

They broke to commercial.

The order of speakers had been drawn by lot. The room still stirring, two Democrats came next, but the questions about the Shut It Down movement were not done. The answer by Maria Pena, the candidate furthest to the left politically, was in substance, Alabama thought, not that far from Scott's, if also less concrete.

"Shut It Down, no. We can't be without a Congress. But it makes sense to think fresh for the twenty-first century. How would the Founders plan a national legislature in the digital age? How could we not consider the prospect?"

She kept her answers short and direct—perfectly sized to be clipped on Y'all Post. David Traynor was now glaring at Pena, as Bakke had at Scott. They were competing for different wings of the Democratic vote. But Traynor recognized in Pena the candidate with the most innate talent. It was she, not the moderate Cole Murphy, with whom Traynor was becoming most concerned. He wasn't fighting Murphy for the center. He was fighting Pena for the party itself.

"I know I'm not supposed to talk to Maria directly," Traynor began. "And we've already seen a breach of the rules." He gave a restrained glance at Bakke and Scott. "But look, Maria, I break stuff for a living. That's what I did for twenty years. Reinvent the economy by building digital businesses. And, Governor, the Founders were extraordinary people in an extraordinary moment. I may have only been in politics a couple years. But I've learned this much already: the folks on this stage are not the Founding Fathers. And I don't pretend to be. The problem we've got in politics isn't that Alexander Hamilton, James Madison, and George Washington came up with a lousy system or didn't imagine the Internet. And the people outside this arena yelling 'Shut it down' aren't going to be coming up with something better. If you believe they will, I've got some old DVD players to sell you."

The audience laughed, and not just Traynor's people. Then the billionaire looked straight into the camera. "The problem we've got in Washington is the way the elites and billionaires and the parties have started to rig the system the Founders created. It's not a deep state like some people will tell you. But it sure is entrenched power. We need to fix that. But don't screw around with the Constitution, because we got ourselves all worked up. Let's keep our damn hands off the Constitution."

"You're right, David," Pena interjected. "Billionaires like you are exactly the problem."

The debate went on another hour, but the anger of these past few minutes seemed to have acted like a ray gun on the rest of the proceedings. And Jennifer Lee, Omar Fulwood, Cole Murphy, and Tony Soto seemed to fade into the background as time passed. Alabama considered Fulwood and Murphy the more interesting Democrats, and he admired the vision Lee tried to articulate about conservatism. But they could not contend in the format.

Mostly, Alabama felt unnerved. While the candidates had been debating for months, this encounter was supposed to be different, more important thanks to its timing and perhaps better because of the arrangement. Alabama had been skeptical. But what transpired left even him a little shaken. Debates had that ability, even after seeing scores of them. This evening felt debasing to him.

Debates were often extolled as a more authentic way of learning about leadership than the consultant-made ads or cartoon tweets that dominated the media now. It was presumed candidates would rise to the prospect of standing side by side and answering questions.

But the events had become another form of entertainment—and this one had proven the worst yet. The cable channels had become addicted to the ratings and revenues the evenings generated, the more tricked-up the format the better. Reality television skills had become a new proxy for leadership. And Alabama, who had spent a career in television, feared where that was taking the country.

It was an oversimplification, he thought, to blame voter anger. The whole political apparatus was culpable. But there was something uglier, some deeper anger, being exposed, like a family that no longer could abide itself. The public was dissatisfied with the country—not just politics. They were beginning to doubt whether America worked as an experiment. They were angry about their lives. They were angry about the people who disagreed with them. The whole notion of governing by letting everyone vote seemed broken. The answer wasn't to shut it down. But for the life of him, Alabama didn't have an answer.

As he wandered through the press room, watching the spin doctors operate, he spotted Steve Unruh standing by himself. The political strategist, who dreamed of a new era of enlightened, compassionate neoconservativism, had a different expression on his face than Alabama had seen earlier. The frown was gone, replaced by something else. It wasn't fear. More a look of shocked recognition, as if Unruh understood something he hadn't realized before. It was the same suspicion Alabama had sensed. That something in the country had shifted, and the nation wasn't taking a detour in its long journey as a democracy. Instead maybe it was headed down an entirely new road. Unruh recognized it now. Alabama saw it in his eyes. In the era of networked connectivity, foreign manipulation of social media, corporations without borders, and a global economy, maybe eighteenth-century notions of democracy had run their course. The proposition hadn't occurred to Alabama seriously before tonight. It did now.

TWENTY

WASHINGTON, D.C.

Peter Rena and Randi Brooks had not seen the debate.

They were busy with Wendy Upton and Gil Sedaka at Rena's town house—trying to shock the senator into understanding just how threatened she was and to discover what secrets she might be hiding.

Upton sat on the sofa in Rena's living room dressed in blue jeans and well-worn boots, her hair down in a ponytail. She looked smaller than usual, and more vulnerable. But she didn't look afraid.

Not as much as Rena wanted her to.

Sedaka, on the sofa next to her, appeared more unsettled.

Brooks and Rena sat on chairs arranged to face them, along with Ang Liu, whom they'd asked to come to take notes and to see how hard you sometimes had to push a client.

They were here for what they called their intervention, the moment when they leaned on a client harder than the client ever imagined possible. For every client hides something. Sometimes even from themselves.

Rena started:

"We're at the end of the second day, Wendy." Just first name, no honorific, no respect for the office. "We've done a biography of you." He explained how they had someone in Tucson looking into her early life, her friends, her sister. They were probing her military and political careers. It was important she know how thorough the invasion of her life would be.

"Tonight we need you to be more candid than you have been up to now." His voice was detached and a little threatening. "We need to go deeper to find out what you have done in your life that could be used against you."

Upton looked back at him impassively.

Rena and Brooks had heard people lie about most things. They had seen people try to hide affairs, drug addictions, sexual identities, even children out of wedlock. They had seen people try to hide habits that had spun out of control, like eating addictions or gambling. They had watched people virtually drive from their mind some terrible act so out of character the person had stopped believing it actually happened to them. They had heard all kinds of rationalizations.

To confront people about these things, they had learned to stage these encounters somewhere personal, in the subject's home if possible, to make these sessions more intrusive and to signal this was not just another work problem you dispatched at the office. Upton, who shared a town house with two other senators, had agreed to come to Rena's row house in the West End. Since his divorce from Katie Cochran four years earlier, the place had taken on the haphazard quality of a bachelor's home that didn't receive many visitors, though Vic Madison had helped Rena make the place more presentable. The cat Vic had given Rena, a large dark-gray British shorthair with striking golden eyes named Nelson, lay sleeping on a chair in the corner.

"Whatever is being used to threaten you, it may be something you did in politics. Something controversial or hypocritical. More likely it's something personal. A favor you did for someone that crossed the line. Or something sexual."

He let that linger.

"Perhaps the incident you are being threatened with comes from a former lover."

Wendy Upton was not married and was rarely seen out with men or women. In an early interview Wiley had unearthed, she was quoted as saying, "That part of my life has eluded me." She had been close to marriage once in the army, she allowed—the only reference to a romantic past they'd found. The relationship hadn't survived, she said, after the two lovers were assigned to postings in different countries.

Upton was still looking back at Rena saying nothing, which seemed to enrage Randi Brooks.

Randi leaned forward to the senator now and interrupted Rena. "You need to understand, Wendy, we're going to be here tonight for as long as it takes." A glance at Sedaka. "And at some point tonight, I am going to talk with Gil alone in the other room." She paused. "Any questions before we begin?"

Upton offered a dry smile. "I assume then you'll stop the dramatics?"

That only made Brooks testier. "I'll drop the dramatics when I feel confident that you're taking this as seriously as we are."

Upton finally seemed to react. "You don't think I'm taking this seriously? It's my life, my career." There was emotion now behind the hazel eyes. "What do I need to do to show you it's serious? Break down? Cry? Confess something? I'm sorry, I don't do that."

Brooks's shoulders pulled back slightly, and she said: "Okay. Then let's get started."

She rose from her chair so she could use her height. She planned, Rena knew, to be very hard, a sign of frustration but, in a way, also a show of respect for Upton's strength.

"Forget any research that was done on you in the past races. It was crap. The kind anyone could get online. Whoever's coming after you now, they paid real money. They hired detectives. They talked to people who hate you. Tracked down every old rumor about you. They've got your digital history—every Web page you ever looked at. Every bit of porn or hate. And we're doing that, too. And I'll tell you now, in our experience, if someone pays enough money, there is always something."

It was hard to know how a client would react. Brooks had seen cases where even a few days of serious oppo were enough to drive someone from public life. That was the case with a congressman from Utah last year who had been pondering challenging the incumbent senator. The incumbent asked his oppo team to take a look at the upstart. Just three days later, the team paused to give the senator a report. He, in turn, sent an intermediary to meet with the congressman. You're more than welcome to challenge the senator for his seat, the congressman was told. But you should know that after less than a week of digging we've got strippers and pills. Only you know what we will find next. "Strippers and pills" meant the congressman, a family-values conservative, was cheating on his wife and taking drugs of some kind. The congressman asked them for a week to think it over. Two days after that, he announced his immediate retirement from public life to "spend more time with my family."

The story had never come out.

On the other hand, Brooks had seen clients for whom no transgression was too great. She once had to tell a governor who had put his gay lover on his payroll that he now had to resign and recognize his public career was over. The man's wife and child were upstairs in the mansion while they met. The governor tried to argue that the scandal would be liberating; now he could live in the open as a homosexual, which would make him an even more effective champion of the oppressed, communities like the LGBTQ.

Finally Brooks told him to stop. We're paid to tell you the truth, she'd said. The truth is you married that woman upstairs, and even had a child with her, knowing they were a political cover story, brought a life into this world as a political lie. What you have done is immoral, and we will not stand by you. You cannot survive this and you shouldn't. The governor resigned the next morning, still believing he could go on.

Brooks looked at Upton and said, "Senator, are you a homosexual?"

TWENTY-ONE

Rena was watching Sedaka. The chief of staff looked like he didn't know how his friend would answer Brooks's question. Because he didn't know? Or didn't know how much she would reveal?

"If you're gay, Senator, or bisexual," Brooks was saying, "you need to tell us now. All the relationships you've had. And why you are not married."

In a quiet voice Upton said, "Love is a part of my life that has in large part eluded me."

The same phrase she had used in the interview Wiley had found.

It sounded both sincere, Rena thought, and rehearsed.

And it set off his partner even more. "I'm not a reporter for fucking Tucson.com, Wendy," Brooks said. "So cut the bullshit. You told me when this began that you wouldn't be intimidated by whoever was doing this. Then don't be. That means we have no secrets here tonight. Or we are done with this and you walk out the door."

Upton cupped her hands in front of her, closed her eyes, and said, "I had a relationship in the army. In JAG."

"Hold on, back up first," Brooks said. "Nothing in college? At all?"

Upton shook her head no.

"We're going to verify that," Brooks warned her, glancing at Liu to make a note for Smolonsky. "So your first sexual relationship occurred in the army? In JAG?"

Upton nodded. "He was another attorney. We tried a case together—on opposing sides. We were both posted in Germany at the time. Then he was sent to Japan, and I was posted in Washington. We talked briefly about getting married. The relationship didn't survive the distance."

Brooks said: "We need his name."

Upton, hesitated, hands still in her lap, rocking forward slightly, then nodded. "Dave Garrod. David. Middle name Paul."

Ang Liu wrote it down.

"Where can we find David Paul Garrord now?"

"Brussels," Upton said.

"Tell us about your time with him. How did it start? How long did it go on? Tell me about how it ended."

Upton told the story stiffly, of a young woman with little experience falling for a superior officer who had a girlfriend in another country and dumped her for Upton, and then both relationships fell apart. It was a distant story from long ago, told the way someone might tell a story about someone else. According to Upton, however, it was the last significant relationship of her life.

They would have someone track this down in the morning to see if Upton was lying about any of it.

"You say this was the most important relationship you had. Were there others? Even casual ones?"

Upton shook her head slightly. There was a moment of quiet. Then Rena, who had not spoken for some time, asked:

"You didn't answer Randi's question. Have you ever had a homosexual relationship?"

"What if I had?"

"That's not the question."

"The question," Brooks joined, "is whether someone might try to use it against you. If you have had relationships with women, we need to know now. We need to talk to them and find out if one of them might have given something to someone and whether it's being used against you."

Sedaka was looking down. He had known someday this was coming, Rena thought, even if he didn't know the truth about his friend's private life.

"Yes, I have." A breath. "I've had experiences with women."

Upton looked Brooks in the eye. "One amounted to a kiss during law school. With a friend, a woman. She considered herself bisexual at the time. We were friends. The friendship deepened. For a few days we wandered on the edge of something else. There were hugs. And one night, kissing. And a bit more. But that was all. It didn't go further. She is married now with children. She no longer, as far as I know, considers herself bisexual."

"But there were others," Brooks said.

Upton took a deep breath. "The other was over a period of a few months when I was in JAG. It was also in Germany. After David. It was brief. We never went out in public as a couple. We are still friends. I cannot imagine she would ever reveal anything about it. I don't believe either of these women would betray those relationships."

Brooks said: "They wouldn't need to. And they shouldn't need to. But we need their names."

"Every name. If there are more than those two," Rena said.

At the suggestion she was still holding more back, Upton simply nodded her understanding. "It's just these two. I will write them down for you, and give them to you tomorrow. But they should hear from me first."

"You'll give them to us now," Brooks said. "We'll give you till noon tomorrow to contact them first yourself."

So they had gotten this far. But it was only a start. Rena got up to stretch. As he did so, he noticed a red sensor light behind the television in the den flickering. The light was part of a system Arvid Lupsa from the office had installed. The system monitored whether someone outside the house might be tracking digital devices inside. It was now possible, Lupsa had explained, for people to monitor the various devices you owned that were already tracking you—your computer, phone, TVs, audio internet devices, even the fridge—watching, listening, counting how often you opened the door. Lupsa had installed the sensors in the homes of everyone at the firm. The flicker was a silent warning. Rena had never seen it flickering before. It meant someone was monitoring them, including perhaps this conversation.

"Do you want to take a break?" Brooks was asking Upton.

"I'm fine. Let's keep on."

"Well, I need a break," Rena said. "Stretch my legs." He headed upstairs and then to the front bedroom window. A glance down both sides of the street.

He saw a car with two men inside parked at the end of the block, just enough light inside to suggest the presence of some kind of larger electronic screen. Rena made his way to his closet and pulled out a lockbox. From it he pulled something dark and heavy—not a gun, which sat in a different lockbox, but an encrypted phone, one that couldn't be monitored. He left his regular phone by his bed, still on, and plugged it into a charger. Then he came downstairs and left the house through the back door.

By the time he got to the street, the car was gone. He'd been spotted, he thought. Upton was being watched. And so, apparently, was he and probably his team.

This had just gotten a lot more serious.

With the encrypted phone he dialed his friend Samantha Reese, the woman he had called from outside Llewellyn Burke's house yesterday.

"Sam, are you in the city yet?"

"Yes, Peter," said Reese.

"Then I think we need you to start what we discussed. First thing tomorrow morning."

They talked over a few details. And Rena went back inside.

TWENTY-TWO

Most of the time the things that destroy a public life are as familiar as old movie plots: Family. Love. Money. Sin. And sometimes, if it's great enough, hypocrisy.

They knew Upton probably had no scandal with money. Rena, Brooks & Associates operated a small credit union, ostensibly for employees, that mostly was used to conduct credit checks on clients, something that was shockingly easy to do now. They knew everything about Upton's finances—what she owned and what she owed. Her net worth consisted of the tavern and store owned with her sister, a small apartment in Tucson, a parcel of land outside the city, some stocks and bonds, and some retirement money from the army and Congress. There was little else.

They had walked through Upton's love life, such as it was.

When Rena returned, Brooks was questioning her about her early days in Tucson.

He said nothing to anyone about the discovery that they were being watched.

"You got through college awfully quickly, two years—while raising a kid sister and running a business. Sure you didn't cut any corners?"

That made Upton smile. "You need to understand something:

I started college at twenty, having missed half of high school. I'd lost four years of my youth raising my sister and running a business. All I wanted to do at school was catch up. College was the first thing I had done entirely for myself since I was sixteen. I couldn't get enough of it."

It was the answer they expected, but they wanted to know if the Wendy Upton they were seeing now was the same one they had put together in their jigsaw puzzle picture of her from documents last night and where, if not, the pieces didn't fit.

Brooks nodded and looked at her partner. "I'm going to talk to Gil in the other room now," she said.

They had two reasons for talking to Sedaka, for his being here at all. They wanted to watch his reactions and ask him questions. They also wanted Upton to see it and feel pressured by it.

Brooks and Sedaka left, and Rena and Liu were alone with Upton.

"Tell us about JAG," Rena said.

"What about it?

"What were the most contentious cases you had?" She named three. Ang Liu wrote them down. "Were you ever threatened by someone you convicted?" She hadn't been. "Which cases did you fail on?" There were a few.

Whoever was watching them was likely the same person threatening Upton, Rena was thinking. Then he tried not to think about it. He needed to focus on the task at hand.

"Tell us about what happened when you began to change your mind about defending soldiers accused of sexual offenses."

"Ahh," she said. "So that's where you are heading."

"Yes, that's where we're heading. We need to know what enemies you made."

"I don't believe I left the service with enemies."

Well, you've got some now, Rena thought. And they're trying to destroy you, and they have people outside my house listening.

"You need to do better than that, Wendy," Rena said. "You

pushed the army to reform itself over sexual harassment. And you think no one held a grudge?"

The army still held a grudge against Rena for saving it from promoting a general who was a sexual harasser.

But she was silent, loyal, unwilling apparently to throw anyone in the service to the wolves. It was admirable. And probably foolish.

She was waiting for him to ask another question.

"The experience you had defending sexual harassers opened your eyes to what was wrong with the system. And you, in turn, began to open the eyes of others."

"You mean Henry Nelson," she said.

Rena said: "And ultimately he pushed harder than you did. And it ended his career."

A look of defiance flashed across her face.

"Henry was moved by his own experience. Maybe my journey gave him permission to act on what he already felt."

"But it ended *his* career."

"I think Henry . . . went about advocating for change the wrong way," she said.

"What does that mean?"

"You were in the army. You should know."

"I don't know."

"It isn't complaining in the service that bothers people. It's how you do it. Henry decided to break the chain of command. But he knew what he was doing."

For all her strength, Rena thought, there was more underneath. He just hadn't gotten to it.

"And you don't think that made *you* enemies, for your part in changing Nelson? His enemies didn't blame you?"

"Not someone who would come after me like this," she said.

Let us decide that, Rena thought.

"What about Nelson? Is it possible he blames you, for leading him down a path that drove him out of the army?"

She was silent, and Rena leaned on it. "Why are you and Henry no longer close?"

Finally a question that seemed to stop her.

"Maybe because we had different jobs by then," she said. "I had left the service. Gone into politics."

"And he had fallen in love with you. And now he was busy blowing himself up. And you didn't help him."

She stared him.

"He didn't want my help," she said.

Rena stared back with a mix of sadness, sympathy, and pitilessness. Then he took a long breath, rose slowly from his chair, and disappeared into the kitchen.

AT HIS BREAKFAST TABLE Brooks was talking to Sedaka.

"You had to know," she said, repeating her last question for Rena's benefit.

"Know?" Sedaka said. "Was I supposed to follow her around?"

She gave him a disappointed look. "You never asked?"

"Would you?"

"You've never seen her with anyone romantically?"

"Wendy is about as private a person as I have ever met."

"Never seen her with a close friend. Male or female."

Sedaka hesitated, and Brooks and Rena exchanged a glance.

"I know you want to protect her, Gil. The way to do that is no more secrets."

Sedaka let out a long breath. Forty-eight, five years younger than Upton, he had spent most of his working life at her side. They'd met as aides on Senator Furman Morgan's staff, Sedaka only a few years out of the University of Charleston. When Upton ran for the House, she'd taken Sedaka with her.

Sedaka was married with two kids, happily, by all they could find—and they had looked. He and Upton appeared to be a classic work couple—married at the office, but not connected outside. She was quiet, forceful, with something vulnerable about her. He was shrewd and smart, a son of South Carolina gentry with a reputation for protecting her politically. He seemed utterly loyal.

"I'm not protecting her. We just have boundaries. One way we support each other is by not getting involved in the other part of each other's lives."

"Two days ago, when this started, we asked you who might want to blackmail her. You said you wanted to think about that. Now you've had time."

"And I've been wracking my brain."

"Not hard enough."

He nodded. "She's been hard on international tax cheats," he said. "But it's a long list. She bucks the party on women's issues. And health. She's worried about climate change, though she can't talk about it."

"And we have a short amount of time. So tomorrow, Gil, we're sending someone to spend the day with you to go through it. Clear your calendar."

When they returned to the den, Liu was telling Upton they would need her complete email history. It was possible Upton's email had been hacked, she explained. That intrusion of privacy had become a feature of Washington in the last two years. As Lupsa put it, "People need to understand email is like skywriting."

"It will be years of them. Tens of thousands," Upton told her.

"It doesn't matter," Liu said.

They had algorithms that would go through them, and only a few hundred would be relevant. They had done this before, this quantifying of a person via their inbox. One can measure how human beings spend and squander their time now from the detritus of their email.

At this, finally Upton seemed to sag. "It doesn't end, does it?"

Rena watched her and decided she wasn't pretending or trying to be strong anymore. And after hours of leaning on her, he now tried to reassure her. "This is going to be all right," he told her. "We will get to the bottom of it."

He liked her, perhaps more than he should a client. She might still be lying or not revealing something, or more than one thing, but he doubted it.

"Are we done?" he asked Brooks.

"For now."

Rena walked Upton and Sedaka to the door. Upton looked at him searchingly. They had not discovered everything they had wanted. But now, he thought, she realized how much she needed them. From now on, she would be more open.

He thought about the men who had been watching them, and how much larger this threat now seemed than it did even a few hours ago. "We'll get them," he said. And he wondered if he believed it.

When he returned to the living room, Brooks was writing in her notebook. Liu looked shock worn.

"She will help us more now," Rena said.

Brooks looked up at him.

"The women and the old boyfriend," she said.

Liu, rubbing her eyes, asked, "Why the old boyfriend?"

"The lost love," Brooks said. "It was a long time ago, but he could be bitter. We need to talk to him face-to-face."

"Why?" Liu said.

"Because of the women," Brooks said. "If she's telling us the truth, the boyfriend and her experiments with women happened around the same time. Maybe that ended the relationship with David Garrod. He may know about it. If it bothered him, maybe he's the source for whoever is making the threat." Brooks looked to see if Liu understood. "I doubt it's going to be that simple. But it's the strongest thing we got tonight."

"You really think a fling with women that long ago could be used against her?" Liu asked. "In the twenty-first century?"

Brooks frowned. "Homosexuality in national politics is uncharted territory. You know how many gay senators are public? One. Senator Fred Blaylish. And he could never run for president because of it."

Rena and his partner had never discussed Brooks's own sexuality. In college, she had discovered her roommate murdered, and it had helped shape her life. She had dropped out of school for a semester and helped solve the woman's killing—and the experience had drawn her to the law and ultimately to becoming an investigator. Rena also was convinced, though Randi had never told him, that she and her murdered roommate were lovers. He watched Brooks's face now and thought he saw a deeper sadness there.

Rena still hadn't told Brooks they were being watched, that his house monitors had picked it up, that he had seen a car outside, and that he'd called Samantha Reese. But he didn't want to do it in front of Ang Liu.

"None of that gets us to the blackmailer," Brooks said.

"The blackmailer is a political enemy," said Rena.

"Then we'll find that in political work," Brooks said. "Probably from her time in the Senate. Tomorrow. We just need to hope we don't run out of time."

"I don't understand why she put up with this tonight. With how tough you were," said Liu.

Brooks, who had been standing up, sat down on the sofa.

"That's the goddamn thing about the people in public life, at least at this level: it's incredible what they will put up with."

"Why do they?" Liu asked.

"That's something I'm not sure I'll ever understand," Brooks said. "Politicians come in different flavors. Different motivations. Public service. Ego. For some, a kind of weird need. But most of these people—at least the ones who get near the presidency—they're different than the rest of us. Someone sometime must have told them, 'You should be president.' And they believed them. They thought, Yeah,

I should be the one who holds the nuclear football with the fate of the world in my hands. And have every moment of my life scrutinized. And have half the world hate me. Yeah, I want that."

She closed her eyes. "What time is it?"

"Almost four thirty," said Rena. "You can both sleep here. I'll get blankets."

"I need my own bed," Brooks said, "and a long shower. I'll see you tomorrow."

Liu said, "It *is* tomorrow."

DAY FOUR

THURSDAY

FEBRUARY 27

TWENTY-THREE

HOUSTON, TEXAS

The Traynor campaign liked to do a rally the morning after a debate. "A sign you're pumped up 'cause you kicked a little butt and ain't sneakin' out of town with your tail between your legs," Sterling Moss always said. "That's the best kind of spin: when you do something, say nothing much about it, and reporters imagine what they're thinking is their idea."

The godforsaken "breakfast rally" was being held at Station 3, a converted firehouse now used for events. David Traynor looked energized, eyes glowing, the intelligence he often hid behind them more visible. He was happy. For all his image as careless and fun loving, he was a driven man used to rising early, working out first thing—speed-reading books while on the elliptical machine—and starting the day on a dead run.

"Yowza!" he said from the dais. "Thank y'all for being here so early."

There were smiles in the crowd, raised orange juice glasses, scattered hoots.

"Quite a night. All those Republicans. And Jeff Scott, he wanted to kill Dick Bakke and go dancing with Maria Pena!" Knowing laughs for that one. "After they were done rewriting the Constitution and getting rid of some of our democratic institutions. Some scary stuff going on."

The laughs turned nervous and were joined by a few chants of "Hell, no, David."

"I'll tell you, working in tech, you see a lot of bad ideas. You learn to smoke 'em out fast—or risk losing a lot of money in a hurry. You need to be able to tell the difference these days between the next big thing and the next big hoax."

That generated some genuine Texas whoops and real applause.

Near the back, two men slipped off their cowboy shirts and were wearing PENA FOR PRESIDENT long-sleeve tees underneath. They were both Hispanic. They moved along the back of the room until they stood next to a big burly man wearing a TRAYNOR FOR THE FUTURE baseball cap. The man in the cap looked like he could handle himself. He had a tattoo on his right wrist and a beard, that chic hipster lumberjack look of a computer coder from Austin, but one who liked a hockey game and an occasional bar fight. The smaller man in the Pena T-shirt started pushing the man in the Traynor cap from behind.

"Fuck, man, what do you think you're doing?" the man in the Traynor cap asked.

"Stopping you white shitheads from ruining the country."

"What the fuck you just say?"

"I said we're coming across the border and we're gonna take this continent back and send your Euro asses back to Ireland where you belong. *Chinga tu puta madre.*"

The first blow caught the mouthy Hispanic guy hard just below the temple.

People around them screamed. Alabama started to climb onto the ABN camera platform near him for a better look.

By then the guy in the Traynor hat was wailing on the little guy pretty good. He had the man on the ground and he was throwing right after right at the smaller man's head, using the wooden floor as a backboard.

There was a lot of screaming. Alabama was surprised the second Pena guy took as long as he did to jump in and try to pull the guy in the Traynor hat off his friend.

The heat of it was over quickly. Security guards grabbed the big man throwing all the punches. Underneath, the little guy in the Pena shirt wasn't moving. There was a lot of blood, and the second man was hysterical.

"You're fucking crazy! What is wrong with you people?" he shouted.

Or it sounded something like that to Alabama. The guy throwing the punches was being pinned by cops and put in handcuffs. The EMS team hovered over the guy who was hurt. By the time they had checked him out and got him a gurney and started rolling it out, it was clear the injuries were serious.

Alabama called New York and said he was breaking off from Traynor and going to look into the fight and the men involved. Too many fights at too many rallies, too many days in a row. That, Alabama thought, was the tip of a real story.

TWENTY-FOUR

WASHINGTON, D.C.

Ellen Wiley started the morning searching video on the Web. She called it "cultural sailing," and it relaxed her.

She'd come in early to find video of a young Wendy Upton, before the senator had become careful and guarded. What was she like before she became the person she made herself into?

She knew a little-known video archive at Vanderbilt University, the lifework of a now-retired scholar who had painstakingly archived the logs of every local television station in the country going back a half century. Wiley could type in a name and find, with fair accuracy, any time a person had appeared on a local television news program since 1972. You still had to track down whether that video existed anywhere on the Web. It was a crapshoot. But Wiley had ways to find those as well.

When she typed in Wendy Upton's name, she came across a couple of appearances by her sister, Emily, the bar owner and singer. The longest, more than a decade old, was from a local Arizona TV show, *Good Morning Tucson*. She found a viewable copy of the appearance in the archive of the University of Arizona student video lab—not exactly public, but not exactly secure if you knew what you were doing.

The program's morning host was asking Emily what it was like to be the sister of the famous Wendy Upton. Later, the show hinted, Emily would sing with her rock band.

Emily Upton was dressed in red cowboy boots, a denim miniskirt, a straw cowboy hat, and a low-cut Mexican blouse. The program's host, Susie Stanton, wore big red glasses and had a younger hunky male sidekick named Todd.

"True that your code name during your sister's run for the Senate was 'Headache'?"

Todd laughed. The audience roared.

Emily tugged at a handkerchief in her hand and smiled tightly. "Might be, Susie."

Stanton made a droll face that seemed to say, now tell the truth. "And did you live up to the name—create any headaches for your sister?"

More laughter, but uneasy this time. Emily, shot mostly from the side, looked suspiciously at Susie and Todd.

It went on like this awhile. Susie Stanton was rolling: "Let's talk about your relationship with your sister when you were kids. She actually raised you, didn't she? She was like your sister *and* your mother. Oh, that sounded a little weird, like the scene in *Chinatown*. 'Sister, daughter, sister, daughter.' Oops."

Todd didn't laugh, and Susie realized the joke had missed. "But you are pretty different, aren't you, you and Wendy?"

After a moment Emily said, "Yeah, she was always a little more disciplined. I was always a little wilder."

"Let's talk about that."

What happened next was subtle. Something seemed to go out of Emily, some liveliness, as she surrendered to the clown's role she had been cast to play—the bad sister—in exchange for the chance to promote her new CD.

"Well, basically, Susie, I'm a college dropout. I became a rock and roll singer. I got married when I was eighteen and divorced when

I was twenty. And Wendy, she was, well, you know, Phi Beta Kappa, a lawyer, U.S. senator. So, yeah, we're pretty different."

Even Susie Stanton looked uneasy now. The shallow banter of the segment had rubbed away and only the cynical gawking behind it remained. After a few more awkward exchanges she invited Emily to sing.

Emily Upton had a boozy roadhouse voice. Wiley imagined she was better than this usually, but Upton's voice was flat and off key. Wiley thought the just-finished, humiliating interview probably had something to do with it. The songs were hard to watch.

Emily Upton had been reduced to a type: the slob political sibling. The other kid, who could never compete with their overachieving brother or sister, so they defined themselves as the opposite. It was a crowded category: Dick Nixon's brother, Donald; Bill Clinton's brother, Roger; Jimmy Carter's brother, Billy. Emily played the role uneasily, complicated by the fact that her sister had also raised her. The competitor was also the protector.

Wiley closed the video and walked into Brooks's office.

"You need to see this."

When Brooks finished watching they went to see Rena.

He didn't need to watch it all the way through.

"Maybe we should be looking more closely at the sister," Brooks said.

Rena said, "Let's call Smolo."

TWENTY-FIVE

Walt Smolonsky got lucky quickly. Maybe because they were finally looking in the right place.

Phil Dixon, the former local sheriff's deputy he'd hired to be their local PI, found something on the sister that wasn't in the records. He'd done it by working old friends in law enforcement. A half-dozen calls in, he came up with rumors of an old drug case—possession with intent to sell. Emily Upton was suspected of dealing. And then the case had gone away.

The arresting officer, Bobby Triska, was still on the force. When Dixon and Smolo reached him, the detective wasn't enthusiastic about talking, but he eventually agreed to see them outside of the office at a Sonoran hot dog place called Guero Canelo in South Tucson, the predominantly Hispanic part of town.

Triska was waiting for them at a picnic table.

He was skeptical of Smolo, the out-of-towner, but remembered Dixon. "I don't get you guys," Triska said. "You want to know about this case, but you're working for Wendy Upton?"

"Way it works," said Smolo. "You find out all the worst things about your own candidate first. So you know what's coming."

Triska glanced at Dixon, then rolled his eyes like politics was some international sport with rules he didn't understand. "Why not ask her?" he said.

"We will. Once I know what really happened," Smolo said.

Dixon tried to be reassuring. "Bobby, he really does work for Upton. And he really is interested in finding out what happened. Either it disqualifies her. Which we need to know. Or it can be explained. Which we also need to know."

Triska said: "Simpler to put the bad guys in jail, isn't it?"

"Is it?" said Smolo.

Dixon got everyone coffee while Smolonsky and Triska talked.

"We had Emily Upton dead to rights. Had one of her bartenders selling from behind the bar. Cocaine. And some Molly. No way she didn't know."

He was a thick man with a shaved head and big ears, and Smolo sensed he seemed stuck and was waiting to retire.

They'd gotten onto the case through an anonymous tip, Triska said. "There had been stories before about Emily, the fuck-up sister. She was trying to put out music CDs back then, make it as a rock star. But she was already too old."

The fact that Emily Upton had never been charged, and the case against the dealer had never been connected publicly to Shiny's bar, had stuck in Triska's craw. Smolo thought he and Dixon couldn't possibly have been the first people Triska'd ever told. But it also felt like it'd been a while since he'd talked about it.

"A tip?" Smolonsky asked.

"That seem fishy to you?" Dixon added. "Or maybe political?"

"This stuff never comes from virgins," Triska said. "You were in law enforcement. You know, where there's smoke there's fire. The time you catch them, it's never the first time they did it. Just the first time they were caught."

Smolonsky asked: "So you had the drugs. You had the bartender. And you had Upton."

"She claimed she had no idea. Of course."

"What'd the bartender say?"

"He was ready to say it was all her—that he was her employee in all things."

"What happened?"

"What happens in the world?" Triska said. "Big people get protected. A different set of rules for everybody else."

"What does that mean?" asked Smolo.

Triska gave Dixon a look. "It means it went away," the detective said.

That earned a frown from Smolonsky. "Explain that."

A sigh, like this was obvious, and Triska in a bored voice said: "We made the case, picked her up, sent up the evidence. Prosecutor wants to proceed. Then it stops. Bartender is arrested and indicted. Not Emily."

"Why not?"

"Big man said there's no case."

"Big man?" Smolo asked.

"Burdick."

"Dick Burdick," Dixon explained. "The D.A. in Tucson."

"You hear Burdick say anything directly?"

"What are you, born yesterday?" said Triska.

"Then how do you know what happened?"

Triska gave Smolonsky a stare that wasn't half bad.

"Because I knew what we had. Knew it made a case. Knew the A.D.A. was good with it"—the assistant district attorney. "And then it went away. Two plus two. I know you do funny math in D.C., but here that adds."

Smolonsky gave Triska a stare of his own, and it was better than Triska's. "But you don't have proof. Only suspicion."

"You guys gonna throw me under the fucking bus?"

The skin above Triska's bald forehead had crinkled up and little beads of sweat were forming. "Dixon, I heard you were a straight guy," Triska said to the local P.I.

"There's no bus," Smolonsky assured him. "We just need proof. Documents. Phone records."

Triska crushed an empty coffee cup and tossed it into a big wire trash can. "Didn't you say you were a cop once?"

"D.C. police," Smolo said.

"Well, be police like you used to be. Track it down. Or do you just clean up powerful people's shit now?"

"Bobby, we're here asking, aren't we?" Dixon said. "We just need as much proof as we can get."

That calmed Triska a little. Smolonsky felt for him. Bringing big cases against family members of powerful people was dangerous. And one thing was true everywhere: cops were at the bottom of the food chain. But that meant you had to make your cases even stronger. Not become bitter if they weren't.

"Look, ask Stroman. He was the assistant D.A. Gung ho for it. Jeff Stroman." Triska paused. "That's what I got. Not paperwork. Or evidence bags. Just what happened. Or my own noose for you to put my neck in."

Now Triska balled up his empty hot dog wrapper, threw it at the trash can, and missed. "I gotta get back to my partner and back to work."

Smolonsky held out a hand and Triska shook it. "I know these stick with you. The ones you can't make," he said. Smolonsky wanted to end on good terms with Triska. He didn't need a disgruntled local cop to make the visitor from Washington a new part of his story of cover-up to protect Wendy Upton. "But I need to ask one other thing. We can keep you out of this, but this last question matters. Anyone ask you about this recently? Anyone at all? Or has it come up in conversation?"

Triska glanced at Dixon, who nodded him to answer.

"No," Triska said. "Not to me."

SMOLONSKY CALLED RENA FROM THE CAR. "Maybe we found something. On the sister."

TWENTY-SIX

WASHINGTON, D.C.

The Ford was parked along the water in East Potomac Park. You could see the sunrise from here, and it was quiet, just a few runners and cyclists. He liked the peacefulness of it. Across the little channel, where there were slips for sailboats, was Fort McNair, where they hanged the conspirators for Lincoln's assassination. Down the road, near where the Anacostia River merged with the Potomac, they were building a new billion-dollar wharf development. Going to ruin the place, the guy thought. Make it all retail and hipster and drive out the poor. So it goes. He would be out of the country in a few weeks. Not his problem.

He looked at the man next to him in the car and made a phone call. "Guy may have spotted us last night," he said into the phone. After a moment he added, sounding irritated: "Whaddya mean, which guy? Guy I'm talking about. The fixer. Guy you had us following. Rena." He listened again and explained, "We were watching his place. Listening. Through monitoring the digital stuff in the house. He had the senator there. It was perfect. They were asking *her* for dirt. She was giving it to us!" The voice on the other end was talking. "Then he went upstairs and seemed to be looking down the street, like he knew someone was there watching the place. Then he came outside. By then we took off." He listened again. "Because it was three in the morning. I'm letting you know now. I know you sleep at night, now that you're fat and rich."

He seemed to be getting instructions of some kind. "No shit," he said. "Yeah, I figured. Looser surveillance. Keep the monitoring."

* * *

Rena and Brooks's team was gathered in the fourth-floor attic conference room. The topic: what they'd learned after two days and nights. The Grid, their digital case-tracking system, was filling up with names of suspected blackmailers who might want to threaten Upton—billionaire donors, trade associations, and political action committees. But they were missing hard evidence linking any of them to making a threat.

"We did an intervention with Upton last night," Brooks was saying. "She acknowledged she has had a couple of sexual experiences with women."

"That's further than she's ever gone before," said Jonathan Robinson, their political communications guy.

"I wouldn't say she poured her heart out," Brooks said.

She looked exhausted.

"And there's an old boyfriend from JAG in Germany," added Ang Liu, who did not appear as worn out.

"I'm tracking him down today," said Hallie Jobe. She and Liu had already talked.

"Ellen and Smolo think the sister, Emily, is a soft spot," Brooks said. "Smolo is on it."

Rena was standing in the corner watching. If he sat down, he thought he might fall asleep.

But he was worried. They were still too scattered; there was too much to do; they didn't have enough time. "Our core job," he said, "is to find who's making the threat. Who feels wounded by Upton? Someone rich. Who hates her that much?"

The answer, he was convinced, was buried in Upton's political work. "Committees. Key votes."

Walt would track the case against the sister in Tucson. But they still had to find out who was using it and why.

And they probably had to do it today. Sometime by nightfall, Traynor and Bakke would likely withdraw their overtures to Upton about the vice presidency. Then it wouldn't matter what they found. The threat would have done its job—and they might not ever know what it was or from whom the threat came. A deft maneuver on the part of whoever was behind this: destroy your enemy with only the possibility of a threat. Whoever it was, Rena had a growing sense they were more formidable than he first imagined.

He looked at Lupsa and Wiley: "We need to use technology to help the political search," he said. "We need to match who gave money to Upton's rivals to who's on this list of people whose ox she might have gored. Can you help?"

Lupsa said, "Already started. I'm writing code that will match who gave to what political PACs with which companies or their parent companies might have been affected by work done by Upton's committees."

When the meeting was over and they were back downstairs, Rena walked into Brooks's office.

"Something I didn't tell you last night."

She was sitting in her desk chair, leaning back, half asleep. "I'm not going to like it, am I?"

"Not a bit."

She smiled, and he sat down.

"Arvid's little monitoring sensors in my house last night were flickering. Someone was tapping the digital devices in the house, probably listening to us as we talked to Upton. I spotted a car outside. When I got out there, they'd driven off."

Maybe because she was so exhausted, Brooks didn't look as alarmed as Rena expected. She didn't like the cloak-and-dagger side of what they did. She was a political animal and she could play that game as hard and as tough as anyone he had ever seen. Harder than he was comfortable with sometimes. But she was a lawyer who used her skills to research people and their organizations—legally. She was not a cop.

Increasingly, however, being an investigator meant being in harm's way. More than it used to. Technology was part of it. It was just too easy to invade people's lives. And that had seemed to intertwine with something else, like a vine that jumps your neighbor's fence and begins to wind itself around everything that grows in your yard. Because technology made snooping so easy, there seemed to be fewer lines that people wouldn't cross. And for those with enough money and arrogance, the laws prohibiting invading others people's lives, and hiring thugs to do it, seemed increasingly irrelevant. People signed terms-of-service agreements every day with a click of their mouse without reading them, handing over most of their lives without a thought. Political hardball was one thing. To Brooks that meant holding public figures accountable for their records and their words. All this—threatening people, blackmailing them, listening to them in their houses, even making things up on the Internet to destroy them—this wasn't hardball. This wasn't a game. This was the culture and its mores slipping out of whack.

"You're not flipped out?" Rena asked.

"I'm too tired."

"This means someone has people probably following Upton. That's how they would have known about us. They're listening to her. And now they're listening to us."

To his surprise, Brooks smiled.

"Whoever it is, they're not from politics," she said. "And they must be worried about us."

Rena smiled back. His partner was always stronger than he expected.

She asked: "They see you spotting them?"

"Probably."

She rocked a little in her desk chair and said, "What do you want to do?"

"I already called Sam. The first night we met Upton. I told her to come to D.C. from Colorado, that we might need her. So last night she was already here. I told her to start. Full on."

Brooks made a concerned face. Samantha Reese did surveillance, body work. So now she would be tailing Upton, too. Two sets of people tailing the senator, their person and someone else's. A perfect recipe for disaster.

"This is getting very cowboy," she said.

"We're still the white hats."

That earned only a small smile. Brooks got up from her desk. She had an appointment with someone on the Hill, but she looked back over her shoulder and said:

"Maybe we should be worried if we're deciding good and evil based on the color of the hats."

TWENTY-SEVEN

TUCSON, ARIZONA

Jeff Stroman, the former assistant district attorney who had tried to prosecute Emily Upton, was not hard to find.

He was no longer with the city but at a defense litigation firm called Fulton, Day & Stroman. It was located in one of the shiny tall office buildings in Tucson's small downtown.

Stroman said he preferred to meet out of the office. So Emily Upton was a sensitive subject for him as well, Smolo thought, just as she was with Detective Bobby Triska.

Stroman picked an old-fashioned diner. They sat in a booth. Smolo explained he was working for Upton, but the job was to find any skeletons he could and to be honest about them. It was possible Upton was holding things back from them. The firm he worked for didn't sweep things under the rug. You protected a client by knowing the truth, and either getting ahead of it or knowing when it was so bad that it was time to tell the client to get out.

The lawyer was more suspicious than the detective. "How do I know you're not lying and working for her enemies?"

"Call her chief of staff, Gil Sedaka," Smolo said, handing over one of Sedaka's business cards. Rena had gotten a batch of them the first day for just this purpose. "If you want to use my phone, he'll be certain to pick up."

Stroman sighed and shook his head. "Ask what you want. I'll tell you what I'm comfortable telling you."

Smolo figured the lawyer would lose patience quickly, so he tried to save time by being direct. "I heard you had a drug case against Emily Upton that was squashed from above."

Stroman took a few extra seconds to answer. "The decision was made not to prosecute. That's what I know."

"Help me, Jeff. If Emily Upton did something wrong, I need to know."

"I'm not volunteering anything," Stroman said. "You tell me what you've heard. I'll tell you if I can confirm it."

This game, huh, Smolo thought. People watched too much TV. "My understanding is you recommended prosecution. The D.A. did not accept your recommendation."

"Which happens all the time. He's the D.A. He scores the wins and losses, knows the court schedule, has the big picture. And he has more experience. That's the D.A.'s job—to make those calls. I brought him what we had."

"Which was?"

"Less than perfect. The bartender was guilty. He flipped on Upton. We needed a little more to make the case. If we'd kept going, I think we would have gotten it. Boss said no."

"Why no arrest for Upton?"

"Good question," Stroman said. "A senator's sister? What could possibly explain it?"

"But you don't have any proof Upton interceded?"

Stroman looked at Smolonsky with quick contempt. "You're going to screw me over with this, aren't you? Smear me to protect her."

Smolonsky gave a sharp look of his own. "Not how this works. I don't care if she's dirty. I just need to know what's coming, what shit is out there and if it's proven or just hearsay. I miss things, I'm screwed."

Stroman was trying to decide if he believed it. He said: "The bartender worked more than one place. He was selling drugs from both. I was sure Emily knew and maybe was getting a cut. That's what the bartender was offering to get himself out from under—Emily. But proving it would have taken more work. Probably sending the bartender all wired up to have a conversation with her. I was told to just go with the bartender. So that's what we did."

Smolo asked a few more questions and got a few more answers, but Stroman was keeping himself out of it as much as he could.

"I need to ask one more thing, and I really need you to answer this one. If nothing else, answer this one."

Stroman tried to look cool but finally shrugged.

"Anyone else asking about this? That you know of?"

If the answer were yes, it was a signal that someone else, the blackmailer, knew about this quashed drug case against Emily Upton and was using it.

"I heard someone was nosing around town. Yeah. But I haven't seen them."

Smolo couldn't decide if the lawyer was lying.

* * *

The D.A. of Pima county, Dick Burdick, proved a harder man to see than a former assistant D.A. now in private practice or a detective second grade whose career had stalled. Smolonsky's initial efforts to see Burdick went nowhere. So he solved the problem of access the way any out-of-towner with connections might, if you were dealing with an asshole and wanted him to think you an even bigger asshole.

Smolo got Rena to call Gil Sedaka, who in turn called Burdick personally with a simple message: Senator Upton would appreciate if Burdick could extend every possible courtesy to Mr. Smolonsky. Less than ten minutes later Smolo got a call saying the district attorney had a sudden opening in his schedule.

According to their local P.I., Phil Dixon, and Ellen Wiley's quick file on him, District Attorney Elton Richard "Dick" Burdick III was a man in a hurry. Burdick came from an Arizona political family, had made D.A. of Pima County at thirty-seven, and had no intention of holding the job for another thirty years. Dixon thought Burdick had his eye on the state attorney general's office, and from there the governor's mansion. After that, maybe the Senate or a lucrative private practice. A twenty-five- or thirty-year plan—with options.

One important element of any such plan was always to remain on the right side of the people who hold the jobs above you.

The D.A. had a kind of permanent half smile, the corners of his mouth pleasantly upturned, and Smolo wondered if he'd had surgical help for that. You could have that done now, Smolo had read somewhere—get your smile shaped. Jesus. He'd heard you could also "live your life out loud and online," in social media. Apparently, some people thought you had to look the part, too, or get enhanced to look it. Everyone had become their own personal casting director. However Burdick's mouth got that way, the man had a great-to-see-ya kind of grin that Smolo immediately disliked.

He walked through the elevator pitch about why he was there—working for Upton, scrubbing her in case of an offer for the vice presidency. Burdick nodded with interest, happy to learn the secrets of the big game; an enthusiastic "glad to help" and a lot of "uh-huhs" and "yeps."

"We're running down the story that you quashed a drug case against Emily Upton after getting a call from her sister's people. Made the case go away."

Burdick's demi grin vanished. "You said you worked for the senator. If you've wormed your way in here under false pretenses, all to make outrageous accusations, you best turn around and go."

"I *do* work for the senator."

"Then what the hell do you think you're doing?"

"What I'm paid to. Getting to the bottom of the worst things that might come at her."

Burdick gave a powerful man's stare: "Look, every case is a judgment call. A balance of resources of this office, chance of conviction, significance of the crime, strength of evidence."

"We heard this was a strong case, especially against the bartender."

The little wheels in Burdick's brain spun. It couldn't be that hard for him to figure out who Smolo had been talking to. "I stand by this call as much as any I've ever made in this office," the D.A. declared. "That doesn't mean every cop or assistant D.A. will understand or agree."

"You never got a call from the senator or her people?"

"Telling me to drop the case? Hell, no. And I resent the accusation. This office is not for sale. Put that in your oppo research book."

Burdick pushed a buzzer under his desk and his secretary entered a moment later—like it was 1975. "I'm afraid I've things to do. Janice will see you see out."

"Hi, Janice," Smolo said.

"IF I HAD TO PICK one guy who lied to me, it'd be the D.A.," Smolonsky told Rena after he got back to Phil Dixon's office.

"I don't know if it matters whether he was lying," Rena said. He walked through the scenarios with Smolo: If Emily had been selling drugs out of Shiny's bar, a place Wendy Upton still half owned, and a strong case against her had suddenly vanished, it could be enough to knock Upton from being a vice presidential choice.

And if there were any record of communication between her and Burdick during that time, it might be enough to beat her in a Senate run. And if the FBI got involved and mounted an investigation, it might charge her with obstruction of justice.

"You could make two and two look like four even if Burdick swore out an affidavit he killed the case on the merits."

Not good math.

And if this were the hidden scandal Upton was being threatened with—that she had intervened to protect her sister—their work wasn't over. They still had no idea who was threatening Upton with it. Smolonsky had unearthed no evidence for that.

Another fact nagged at Rena, too. Upton hadn't mentioned this drug case to them.

He wanted to confront her. But he wanted Brooks with him. And she was still out someplace.

TWENTY-EIGHT

WASHINGTON, D.C.

Randi Brooks was not a gumshoe. Not like Peter, or Smolonsky, or Hallie Jobe. She'd never been a cop or carried a gun—or even shot one. She wasn't a computer hacker like Ellen Wiley or Arvid Lupsa. She didn't understand the Dark Web. And she certainly didn't want to visit it, thank you very much.

She was a lawyer. Proudly. Double Ivy, Cambridge and New Haven—and the Dalton School in New York City before that, where, as a scholarship girl, she had also acquired a healthy distrust of the very wealthy. She was good at following documents and logic. She believed in the story they told. And, as Peter often said, she was the most relentless researcher he knew. For she believed that if you followed the documents all the way down, you could see just what people really do. How far they will go. Documents don't lie. They don't smile. They don't flirt. They get jobs done—the dirty, cold, greedy jobs you hide in the fine print and don't admit to in person. You just had to know how to find the right documents. And how to read them. And Randi surely did.

She wanted to know which documents answered the puzzle of who was threatening Wendy Upton. That's how they would solve this. And for this, friends could definitely help, especially women, whom she found easier to comprehend because they were complicated in ways she understood. And she thought women didn't lie as easily, or at least they were more tortured when they did. Yes, friends could help.

Judy Worthington was one of those friends, an old acquaintance from the other side of the aisle, chief of staff for Republican Senator Arnie Nelson of Arkansas. She and Worthington were similar in age, Judy a little older, and had risen through the Senate ranks together, Judy as a Senate chief, Randi as a committee counsel. They were from different parties, but they'd come up at a time when women in senior positions were rare enough to consider themselves members of a shared tribe. And she knew Judy thought the world of Wendy Upton.

They had a reservation at the Monocle, one of the oldest and most venerated meeting spots on the Senate side of the Hill. They were shown to a table at the back, caught up on old friends and—in Judy's case—kids and a grandchild. And she heard about the progress of Worthington's most personal legislative cause, Alzheimer's research, inspired by the illness of Judy's mother-in-law as well as Senator Nelson's mother. Worthington had been working on the bill for more than ten years, which to genuine Senate veterans was not all that long.

"We haven't had a meal during the week together in years," Worthington said. "Why are we here?"

"I wanted to fix that."

"Okay. We've fixed that. Why are we here?"

Brooks smiled at her friend's candor.

"I want to know who Wendy Upton's enemies are."

Worthington stared at her a long moment. "Of course you can't tell me what you're really working on."

"Of course not. But I'm here to help Wendy Upton. Not harm her." Brooks matched Judy's stare with her own. Women like us, it said, don't lie to women like us. "Help me, Judy, help Wendy. I'm not a Democrat here or a Republican."

"You were never a Republican, Randi. You were someone who tried to beat Republicans."

"Who are Wendy's enemies who might try to harm her? I mean mortal enemies."

"I wouldn't call them enemies, exactly," Worthington said.

"Whatever you might call them, who are they?"

"Well, they mostly wear pants," Worthington said with a sour expression. "And most of them are on the far right of my own party."

While members of Congress in both parties now were more politically extreme than in the past, they were usually not as extreme as their constituents. And their staff tended to be more politically moderate than their bosses. All this was the opposite of what it was a generation ago, when the senators tended to be moderates and their staffers more hotheaded.

The waiter appeared with water but not a lot of patience, a man in his sixties wearing a tuxedo and a glower. The Monocle was old school, not a place where the wait staff introduced themselves, said they would be your server, and asked how your day had been.

He left with their orders and Worthington said, "Well, I put Dick Bakke at the top of any list of enemies of Wendy's."

Brooks didn't dare tell her that Bakke had secretly offered Upton a place on his campaign ticket. "Who else? Who challenges her directly when they're in conference?"

Conference referred to the meetings all Republican senators had with each other in private. Usually, chiefs of staff attended, too, which meant Worthington was there. Conference was one of the few places senators were blunt with each other. Word was the meetings had become increasingly ugly as the GOP had begun to fissure.

"Guy Filippo was once really terrible to Wendy," Worthington said. Filippo was the junior senator from Wyoming. "Upton had refused to vote the party line on a women's-health issue. I don't remember the particular vote anymore. Guy, who is as dumb as a box of rocks, told Upton there needed to be some accountability for women breaking with the party on this issue. He suggested she be stripped of her seat on the committee."

Brooks gave a disgusted look.

"I mean, 'accountability for women'?" Worthington said. "Ever hear someone say there needed to be accountability for men, like it was a gender problem?"

"What happened?"

"Wendy got that voice she has, you know, the one where she gets hyperarticulate and sounds like the most adult person you ever met." Brooks nodded and Worthington continued. "And she said something like, 'Senator, as a matter of this institution's rules as well as law, I am not accountable to you. Not as a senator, and certainly not as a woman. As I assume you know from taking the oath of office, senators are accountable to upholding the Constitution, to upholding the law, to serving the voters of their state, and to their own conscience—in that order.'"

Worthington's eyes went wide. She loved Upton.

"Then, get this: she told Filippo if he tried to punish her for her vote, she would be delighted to make his threat public and test their differing theories of accountability in the next election—including in Wyoming." Worthington formed her mouth into a circle shape and raised her eyebrows, and silently mouthed the word *wow*. "It was pretty fucking awesome."

"What did Filippo say?"

"Not a word. I think the only thing I heard was the sound of his testicles receding." She paused to let the insult settle. "In fact, the old rat hasn't been able to look Wendy in the eye since. Or virtually any other woman in the GOP. The man is a human hairball."

The food arrived. The two women had both ordered Caesars, Brooks's with steak, Worthington's shrimp.

"What about legislatively? Any big donors Upton has tangled with on committee? Any heavy pressure on lobbying that looked especially intense—like she had hit a nerve?"

Sometimes the only sign you got up here was when a lawyer showed up with new language to put in a bill, along with an attitude that the language was not negotiable. Someone whose boss had dropped real money into a PAC anonymously. The day of reckoning came when the guy in a suit was in your office with a piece of paper and draft language and said, 'Put this into bill SR 9024, section 48, paragraph 3, line 2.' And it was a change in the law that would create a loophole for companies that fit a certain description, but if you looked hard it turned out there was only one such company in the world, and it was owned by this one anonymous donor, and the language you couldn't parse saved him billions.

Worthington's expression became more intense: "She hates corporations hiding profits overseas, moving jobs, and using exotic tax schemes. She really got serious a couple years back about something called basket trading. That one involved some heavy hitters, the really major donors."

"Remind me," Brooks said, pretending she might have heard of it.

"It's a corporate tax evasion scheme. I think it's called basket trading. Maybe it's 'bundled trading.' Whatever. It's this complicated thing where hedge funds and banks were conspiring with each other, passing money back and forth, making it look like the hedge fund was investing the bank's money when it was really its own funds. It helped the hedge funds avoid millions in taxes. Came up in Wendy's subcommittee. She came down pretty hard on it. Found billions in back taxes owed. Really, billions. That would be enough to make someone hold a grudge."

"It might."

"She's also been hard on hiding profits overseas, too. Worked with Jonathan Kaplan on some legislation to close those loopholes." Kaplan was a Democratic senator from New Jersey. "And she angered a lot of people on health care. Quietly, you know, she is trying to protect women's health. Even my own senator would probably call Wendy soft on abortion."

Then Worthington got a worried look. "Randi, what are you really up to?"

"I'm looking for something—a moment, or a piece of legislation—that might cause someone to hold a grudge against Upton. A grudge with no limits to it."

Worthington shook her head sadly. Like a lot of longtime veterans of the Hill, she barely recognized the institution she loved. It was like watching a family member go through a personality transformation after an illness, and nothing you did to stop it helped. A lot of her friends who had dedicated their lives to public service had reached a point they called "the dark woods," like the title of the scary book by Ruth Ware. They were lost and wondering, Do I stay and try to change things? Or am I deluding myself and part of the problem? People talked about it endlessly.

"You know, of course, it could be personal," Worthington said. "There isn't a better person up here than Wendy. But I've never seen her with a man or a woman—or anyone socially. There is a secret there, Randi."

Brooks looked back blankly at her friend, recalling Upton's painful closed-down quality last night as she described her private life.

Worthington was saying, "I don't know if Wendy has skeletons in her closet or not, and I don't care. Some people find her a little holier than thou. Mostly she's just tough. But some people hate her because she doesn't fit their definition of how a woman should behave."

"How should they behave?"

"She isn't deferential enough. She actually talks in meetings. And even interrupts if a man isn't listening."

"Wow. What a bitch." Brooks said.

TWENTY-NINE

Brooks called Rena from outside the Monocle. "Don't come back here," he told her. "Meet me at Upton's office."

Smolonsky had found something about the sister in Tucson, he explained. Upton had agreed to see them, though he hadn't told the senator what it was about. Meet him inside the Capitol Building.

Maybe, just maybe, he said, they were getting near a solution.

They met in Upton's "hideaway" Senate office in the Capitol, away from staff and constituents, away from one's official rooms in the Russell, Dirksen, or Hart Office Buildings.

Upton sat on a small sofa, Rena and Brooks in chairs facing her. Rena walked through what Smolo knew of the case against Emily.

Upton began shaking her head slowly. She knew about this, Rena thought. He felt a cool liquid anger rising in his throat. She'd said nothing about this last night. And that was unacceptable. If Upton didn't begin to reveal *everything*—starting right now—maybe they really would have to walk away. And that would be a disaster for everyone.

"I never intervened," Upton said. Her head was bowed. Then she lifted it toward the ceiling, eyes closed.

"It sure as hell looks like you did," said Rena.

Upton's eyes opened, and she was looking at him.

"We've got a cop who says the case was killed for political reasons," he said. "A prosecutor who doesn't deny it, and the district attorney, who does deny it, looks to our people like a self-righteous liar. All our instincts tell us this case was quashed from the top."

Upton took a deep breath. "I did the opposite of intervening,"

"I have no idea what that means," Brooks said.

"It means I never spoke to the D.A., Burdick. Look, yes, I heard about the case. A friend in Tucson called Gil. I told Gil to make it clear to the prosecutors I was staying out of it—that they should follow the law wherever it took them. Like any other case. No special treatment."

The pain from that memory flushed suddenly in Upton's face. "This wasn't the first incident with Emily. There was an arrest that's sealed. She was seventeen, and I was twenty-three. I had just started law school. I asked a friend in the sheriff's department, a guy who worked as an off-duty bouncer at the bar, if there was anything he could do. Emily was selling pot, or had enough to charge her with selling, which would have been a felony. They dropped the charges down to possession. That was a long time ago, and it took them about two seconds to agree."

Upton was shaking her head slowly. "But this time I said no. This was the time I stopped telling myself Emily would change—that she would grow up. I decided this was who Emily was. And I was not responsible. She was an adult, and I had to stop trying to fix her." Upton closed her eyes again and exhaled. She wasn't looking at them when she said, "Maybe if I were really her parent I would have reacted differently. But I didn't."

Then tears welled up in her eyes and started rolling down her cheeks, the first ones they had seen since any of this had begun four days ago. Now that they'd come, the tears flowed and flowed.

"I wasn't proud of this. It wasn't the best day of my life." She didn't wipe the tears away. She looked at the two of them and said,

"I knew a part of me was only protecting myself. Did I really think it would be good for Emily to be convicted of drug trafficking? I didn't just refuse to intervene. I hid from this. I didn't even call her."

"But the D.A. dropped the case," Brooks said.

Rena kept his eyes on Upton. She held the backs of her hands to her face now to dry her cheeks.

"So it sure looks like someone intervened," Brooks said.

"The D.A. in Tucson, this man named Burdick, is not one of my favorite people. I have never spoken to him about it. But it's absolutely possible he thought I would be in his debt. Officially, I was told there were problems with the evidence—no proof Emily was involved and not a strong case to get it. I thought she got lucky, frankly. But I never asked. I stayed as far away as I could."

Brooks glanced at Rena, wondering what her partner's famous intuition was telling him.

Upton was shaking her head as if it were all an ironic joke. "You think this is what they have on me? What they think will destroy me? Something I didn't do?"

"It may be," Brooks said. "If it is, and you're telling us everything, I think we can get in front of it."

"You mean my abandonment of my sister is my defense?" Upton grimaced. "Extolling that as a virtue strikes me as worse than the abandonment itself."

"Would you have gone to court with her if it had gone to trial? Stood by her every day?" Brooks asked.

Upton's grimace turned into look of miserable uncertainty. "To be honest, I don't know. I knew that was what I should do, though I suspect someone would have told me to simply drop my sister from my life entirely. But a part of me would have felt sitting in court with her was cynical, too. Just for show. Honestly, I didn't know what I was going to do. We never got that far."

Rena, who had been quiet, spoke for the first time in a while. "The fact that you feel conflicted makes me think I believe you."

And Upton turned to him, realizing only then that she didn't have his full confidence.

"But you should have told us all this yesterday. Or the first day," he said.

"I was trying to walk through the things I had done. Not the ones I hadn't." She paused. "It isn't easy, imagining everything in one's life that could be turned against you. You live trying to be one way. You don't see how others see it."

Politics was not his chosen world. But Rena was reminded then that politicians are just as human as anyone else. Despite their years of preparation, the hyperbole and evasions that surround them every day, and the layers upon layers of armor they learn to wear to steel themselves for power, they're still just people. It was simple and obvious, and at the same time, at that moment, surprising.

THIRTY

WASHINGTON, D.C.

There was no way, however, they could accept what Upton had told them at face value. That's how you get made a fool of.

To survive in Washington it was better to follow what Ronald Reagan had said about the Russians and "trust but verify." Or better yet, follow the advice about family from the City News Bureau of Chicago: "If your mother says she loves you, check it out."

As Rena and Brooks were meeting with Upton in the Capitol, Maureen Conner was with Gil Sedaka in the Dirksen Building, trying to go through the committee work that might narrow down the list of enemies. Brooks texted Conner while Rena asked Upton a few more questions. They needed Maureen to verify Upton's version of what happened with her chief of staff before the Senator and her aide had time to coordinate.

Conner was able to check some of the details of what Smolonsky had learned on the Grid. Then she walked Sedaka through the bare bones of it, giving away just enough. She didn't reveal Upton's response.

"You remember it?"

He sighed. "One of the worst days of her life. She cut Emily loose. And it nearly killed her."

"Cut Emily loose?"

"I called the U.S. attorney and asked him to convey to Burdick, no special favors. Treat Emily like anyone else. That's what Wendy told me to do. She was cutting Emily loose. Not trying to protect her."

"Why'd you call the U.S. attorney? Why not Dick Burdick? He was the D.A. on the case."

"Because if I called Burdick, it would've looked like the opposite of what it was. To do the right thing here, I also needed to do it at arm's length. And involve as many witnesses as possible."

It would be easy enough to check Sedaka's story by calling the U.S. attorney. Smolonsky could do it.

"The irony," Sedaka was explaining, "is that Wendy has been punishing herself for this ever since."

"Punishing herself?"

"The thing about Wendy, watching her up close all these years." Sedaka paused, worrying he wasn't being clear. "It's not easy up here to be virtuous *and* effective. "It takes real effort. To keep that balance." He paused again. "I don't mean like it's the battle between good and evil. But maybe it is."

Sedaka seemed to be slipping into a kind of nostalgic reverie about Upton's career. Maybe because he thought it was about to end.

"And you don't always succeed trying to figure out what's the right thing to do. You can seem like a moralistic jerk while you're doing it. People tire of that up here. You can have integrity, but you have to be pragmatic. Wendy and some of her close allies up here, they talk about that. Susan Stroud did. What's the right thing to do? That's not a moral question; it's a practical one. What will get the best result? And the answer is not always obvious. You have to know how to pull all the levers. Moral arguments don't get you very far. They're not priests up here. They're politicians."

"No," Conner said. "They're not priests."

"And this place, the Hill, it changes people. And not in a good way," Sedaka kept on. "Of all the thousands of members of the House and Senate, over all the years, maybe only a handful ever made it a better place. Really, only a handful."

He wasn't looking at Conner anymore.

"Wendy is different. She could be a historic figure. I really believe that."

GIL CALLED WENDY after the investigator left. "You okay?"

"Holding up." She sounded as if she had been crying. That was something he couldn't remember seeing her do in years.

"You want me to come over there?" She was still in the Capitol hideaway office.

"No, I have things to do tonight, Gil. Thanks."

AT HOME SEDAKA TOLD HIS WIFE, Charlotte, about the day and the questions asked and the little progress made, just as he had told her this morning about the long night of questions from Rena and Brooks. She stared at him, resenting his commitment to Upton but not resenting the senator herself, whom she liked. "You're in the arena," she said, quoting an old line from Teddy Roosevelt about life in politics.

"I always thought that was a reference to Roman gladiators, who fought to the death for the sport of rich spectators."

"Oh, I think it was," she said.

THIRTY-ONE

RICHMOND, VIRGINIA

Michigan governor Jeff Scott stood at the microphone. The flags of his home state, the United States, and the United States Army hung, as always, from poles beside him onstage. Scott grinned into the lights, the crowd a deep sea of silhouetted shapes. It was the last event of the night. Then home to Michigan on a late charter.

Everyone was on high alert. The whole world was doing stories, it seemed, about the chaos of American elections. "Bloody Liberty," *Le Monde* called the fights at U.S. campaign rallies the last several days—"Liberté sanglante." There had been stories in government-run media of the rightist regimes in Brazil, Poland, Hungary, Turkey, Russia, and even Austria, contemplating the decline of conditions for American democracy. The hint, barely veiled, was that the United States needed stronger leadership if it wanted to put the country back on a path toward security and prosperity, what some called "neo-democracy."

"Has the 20th Century Liberal Democratic Republic Outlived Its Value?" an essay in the new nationalist French paper *Le Front* asked, in a translation reprinted in the new intellectual weekly the *Washington Chronicler,* financed by Karl Sabanoff, the billionaire sports and real estate magnate. "We may no longer need Americans to light the way as a beacon for Europe's political structures. But we need their economy to be stable enough to help our own ships navigate calmer seas."

Whatever one thought of the international right wing telling Americans how to vote, the reality was that it had been an unnerving week. Four violent incidents in four days—the fight at Pena's rally, the brick thrown at Dick Bakke, the brawl at the Omar Fulwood event, and then the ruthless beating of a man in a Pena T-shirt by a Traynor supporter this morning. The story had built all day.

Jeff Scott's campaign security, a firm recommended to him by one of his backers, employed all former Special Forces soldiers, tough men well and efficiently trained. They had high-power scopes mounted in the rafters of the Virginia Commonwealth University Stuart C. Siegel Center.

"Road Runner Four to Command," the team leader stationed in the southeast rafters said.

"Command."

"We have three possibles, moving east in section 104. Wearing dress shirts with what appear to be Pena for President T-shirts underneath."

"Copy that, Road Runner Four," Command answered. "We are sending friends their way. Keep monitoring."

Road Runner Four, monitoring the southwest rafters, issued the orders to his men. "Southwest One and Three, keep eyes on these three possibles. Southwest Two, Four, and Five, keep scanning for others."

Road Runner Four watched through his own scope as the security team now came from two directions at the three suspicious men. Two men were grabbed by six trained former soldiers and began to be led away. There was a mobile police unit waiting outside the auditorium. But the third man broke free and began to run.

Road Runner Four watched as the man climbed over people in their seats to higher rows.

"Road Runner Four to Command, we have a runner," he reported to his superior.

"Copy that."

The man didn't run long. Maybe twenty seconds. But there would be video.

"Runner is in custody," Road Runner Four said into his walkie-talkie.

"Roger, Road Runner Four," said Command, watching monitors in a communications room in the basement. "I will inform the city police."

In a half hour the Scott campaign issued a press release headlined SCOTT SECURITY TEAM FOILS POSSIBLE ATTACK AND DETAINS SUSPECTS AT CAMPAIGN EVENT. The press release noted that the people detained and handed over to police were wearing the same pro–Maria Pena T-shirts as the suspects in the beating at the Traynor rally earlier that day. Friendly media throughout the day would extol the superior security work of the Scott team.

* * *

Rena was in his den reading. Or trying to.

Nelson, the gray cat Vic had given him, was fighting for Rena's attention with the book in his hand, a history of the chaotic 1860 election.

When the phone rang it was Matt Alabama, routed through to Rena's encrypted line.

The correspondent knew nothing of Rena's work for Wendy Upton. Washingtonians are used to compartmentalizing their lives—keeping secrets from friends, even loved ones. It was something people took more seriously than most Americans would have believed.

"How are you, Peter?"

Matt wanted to talk. Something was bothering him.

"Dandy. How 'bout you?"

"I feel like a psychiatrist trying to diagnose an insane patient and I can't read the symptoms," Alabama said.

Rena sat up. "Whaddya mean?"

Alabama told him about the incident at the Scott event, the apprehension by Scott's security team of people planning to disrupt the rally.

"The more I think about it, the more I'm getting paranoid."

"Paranoid about what?"

"About how it looks good for Scott. His people captured rioters before they had done their dirty work, something no other campaign managed to do. All the others had their rallies upset. So Scott looks like a victim, too, of the protesters, but also a hero because his team stopped these people before they did any harm."

Rena was quiet.

"Maybe I'm getting too cynical," his friend went on. "No candidate would risk it, sending people to attack other people's rallies. Certainly not the people who run Jeff Scott's campaign. Jack Garner is too smart for that." Jack Garner was the campaign veteran managing Scott's campaign. He was an old Washington hand.

Rena said nothing.

"You there, Peter?"

"Just thinking about what you're saying," Rena said.

"Your thinking gets in the way of your talking."

"Not for most people," Rena said.

"True that," said Alabama. The reporter sighed but didn't laugh. It was late and they were both tired.

"Hope to see you, buddy, when I get back in town," Alabama said.

"Soon, I hope," said Rena.

Then he called Randi.

He told her about what Alabama had said. She already knew, of course, about the arrests at the Scott rally. Randi was glued to the news most of the time.

"We should try to see if these attacks on the rallies are connected," said Rena. "See if Alabama's paranoia might be justified."

"Wouldn't the police already be doing that?"

"They wouldn't be looking for it," Rena said. "For some connection between people arrested in different cities."

"Jack Garner is too smart to take the risk of pulling a stunt like this," Brooks said. Same thing Matt Alabama had said about Scott's campaign manager.

"What about the people behind him? Lower down? Or his backers?" asked Rena.

Jeff Scott's major backers were the hedge fund and Silicon Valley magnate Wilson Gerard, the Aiken family from Illinois, and the Trice family in Arizona.

"Are we now investigating scuffles at political rallies?" Brooks asked.

Their to-do list was already too long.

When he hung up, Rena glanced out the window to see if there were men watching the house. He hoped there were. Because it would mean they were still worried about him. Maybe he should just run out there and grab them. Maybe their presence was the only secret he knew.

They still hadn't found out what threat was looming over Upton. Every lead they had surfaced had come up dry—the JAG attorney Henry Nelson, sister Emily Upton, even Wendy's love life. They'd contacted the two women Upton said she had had affairs with years earlier, but neither said they had been contacted by anyone else. They'd also tracked down the lone boyfriend from long ago, Dave Garrod. He appeared to bear no grudge against Upton. He also confirmed Upton's story that she and Garrod had once considered marrying. He said he'd loved her at the time, but thought something felt missing for her. She didn't love him, he thought. But he admired her still.

Rena needed sleep, at least for a few hours. Almost everyone else was still at the office. Wiley and Lupsa were combing the Web looking for something they missed. Robinson, Conner, and Brooks were delving through Upton's legislative career—with the help of software Lupsa had written that matched names of donors to rival campaigns to targets of hearings and Upton's legislative votes. Hallie Jobe was still going through Upton's career in JAG.

He wasn't sure how much good any of it would do. He figured sometime tonight Upton would get a call from both Traynor and Bakke pulling the plug on their offers. If they did, hopefully it would never come out that she had been threatened. And he was beginning to wonder if whoever was threatening Upton had anything at all. Maybe it didn't matter. The threat itself was the threat. Upton would be smeared with rumors that weren't true. And that would be enough. The facts wouldn't matter.

DAY FIVE

FRIDAY

FEBRUARY 28

THIRTY-TWO

GRAY HAWK HUNTING LODGE
OGEMAW COUNTY, MICHIGAN

Senator Llewellyn Burke's black Escalade pulled up in front of the stone and wood hunting lodge just after sunrise.

The building was new, but it had been built to look old.

The Gray Hawk Hunt Club was the most exclusive private hunting preserve in the Midwest—eight hundred secluded acres surrounded by a ten-foot electric fence, hidden in the Michigan woods just ninety minutes from Detroit. The main lodge, which sat above the lake, included a "saloon," a main dining room, and a series of private "salons" where business could be conducted. There were various bungalows nearby for overnight guests and a second dining room on the lake called "The Renegade," used for private dinners and heated by Franklin stoves. The club was owned by an anonymous group and offered only one hundred invitation-only equity memberships for an "initiation price" rumored to be $1.4 million, plus an annual operations fee of $250,000. But there was little argument, among those lucky enough to have been invited here as guests for a meal or to hunt white-tailed deer, that Gray Hawk was the most elegant of the 136 controversial private hunting preserves in Michigan.

Senator Burke was visiting this morning at the invitation of

Michigan governor Jeff Scott, the decorated army veteran who, at age forty-one, now aspired to be president. Senator Burke's wife, Evangeline, had been invited, as well, to join them for breakfast after the two men had an early meeting. Senator Burke had sent Evangeline's regrets.

As his car pulled up, Senator Burke noticed that Governor Scott's wife, Elaine, was not waiting on the front porch.

But he did see Scott's campaign manager, Jack Garner, who went inside before the Escalade stopped.

Scott rose to greet Burke and shake his hand. "Senator," he said warmly. "Lew," he added, as he clasped a second hand over Burke's.

The gesture was friendly if choreographed—and vaguely threatening, Burke thought. Scott's hand now enveloped his own and could control it. Politicians loved physical demonstrations of power.

"I was thinking, as I was waiting for you," Scott said, "I don't know we've really had time alone before. Without anyone else in the room, I mean."

They had met before, of course, many times. But Scott was right. This was the first time the senior senator and the young governor had ever been one-on-one for what Scott had promised was just a personal visit. No agenda. Just "two men who oughta know each other better getting the chance."

"Shall we go in, Senator, or would you like to sit here on the front porch?"

"Whatever you prefer," Burke said.

The more Scott chose, the more Burke would learn about him.

"I'd love to take a walk, actually, if you'd like," Scott said. He was polite and respectful. "It's so beautiful here."

Walking had become the new meeting venue of choice at Davos and other gatherings of the powerful, who believed it led to more creative thinking.

"Then let's walk."

"Splendid."

Scott put a light hand on Burke's shoulder and they headed down the steps and onto a path leading to the deep woods.

"I don't know if I've told you before, Senator, what a hero you are of mine. I just admire how you've made your way in politics, how you've always seemed true to your beliefs. There are so few people in public life like that."

And Scott offered the smile that had quickly made him famous. It was a little-boy grin on a grown man's face, sweet and mischievous and a little elusive.

Scott had recognized the magic of his smile on people for as long as he could remember, delighting moms and teachers and big sisters when he was a boy, later intriguing women when he had come of age and drawing men to follow him in combat. Scott's charm was so confident and easy, Burke, too, felt its magnetic pull.

He could have been a movie star. But Scott was more than that. He was a real-life war hero who looked like a movie star. In Iraq, he had saved men in battle at the risk of his own life. That had won him the second-highest medal that his country offered for heroism in combat, the Distinguished Service Cross. Then he'd come back to the U.S. and started a company to help veterans, which made him a millionaire. Then, with no meaningful executive experience beyond his officer field training and being a front man for the veterans group, he ignored the Michigan GOP's request that he run for Congress, "jumped the line," and ran for governor. Now, after a single term, he was running for president.

He wanted to "strip down and remake the GOP and the rest of the country," he said, "get the nation fit again," even if it meant "putting it through basic."

He was tall and broad. Even out of uniform people guessed he'd been either a soldier or an athlete. He had dirty-blond hair, and his head tilted down slightly, a habit he had from being bigger than most people. His face was rugged and impish, and it was not uncommon for women to stare.

"Senator, I'd like us to be friends," Scott said. "We don't know each other as well as we should. I'd like to change that. I'm not necessarily the character you see on TV." They walked a few more steps without Burke reacting, and Scott added, "We all have characters we play, right?"

Burke still said nothing, and Scott went on: "I think there is a good deal I can learn from you, Lew, from your experience and your wisdom. I hope you might be willing to teach me. I know I've moved quickly in politics, but I don't pretend to know everything. I respect experience. I was a soldier, and I believe in the chain of command."

"That is the kind of thing older men usually like to hear," Burke said with a smile. Then, in an earnest way that was genuine but also careful, he added, "But the older I get, the more I find I can learn from the young. When we stop being students, we begin to die. Don't you think?"

Scott stopped walking. He nodded and grinned. Oh, that smile. "See, I'm learning from you already."

Then he put his hand on Burke's shoulder again. "Lew, to me, being friends means being honest. I want to be honest with you, if you'll permit me."

Something in Scott's tone made Burke cautious.

"By all means," Burke said.

"I didn't ask you here today to plead for your endorsement of my candidacy," Scott said. He'd started walking again. "Maybe in time. I certainly hope so. But I did want to discuss your thoughts about the field of candidates."

Burke kept walking and said nothing.

"This is awkward, but I promised to be candid," Scott continued. "I know, Senator, that you would have a hard time supporting Richard Bakke—"

Burke interrupted his host, an uncharacteristic display for him of ill manners. "Why do you think that? Dick is a member of the U.S. Senate. We've worked together. We're colleagues."

Scott stopped. "Are you thinking of endorsing him?"

Burke said: "Putting aside the fact that I could endorse you instead, Governor, is there a reason I shouldn't endorse Senator Bakke?"

Scott smiled differently now, a smile of recognition rather than charm. The patrician and pleasant Burke was not just careful, Scott was thinking. He was also shrewd, and Scott was seeing it close up for the first time. This old dog was going to be harder to manage than he'd realized. He should have known.

"Since I am being honest, I'll just come out and say it," Scott said. "I thought you wouldn't endorse Dick Bakke because you don't like him." He paused. "If he wins the nomination, of course, that's a different matter. Then we all come together as a party."

The timing of this meeting was no accident. They both knew Burke would have to decide about an endorsement soon. The Michigan primary was eleven days away, and if Burke declined to support Scott, his home-state governor, it was a statement within the party. If he endorsed someone else, it was an insult.

What was less clear, as the campaign had progressed and Scott's success grew, was whether Burke, for all his own popularity, could afford to distance himself from Scott—let alone disrespect the governor by endorsing someone else. That was the subtext of this meeting. Burke had suspected it. Now he was sure that it was Scott's message: *Time to choose, old man. And see how much power you have left.*

Burke looked into the woods. He and Scott were walking side by side, their strides not quite in tandem.

"An endorsement is more complicated than whether you like someone," Burke said. "But of course, you know that, Jeff. It's also a matter of *where* you agree and disagree with someone. And whether either of you can compromise."

Burke disagreed with Scott—and with Bakke—on almost every issue where Republicans could differ. On climate change, social policy, how to reform the military, how to reform domestic policy. Scott was doubling down on Dick Bakke's antiestablishment, revolutionary

GOP rhetoric, but adding charisma—and even some winking sense that he wasn't serious about any of it. Llewellyn Burke had no idea what Jeff Scott really believed. Dick Bakke, for all his loathsomeness, was transparent and sincere. And it was increasingly likely that one of these two candidates would win his party's nomination. It was some choice: A misguided and unlikable true believer. Or a dashing, ruthless, and perhaps cynical young neophyte, for whom everything seemed like a means to an end.

"There are other questions that matter to me," Burke said.

"Such as?"

"What kind of people does a candidate hire around him? How will the candidate react to the inevitable crisis? What is their capacity to grow? To learn? To listen? No one, Jeff, is prepared to be president the day they begin."

Jeff Scott had a practiced look of concerned concentration on his face. "Well, I hope home-field advantage, Lew, is worth something," he said. "Us both being from Michigan."

"Of course. You're a very popular governor and you've touched something in the people of Michigan. In the whole country."

Scott stopped walking. "What would it take to win your endorsement, Lew?"

Burke stopped, too. He had wanted to avoid this moment, setting terms—ones that Scott might meet, boxing Burke into a corner.

"Our country's in trouble, Jeff. I want a nominee who can help us heal."

Scott's smile returned, slowly at first, then fully flowered.

The charming, mischievous movie star smile, sweet but knowing and with just a hint of menace.

"This is where it starts, isn't it," Scott said.

Burke wondered what Scott was talking about.

"What starts?"

"The hunger for public service," Scott said. "It starts at home.

When you're young. Listening to your neighbors. Talking about their dreams. It's like a first love—discovering you want to help people. And learning you can do it by leading them."

They were at a private hunting lodge—a place where billionaires met, catered to by servants. But the billionaires who built this place were beginning to back Scott. That was why they were here—so Scott could remind Burke without saying a word that he had their backing.

"Gray Hawk isn't exactly where *the people* are," Burke said.

"Oh, I know. I just think when you're away from Washington, you can be more honest."

There was that word again. Scott used *honesty* in a way that had too many meanings, thought Burke. Scott leaned toward him. "I know you wouldn't be part of these rumors encouraging a cross-party ticket. Maybe with Senator Upton. I cannot believe you would."

How much did Scott know about the offers to Upton? Burke's mind tried to move quickly around the possibilities.

"You think it would be unwise if the country had a bipartisan ticket?"

Scott was smirking. "Well, it would be suicide for Senator Upton. She'd never belong anywhere again."

"Some think a bipartisan ticket might help the country heal," Burke offered. "If you win the nomination, you could pick one, too."

The laugh that came out of Scott began low and was deep and unexpected. "That depends on what kind of healing you want," he said.

"Is there more than one kind?"

Scott began walking again—and Burke had to hurry to keep up.

"Senator," Scott said, "things are changing. That's a fact. The party's changing. And its leaders need to change with these new times. If they don't, they become leaders out of time and get left behind." Scott glanced at Burke. "If someone is a leader out of time, they've lost the feel of their people. It's like a commander losing the feel of the battlefield. The enemy starts to move in a way you don't expect. You aren't sure what they have in mind. Then you don't know where to place your own troops. It's a terrifying, helpless feeling." Scott quickened his pace. "It happens at some point to everyone. All political careers end with someone being left behind and no longer having power." He stopped and turned to Burke, whom he had purposely kept a half step behind.

"I think there are two kinds of leaders, Lew. Those who shape their times, and those who adapt. Very few leaders are true shapers. Reagan. Teddy Roosevelt. Lincoln. Washington. Maybe Andrew Jackson. Most of us must listen and adapt."

Burke waited for Scott to come to his point.

"We need to understand our time, Senator. To lead, to channel our people. Not get caught behind."

Scott paused and then, his voice low and intimate, said, "This is not the same America we grew up in. Or the same Michigan. We need a new Republican Party or the party will die. I hope you can be part of that. You said you wanted to learn from the young. I think we can teach each other. I hope we will."

He put his arm lightly on Burke's shoulder again.

Burke looked up and realized they were back at the lodge. The trail they had taken was a loop.

Burke held out a hand to Scott. "Governor, you said we should know each other better. I am glad that is beginning to happen."

Scott took the hand and looked Burke in the eye, trying to read the older man's meaning. He said, "Too bad your wife couldn't make it this morning. It would have been nice to have breakfast, the four of us." He only paused a half a beat. "I think your car is waiting."

"Maybe next time," Burke said.

"I hope we see more of each other, and establish an honest friendship. That's rare in politics. But after family, friends are all you have in life."

"Another insight from a thoughtful young man," Burke said.

FROM THE ESCALADE Burke called his wife, Evangeline.

"What did he want?"

"To threaten me."

"How?"

His wife rarely sounded surprised when they discussed his life in politics, and he often wondered where he would be if Evangeline Harris, the startlingly intelligent southern belle he'd met at Princeton, had not agreed three decades ago to marry him.

"If I don't support Scott for president, I'll be challenged in my next primary. And Scott is pretty sure they can beat me."

"Did he say that?"

"Not those words. But as Dad used to say, listen to what a man means, not what he says."

Burke's wife took a moment before asking: "How much do you think he can really hurt you?"

As the Escalade drove off, Burke looked back through the rear window. Scott was waving.

"If they find the right person to challenge me, I'm beginning to think I'll be history."

"Lew, no."

But Burke hadn't finished his thought. "That's what Scott threatened me with: being a man past his time."

On the other end of the line Evangeline Burke was silent.

THIRTY-THREE

1820 JEFFERSON PLACE
WASHINGTON, D.C.

Samantha Reese was waiting for Rena in his office when he arrived. She was sitting on his sofa with Randi Brooks.

"You found something," he guessed.

She nodded grimly.

Rena had first called Sam Reese in Colorado four days earlier, the afternoon he and Brooks were summoned to Senator Burke's house to meet Wendy Upton, and asked her to fly to D.C. in case he needed her. Two nights ago, the night they were interrogating Upton and Rena discovered someone monitoring his house, he asked Reese to start following Upton twenty-four hours a day.

Rena sat down beside her now.

Sam Reese was no ordinary person. She was one of six women to have completed the Army Ranger School and a celebrity as an Olympic-caliber athlete. She was a biathlete—the cross-country skiing and shooting sport. But not long after her Rangers accomplishment, Reese became frustrated with the assignments the army was offering her and was set back in her Olympic training by an injury. She resigned her military commission and moved back to Colorado. She owned a gym now in Snowmass, rehabbed her injured leg, and amused herself leading a small group of other former military women who took occasional jobs doing surveillance and security. People rarely spotted women doing this kind of work. They always looked for men.

"What'd you find?" Rena asked.

Reese was tall, five ten, in her early thirties, with sun-washed brown hair and the sculpted lean but muscled look of an athlete. The strength in her arms and legs, however, was hidden by her clothing, a dark blazer over a blouse with slacks, like a check-in clerk's at a hotel, an outfit chosen to be easily forgotten.

"Maybe nothing," she said, taking her time. Brooks, impatient, shifted on the sofa. "There's a woman she's been with. A lot. Night and day."

Wendy Upton had told them there was no one romantically in her life. That part of her, she said, had been all but shut down.

Rena was shaking his head. Was this the secret that could destroy Upton's career, he wondered? That she had a current lover, not just a couple of gay experiments in her long-ago past? Did someone think they could use this as blackmail to keep her from the race? And possibly drive her out of the Senate?

The answer wasn't as simple as whether the country would accept a lesbian as vice president. It was, instead, whether Bakke or perhaps even Traynor would take that risk. If history was any guide, the answer would be no.

It was hard for presidents to know what to look for in a running mate. Often they sought balance. If you were old, pick young—Eisenhower picked Nixon; if a northerner, pick a southerner—Kennedy tapped Johnson; if a conservative, pick a liberal—Carter chose Mondale. There were exceptions, but balance was the first norm. Yet even then it was hard to know how much a veep really helped, whether the balancing act actually won you any new states, except maybe the VP's own.

The only sure thing, the only incontrovertible truth of vice presidential selection, is that a poor VP pick could hurt you. The reason was simple enough. In the basic calculus of politics, if there was a problem or scandal involving a veep, the head of the ticket would have to spend weeks "off message," defending their running mate from whatever accusation had erupted. Worse, they'd have to explain why they had not more carefully vetted their choice. That was why, ironically, the people picked as VP were often cleaner, and blander, than those elected president.

"You have pictures?" Brooks asked.

Reese held up her phone. There was Upton with a dark, rather elegant woman, a brunette who looked somewhere around forty.

There were different shots from different times, usually at night.

"You know who she is?" asked Brooks.

"We did a little Internet hunting, but I figured we'd use your team to be sure. We just wanted to establish they had spent the night together and that there was a pattern. Last night they did."

"I'll get Arvid," Brooks said, meaning Arvid Lupsa, one of their two Internet sleuths. She leaned over her phone to send him a message.

Rena asked: "Your team have eyes on her now?"

"On the hotel where our mystery woman's at. Waiting for her to come out. And on Upton, who's at her office."

Brooks looked up from her phone at Rena. "What are you thinking, Peter?"

Rena had a penchant for what Brooks considered dramatic acts, but he looked back at her, lost in thought, and didn't answer the question. She sensed, however, that her partner was beginning to form a plan.

Lupsa arrived, and Brooks explained the pictures on Reese's phone. "Text them to me," he said cheerily, "and then we'll go people searching." His face had lit up. "I've got some new facial recognition software. The stuff is really improving."

They followed him to the office he shared with Ellen Wiley. Lupsa had three large computer screens arranged in a semicircle on his desk, a multitasking paradise. Reese, Rena, and Brooks hovered behind Lupsa. His fingers danced over a keyboard. Brooks, who still looked at the keys when she typed, marveled at his speed.

On his center screen, Lupsa scanned the images of the woman in Reese's pictures with whatever software he had been referring to; he clacked more strokes on the keyboard; then they watched as the software seemed to scan through countless pictures from the Web at a pace beyond their meager human skills.

"You looking for pictures she's tagged of herself on Y'all Post?" Brooks asked.

Lupsa said, "More than that. This is using more sophisticated facial recognition software to scan any pictures of her on the Web, whether they are tagged with a name or not. It's also reading her facial imagery closely enough that we'll get results when she might look much younger."

In less than a minute the following words appeared on the screen: IMAGES OF SARA BERNIER. Underneath were numerous pictures of a woman who looked like the ones on Reese's phone.

A few moments later the words IMAGES OF SUZANNE BRENNER appeared and, underneath them, other pictures of apparently the same woman.

Then came IMAGES OF ELLA BRUENER and more pictures of the same woman.

"We have a bingo," Lupsa said with a soft thrill in his voice.

"Three bingos," said Reese.

Brooks was leaning in, squinting. "Why would this person have multiple names? You sure your software's working?"

"She has aliases," Lupsa enthused. "It's the same woman, I promise. Your senator is spending time with Sara Bernier, aka Suzanne Brenner, aka Ella Bruener."

Brooks was giving Rena a look. "Now who would use aliases?"

Rena stared back.

"Spies, criminals, and undercover cops," said Reese.

"And which one is she?" Brooks said.

"Can you tell?" Rena asked Lupsa. "Can we figure out who she works for?"

"I'm going to do some pairing so we might find out," Lupsa said.

"Pairing?" Reese asked.

"Look for who she has ever stood next to in pictures. Who are her friends? Who does she associate with? No one is anonymous. Not anymore."

There was more keyboard clicking, and the trio of observers leaned back from Arvid's computer as it searched. Hundreds of pictures seemed to scan by on his screens, there a moment and then gone, as the algorithm placed a photo next to others, saving the matches in thumbnail size on the side of the screen and then moving on to look for more matches.

Ellen Wiley wandered in and asked what they were doing and if she could help.

Reese, on her own phone, started typing in the name *Sara Bernier.* Brooks smiled at her and said, "Sam, don't waste your time. Ellen should do it. She's got more tools for that."

Brooks gave Wiley the names, and Wiley began hunting for businesses associated with the woman in the picture—by all of her various names.

Lupsa was looking for people with whom the woman might have ever had her picture taken.

Rena had a pensive look. "What are you thinking?" Brooks asked him. "And why do I already not like it?"

He smiled vaguely.

"Let's see what they come up with."

It didn't take more than a few minutes before Lupsa called for them to come back. They clustered around his monitors. There were several pictures of a middle-aged man standing next to the woman called Sara Bernier, though in two of the images she was tagged under the name Ella Bruener.

"Ari Belmondo," Lupsa said of the man in the pictures. "Ellen, you got that?" he asked Wiley in a raised voice.

"Ari Belmondo," Wiley called back happily. "Got it."

Now there were pictures of another man on Lupsa's screen, also in pictures with Sara Bernier, aka Ella Bruener, aka Suzanne Brenner.

"François Gui," he called out to Wiley, adding "G-U-I" so Wiley had the spelling.

"François Gui," Wiley repeated back.

A few moments later, she said, "Ooooooh. Yeahhhh."

"What?" Lupsa demanded.

"François Gui, former French intelligence officer."

"Ooh la la," Lupsa said in a poor French accent.

Wiley called out, "Gray Circle Consultants."

"Yes, yes!" answered Lupsa. "Gray Circle."

Brooks, tired of their banter and stupid accents, said, "What is Gray Circle? And who the hell is Sara Bernier?"

Wiley walked over to Brooks, her old friend, holding a laptop. "Why don't we all go down in your office," she said to Brooks, "and Arvid and I can explain it to you?"

THIRTY-FOUR

"Gray Circle is a French and Israeli security company," Wiley said. "They have a couple of subsidiary companies. One is called Vigilas. Another is Canopy. They do slightly different things, but they're all part of Gray Circle."

"And what does Gray Circle do?" Brooks asked.

"That we can tell you up to a point," Wiley said. "But I think you'll find it a little different than what you were expecting."

Wiley opened her computer to another window and showed them more. "Gray Circle is a consulting firm run by a group of former French, Israeli, and a couple of American intelligence officers who've moved into the private security business." Wiley smiled. "And they even have a website, if you can believe it. I guess even former spies need to do some marketing."

They stared at Wiley's little screen. The Gray Circle website said the firm offered "seven dynamic kinds of service." The first one was called "Creative Intelligence."

Underneath that heading were the words: "Tailor-made solutions based on high-quality intelligence, cutting-edge technology, unique expertise and out-of-the-box thinking."

Brooks offered a lawyer's scowl. People trained in legal buzzwords have special radar for the bullshit of other professions.

The other headings were even more ominous sounding. HARVESTING IN THE CYBER WORLD. Under that heading were the words, "Innovative tools and methodologies to handle massive amounts of data, unearth useful information for clients, and map all potential sources of interest by traveling the deep parts of the online world, including typically inaccessible areas of the Dark Web."

"Shit," Brooks said.

"What?" Reese asked.

"These guys are promising to dig up shit on competitors, even going into the Dark Web to find it. These guys are no joke."

The Dark Web was where you found illegal activity. There were two reasons to go there. Either to find out if someone you were investigating was dirty, or to find things that you could use to blackmail people.

The last of the seven "services" offered by Gray Circle, however, was the one that most caught Rena's eye.

It was labeled PROACTIVE RESEARCH. Underneath those words it read:

"We overcome limited access sources with a can-do dynamic approach: We employ methodologies from the social engineering fields that allow us to move freely around limited access sources and extract valuable information, both in virtual and physical environments."

Wiley met Rena's eyes. "You understand, Peter?"

"I do indeed," he said almost in a whisper, glancing at Brooks. Her expression had become grave.

"Well, I'm glad you all understand, because I don't," said Reese. "What the hell does that bullshit about proactive research mean?"

Reese was an expert in "physical" security, surveillance, and protection, so-called body work.

"It's espionage language," Rena said. "Code."

"For what?"

"For spy methods. For setting people up. Sending people in undercover, having them pose as friends or business opportunities. And then either spying on your subject while pretending be their friend or putting them in compromising positions so they begin to work for you. In other words, setting them up to be double agents. The things spies do."

They had talked about this, Rena, Brooks, and others at the firm. At some point in the near future, they figured, the business of private investigation and backgrounding would become so big and lucrative, it would begin to attract people from the clandestine world. Rather than being the province of former law enforcement professionals, who worked within the legal realm, it would begin to attract ex-spies who worked outside the parameters of the law. Intelligence services didn't investigate crime. They were involved in something else, a form of warfare that was often illegal. They would create sting operations and entrapment methods so they could use and control those people.

"You mean this firm is engaged in setting people up so they can blackmail or extort or control them? Honey traps and all that?" Reese asked.

Rena nodded. The tools of covert intelligence included getting close to people and then putting them in compromising situations by offering them bribes, using sexual seductions called "honey traps," involving them in crimes, or doing them illegal favors. Once you had wooed someone into doing something wrong, then you could control them with the threat of exposure. That was the code meaning of the term *proactive*. You didn't have to find something wrong. You could create it and ensnare your target into it.

Wiley was laughing at the screen.

"Gray Circle even identifies some of its top people on its website."

There were pictures there of François Gui and Ari Belmondo.

"Why the hell," Reese asked, "would they do that?"

"Because some of these names have a lot of credibility in the spy world," Rena answered.

"And they advertise?" Reese said. She was incredulous.

Lupsa said: "Not in the conventional sense. You'd never find this website unless you were looking for it. But if you were, it would be because you wanted to check these guys out, because you wanted to know if they were the real deal. So this site is marketing, just like any other company's. Only most people would never go here, because they don't know it exists. You would only get here if you already knew about Gray Circle and wanted to verify some things. They probably have to give you their Web address."

"Jesus," murmured Reese.

Incredibly, Gray Circle even had a "Who We Are" page that listed the names and biographies of the firm's principals and board of advisers, some of them former prominent figures in French and Israeli intelligence circles.

Reese pulled out her phone and began scanning the Gray Circle website for herself, up close. About twenty seconds later, to no one in particular, she said:

"And here in the background of one picture is our girl. She's not named, but in the third row, you can make out her image." She used her fingers to expand the image, which got blurrier.

"Let me check," Lupsa said. He had brought his own laptop into Brooks's office. "Wow, you're right, Sam. And with the human eye, no less."

"Why would they ever put her on their website?"

"I'm not sure anyone was looking for her picture there before," said Wiley. "It didn't come up when the algorithm was scouring pictures of her from the Web. But it's not like this is a secret government agency. They want people to hire them. They need some presence."

"I've seen this before," Rena said, "former spies offering their services to large corporations. They do need some presence. They just don't get too specific. And they use a lot of euphemisms."

"And even aliases."

"No, her real name is Sara Bernier, I think," Lupsa said. He was still searching more deeply into the Web to find out about their mystery woman.

Wiley asked: "Why would she use a real name?"

"We don't know that she did. But she probably would have in case someone ever checked the names of anyone meeting Upton more than casually. It's better to use your real name. If you use a fake one, an alias that's not real, you're breaking the law, and it's pretty easy to get found out."

"So Gray Circle is looking into Upton," Wiley said.

"Or a Gray Circle operative has befriended the senator," Reese said, "and spent much of the last week with her, including overnight."

So they had made a discovery. Gray Circle was all over Wendy Upton. Had that firm been hired, perhaps by Bakke or Traynor, to vet her? And then she and Sara Bernier had become friends? Or was this something else?

Brooks was shaking her head. "The real question is who hired Gray Circle."

Rena was looking at Reese. "Sam, you said you still have eyes on Bernier and Upton, right?"

She nodded.

"Then let's go."

"Peter, don't do anything rash," Brooks said.

But he didn't answer.

"Goddamn it," she said raising her voice. "I don't like it, whatever it is."

By then, however, Rena was gone. Reese was hurrying after him.

THIRTY-FIVE

They parked halfway down the block from the Sylvan Hotel, not far from Georgetown Law Center, Rena behind the wheel of Reese's rented Ford, Reese in the passenger seat.

About twenty minutes passed before they saw someone who looked like Sara Bernier emerge from the hotel.

"On the move," Reese heard one of her team confirm through her earbud.

Reese nodded to Rena, and they slipped out of the Ford and headed toward the hotel on opposite sides of the street.

Reese could see the tall, dark-haired woman from the photos moving toward her, glancing at her phone and swiveling her head looking for a car she'd ordered. A black Lincoln moved slowly up the street. Bernier looked in, but there were two people inside, not one. Two women, the second person sitting up front next to the driver.

Reese moved up close behind Bernier.

"Sara, my name is Samantha Reese." She said it in a voice that was so gentle and familiar, it sounded almost intimate. "I work with Wendy Upton. She needs to see you. Would you get in the car?"

Bernier turned and Reese gently touched her elbow in the reassuring but authoritative way a doctor might guide a patient during a medical procedure in the office. The back door of the Lincoln opened.

"Please don't worry, Sara. You're in no danger. Wendy really needs to see you."

The woman from the passenger seat was now outside the car standing next to Bernier. She placed a hand on Bernier's back. Her touch was much less reassuring than Reese's but just as insistent. Bernier tensed, then hesitated. She wasn't a French government agent anymore, and she wasn't in her own country. Slowly, surrendering, Bernier bent into the car. Reese slipped into the backseat beside her. The woman who had laid hands on Bernier returned to her seat up front.

And in the back, next to Bernier, having entered the Lincoln from the street side, sat Rena.

"Hello, Sara. My name is Peter Rena. I work for friends who are concerned about Wendy Upton."

His voice was flat—not particularly friendly but not threatening.

Sandwiched between Rena and Reese, Bernier was afraid, but she had enough training not to panic.

Reese put a hand on Bernier's bag. "I'm going to need to hold your phone, Sara. You'll get it back."

Now Bernier reacted: "What do you think you're doing?" She tugged at the bag.

"You're safe," Reese said. "This is just so we can talk." She placed her hand on Bernier's. The Frenchwoman let go of the bag.

Then Reese put Bernier's phone inside a black case, one that blocked any device potentially tracking Bernier's location or movements. To anyone monitoring the phone, it would appear as if the device suddenly vanished.

Rena said: "Wendy's not available this minute. So let's talk awhile. We're just going to drive around. Then see Wendy. Then we'll drop you back right here."

"Who the hell do you think you are?"

"I thought I told you. My name is Peter Rena. I do what you do—security and background work. We—all of us here, except you—have been hired by friends of Wendy Upton to find who's threatening her."

"This is a kidnapping" Bernier said. She was trying to sound outraged. "I'll call the police. And I'll sue."

"By all means," said Rena. "We'd welcome the police. That would mean news coverage. And a public record of what we want to ask you about. That would be excellent. So would a lawsuit."

He paused for a moment to let that sink in. "We'd especially look forward to the disclosure phase. Maybe I don't need to ask you anything at all here. We could call the police now, and you and your people could file the lawsuit against us today."

Bernier was watching him.

"But I'd insist you make the call right now so we could be sure it actually happens. Maybe we should file the complaint against you. Or. . . ."

Bernier waited, but Rena didn't finish.

"Or what?"

"Or we could just talk instead. You could answer a few questions. And when we're done you get out and you'd be free to tell anyone you need to about this."

Bernier looked somewhere between thirty-five and forty. Lupsa had unearthed what he could quickly about her and sent it in an encrypted file. But, she had three different birth years listed. The file said she was French but had studied in the United States. After traveling as an actress briefly and selling pharmaceuticals, she had joined the French security services. As a cover, she appeared to have worked as a consultant to a health care industry trade group and as a fund-raiser for a nonprofit. She had social media profiles under all three of her names, one featuring her life as a health care consultant, another as a fund-raiser, and a third under what appeared to be her real name, but that one was vague on detail.

She was, by anyone's definition, a beautiful woman, her face angular and refined, her hair a dark chocolate brown, nearly the same color as her eyes. She could have been taken for French or perhaps Turkish or Iranian, Rena thought, and even now, trapped between Reese and him, she had an elegance that her fear hadn't entirely erased.

"What do you want to talk about?" Her English was fluent, with just a hint of a Parisian accent.

"Mostly, your time with Wendy."

"What do you want to know?" She was calming now.

"Simple things. When did you meet? How long have you known each other? Who hired you? How did this all come about—at least as much as you know about it?"

Bernier was an operative, not a strategist, chosen most likely for her charm and some measure of being adaptive, Rena reasoned. But this—getting caught and put in the back of a car—was almost certainly beyond what she'd experienced, even if she'd had training for it. No matter what you see in movies, most spies are never grabbed. He was counting on Bernier, now that they had her, to be calculating how to minimize the damage.

"That is a lot of questions," she said.

"We'll go one at a time," he told her.

THIRTY-SIX

Hallie Jobe found Randi Brooks at a table hovering over a computer with Ellen Wiley.

"I found something," Jobe said. "A letter Wendy Upton wrote not long before she left the Judge Advocate General's service to work for Congress."

"What's in it?"

"It's long story," Jobe said.

She sat down across from Brooks. "I had to do some digging to know what it meant. Good thing I did."

Brooks was quiet as Jobe walked her through it. The letter Upton had written vouched for a Kuwaiti man who had been imprisoned in Guantánamo Bay, Cuba, for eleven years. Upton's letter argued the man be set free.

The man in question had been a member of the Kuwaiti elite. His father had been a fighter pilot and even flown in squadrons with Americans against Iraq in Desert Storm in 1991. The son had studied engineering in college and during his summers taught villagers in poor areas how to dig clean-water wells. He was spending the summer of 2001 teaching people in Afghanistan. When the Twin Towers came down and the Americans arrived in Afghanistan to root out the Taliban, the young man, like thousands of other non-Afghans, had tried to leave the country and get back home.

"Finding out who was Taliban and who was not was like spitting in the dark," Jobe said.

At the border, American military personnel were improvising, paying men five hundred dollars for every member of the Taliban they could identify. "Someone picked out this young Kuwaiti." He was renditioned to Gitmo. A year later, the man who had pointed him out was discovered to be a fraud. An Afghan judge said his testimony could never be used in court.

"The thing was," Jobe said, "that meant the Kuwaiti kid in Guantánamo could never be brought to trial on that evidence. But by now he he'd been through the whole playbook of enhanced interrogation—sleep deprivation, light deprivation, waterboarding, all that. We were reluctant to set those guys free."

Instead, his jailers doubled down to get a confession. "The interrogations continued, and maybe intensified," Jobe said. Another decade went by. Finally, Upton took up his case, Jobe explained.

"Getting a Gitmo prisoner free is no picnic," she said. "Not only do you have to establish the person's innocence, prove his support of the United States, and persuade the State Department of those facts. You also have to satisfy the Department of Defense that if the guy were let go, he would remain a supporter of the United States and its allies in the future. That means you have to persuade people that this guy, who had suffered all this mistreatment in prison, would never do anything to support jihadists or our other enemies."

It was an almost impossible test to meet.

"Upton did it for this guy. She really went to bat for him. It was a tragic case."

"Why is this bad?" Brooks asked.

"The man has just been arrested on suspicion of helping jihadists," Jobe said coolly.

"Now, all these years later?" Brooks said. "How do you know?"

"That's what's interesting. I found the letter and called one of my JAG sources. He said we weren't the first people to call him about this letter."

"What?" Brooks said. "Someone else called him about this?"

A trace of a droll smile was forming on Jobe's beautifully sculptured face. "And this is the good part. The guy who called had to identify himself. He said he was vetting Upton for one of the campaigns. The military wasn't all that helpful. Asked for the man's employer."

"Don't drag this out, Hallie. I'm so tired."

Jobe gave Brooks a pat on the hand across the table. "My source said the man who called him was named Dan Becker, and he worked for a company called Vigilas. Some kind of private investigation firm. My source was upset that private eyes were poking around. Said he didn't think that's how we ought to run our campaigns."

"What about you?" Brooks asked.

"Apparently I am a beautiful black woman. Not just a private eye. And we're friends."

That earned a look from Brooks. "You have that letter?" Jobe nodded and handed it over. Brooks began to read it; then she stopped, remembering something.

"Vigilas. Wasn't that one of the subsidiaries of Gray Circle?"

She typed the name of the website they had found for Gray Circle, the one no one would know was there unless they were looking for it. Buried near the bottom of the "About" page was the reference she recalled to "our affiliates Vigilas and Canopy," which provided additional services.

It was not unusual for people in politics to be attacked for things they had done that were noble at the time they were undertaken. Nothing about Upton's letter was dishonorable. Just the opposite. But it could be easily used as a weapon to harm her if it were framed the wrong way. A skilled consultant could twist the letter into looking like evidence of Upton's poor judgment or, even more bizarrely, raise doubts about her patriotism.

If Brooks were Upton's consultant, she thought, she would want to get the defense of this Kuwaiti man out early, as part of the biography introducing Upton to a national audience—to suggest that Upton was a woman of unusual courage. That was a basic rule of political consulting. Framing and timing were critical. But that was not Brooks's problem now.

Who had hired Gray Circle, she wondered. When Brooks and Rena figured that out, they would have their blackmailer.

Then another thought occurred to her. The blackmailer, whoever it was, didn't have *one* thing on Upton. Maybe because it wasn't clear there *was* one thing that was devastating enough on its own to destroy her.

Instead, whoever was trying to blackmail Upton was trying to come at her with several things. The blackmailers were now inside Upton's life. And they were just going to keep coming and coming.

She thought about Peter. She shuddered to think what he and Sam Reese might be up to. When he dashed off like this, he didn't ask permission or explain his plan. She worried that her partner—the soldier that the army no longer wanted, the loyal American increasingly brokenhearted about his country—was becoming more ruthless. She feared for him a little. But at the moment, she was glad he was doing something. She just hoped it wasn't illegal.

THIRTY-SEVEN

"Your real name, to start," Rena said.

"Sara Bernier."

"Born?"

"Paris."

"Date of birth?"

Bernier resisted even on some of the basics. Rena took it as a sign she had at least some training for this kind of encounter. Fight your interrogator over simple things. Stop them—in effect—at name, rank, et cetera.

Rena also knew, however, that the gulf between training and the real thing was vast. Most people who undergo questioning—during a deposition, by police, or in other circumstances—do so for the first time. For the interrogator, however, it's their job.

In the front passenger seat, Reese's operative typed on a laptop, checking Bernier's answers.

"What service did you work for?"

"Pardon?"

"In France? Which government service?"

Bernier didn't answer at first, and Rena explained her predicament to her in a little more detail. "Sara, this is a legal situation, now. You appear to be engaged in an extortion scheme against a United States senator. That is a crime in the District of Columbia, a violation of D.C. statute, and because Senator Upton is a federal elected official, it is also a federal crime. If you lie to us now, given that we are acting on her behalf, you are compounding that crime."

Rena wasn't sure if his last statement was strictly true as a legal matter, but Bernier was pissing him off, and he figured she wouldn't know.

Still he didn't give her a lot of time to think. "Again, if you prefer, we can drive you to the police now and explain what has occurred and you can be arrested, and your company and your client charged, and you can file your suit against us. What did you say you would allege? Kidnapping?"

He waited a couple of beats. "But remember, *we'd* be bringing you to the police to ensure that you didn't flee. Not really much of a kidnapping, is it?"

He watched her think. Reese watched her, too.

"Or, as I said, you could just answer some questions. And when we're done, you can go. That wouldn't be much of a kidnapping, either. And just to be clear, Linda in the front seat up there is recording our conversation, so there's a record. Should we talk? Or go to the police station? Whichever you want."

Bernier thought about it longer than Rena expected.

And slowly said: "What do you want to know?"

"So, to be clear, you're agreeing to talk to us?"

Bernier nodded.

"Please say it so Linda can record it."

"Yes."

"Thanks. I was asking what government agency you used to work for."

Bernier muttered, "DGSE."

The General Directorate for External Security, the French military spy agency. She had to guess they knew this already, that Rena was testing whether she would lie to them.

"When did you begin to work for Gray Circle?"

Bernier didn't answer.

"Okay, Sharon, let's go to the police station," Rena said to the driver. "But I'm still not sure between Capitol and Metro."

Then, to Bernier, Rena said: "Sara, Capitol police will be more protective of the senator. So you'll have the presumption of being some kind of terrorist threatening her. But Metro D.C. cops will mean more publicity. And we'll be there longer. It's kind of a mess at Metro. Processing takes hours. But we'll get a lot of publicity. The local TV stations and the newspapers monitor the activity there. So this will be a story on the six o'clock news and the wires and the *Tribune*. We've got our version of the story ready."

"I think you have made your point, more than once, Mr. Rena." She pronounced it *Reeena*.

"It's Ray-na," he corrected her. "As in ray gun. Or X-ray."

He wanted to irritate her.

They had reached that point in the interrogation now.

"I will answer some questions," she said.

She was not as worn down yet, or as frightened, as Rena wanted, so he went at it gradually, one question at a time, so incrementally that the information would seem trivial. Breaking it up like this, Rena knew, also tended to make a subject lose track of time. When did you leave the French security service? When did you go to work for Gray Circle? Who recruited you there?

They showed Bernier the pictures of her with François Gui and Ari Belmondo, and the picture of her on the Gray Circle website.

Slowly, she told them a story. Some of which had to be true, Rena figured, because they'd already revealed they knew some of it. How much of what she said was the truth? Rena watched and listened.

In the army, he had been regarded as among the most skilled interviewers in military intelligence. He was careful, intuitive, and extraordinarily patient. And he was in his element now.

But Bernier was good at being false with people. That was her job. She had a daredevil spirit, typical of those who operated undercover, and she was still more in control of herself than she pretended. She was also, he sensed, not as smart as she believed herself to be—or as she needed to be today.

She was certainly beautiful, and Rena could see that she used her beauty to keep people at a distance, making herself appear more formidable. But he also saw that once she no longer had that shield of mystery, she felt vulnerable. That was her secret, and they'd unlocked it.

Rena listened and asked questions that went back over the vagaries until more detail was filled in. He pretended to be easily confused—so she had to explain things more than once. That began to expose her fear—that she was not smart enough for this. And that was important for what was to come next.

"How long have you known Wendy Upton?"

She would know they could get Upton's side of the story, if they didn't already have it.

"About two and a half weeks," she said.

That meant some fifteen days before Upton was threatened—long enough for a cautious Upton to be swayed into a relationship with Bernier, but not long enough perhaps to have second thoughts about it. That had all the earmarks of the timing of a honey trap.

"Where did you meet?"

"At a reception."

"Where? What reception?"

"For a youth group, Young Statesmen of America."

"How did you meet there?"

"We were introduced."

Despite her growing discomfort, her short answers were a sign she still was exercising some control.

"Who introduced you?"

Bernier gave the name of a GOP donor.

"And how do you know him?"

François Gui had introduced her to him, she said. The donor was a client of the firm, she allowed, to whom she'd been introduced as a health care consultant.

"So Gui recruited you to get close to Upton?"

She had made a mistake. And she recognized it. She nodded.

"Should I take that as a yes?"

Bernier didn't answer verbally.

"What did Gui tell you to do?"

No answer again.

Softly, with a menacing gentleness, Rena said: "What did Gui tell you to do?"

"To talk to Upton about health care legislation."

Rena shook his head as if he were disappointed. "Sara," he said.

"To win her trust, too. As any lobbyist would."

"You mean to seduce her? To sleep with her?"

Bernier stiffened. "To win her trust. If I could, to be her friend."

"Were you told to try to sleep with her, to become her lover?"

Rena's voice had become so quiet, the words were barely more than air passing between them, and he leaned closer so Bernier could hear.

Her eyes now registered some new emotion, something close now to true panic. This had gone further than she'd expected, and for longer. This man Rena had used her short, elliptical answers against her, and she had lost track of time. They had long ago left the city and were well on their way now toward the Chesapeake Bay to the east. They had been driving more than an hour, perhaps closer to two.

After a deep breath she said, "You don't understand. You only see how this started. I've been honest with you. I was sent to meet her, to become her friend. That's all." She stopped and looked into Rena's eyes. "But . . . then. Look, you know her. You work with her. Wendy is—how to put it—extraordinary. An extraordinary person. You recognize you will meet someone like her, someone so different than everyone else, only a few times in your life. You know you are in the presence of someone special, someone who—makes you want to be better."

Rena let silence hang between them and waited to see if Bernier would fill it. He wanted to know if she was inventing this or struggling to articulate something true. The best way was to say nothing, to watch. When people lie, silence becomes a kind of insufferable weight, in its own way unbearable, because they don't know if the lie has worked. "What I'm trying—I don't know how to say it, but—I have feelings for her. It's not an op anymore. Not for me."

Rena watched, and Bernier tried to see out the front windows, to place where they were. They had turned off the highway and were on a county road now.

"You're her genuine lover? Is that what you're saying?"

Bernier didn't answer. And they drove awhile longer in silence.

In a mile or so they turned onto a smaller country lane and then down a dirt road until the car slowed down and stopped.

"Where are we?" Bernier asked.

Reese answered: "Someplace where we can take a break, get something to eat. There is a house here, a cabin, on a creek. It belongs to a friend of mine."

"Am I a prisoner?"

"Not at all. We'll take you back anytime."

"And go to the police?"

"And go to the police," Reese said.

"But I've answered your questions. You said I could go home."

Rena, without looking up at her, said: "You've answered some. We have a few more. But if you want to stop, we can call the police and both tell our stories."

AS THEY WALKED TO THE CABIN, Rena texted Brooks asking what more they had learned he could use.

THIRTY-EIGHT

1820 JEFFERSON PLACE WASHINGTON, D.C.

They had brought their computers into the conference room—Brooks, Wiley, Lupsa, Conner, Robinson, and Liu.

Being together helped them coordinate and work faster as they combed through the fragments of Upton's life that could be used to harm her. Had any of the campaigns potentially threatened by her candidacy—or any of the consultants they'd used—ever hired Gray Circle? Could they link any of the PACs that subsidized those campaigns, or their contributors, to Gray Circle or to its subsidiary Vigilas? It was a wide net.

We live in a surveillance society now. True privacy has been destroyed. Everything about a person be can be collected—and sold. But it is corporations doing the surveilling, not governments, and if you have the skills, you can turn it around and use all that to learn about the corporations themselves. Surveillance can work both ways.

Conner and Brooks were poring through court filings and government records, looking to see if Gray Circle's name ever surfaced in a lawsuit involving any of the companies or people associated with any of the campaigns. Robinson and Liu were hunting campaign filings, including Federal Election Commission files, checking whether any political campaign had ever used Gray Circle. Most likely, they'd be hidden inside a payment from a campaign to a law firm and the law firm to Gray Circle, obscured, buried. But maybe someone had been careless. Lupsa and Jobe were looking at anything they could find about Vigilas and Gray Circle everywhere else. Smolo was looking for any signs that Vigilas and Gray Circle were in Tucson. Wiley was helping everyone.

Only Rena had not been dragged into the vast digital ghost trail. He was with Bernier.

Randi Brooks was searching for Vigilas, Gray Circle, and its other subsidiaries in congressional subcommittee transcripts. There were dozens of such hearings a year, and she didn't know how many years she might need to go back.

Around 3 P.M. a reference in a document caught her eye. In testimony before the Subcommittee on Taxation and IRS Oversight, a Senate Finance subcommittee that Upton chaired, Brooks saw the name Amadeus Corp.

She had seen that name somewhere else, she thought. She went to the Grid, where all their findings were compiled. She blearily entered the name *Amadeus*.

And there it was.

In a filing buried in State of California disclosure documents, a statement that Amadeus Corporation had once hired Vigilas in a lawsuit challenging a decision by the California State comptroller.

The filing was obscure—and by itself meaningless. But not when combined with what Brooks had just discovered in the Senate subcommittee transcript.

Amadeus, the Senate transcript showed, was a subsidiary of Valerian Investments. Four years earlier, the Senate subcommittee Upton chaired had investigated Valerian in connection with the complex tax evasion scheme called basket trading. Basket trading was the technique Brooks had learned about from her Senate friend Judy Worthington and flagged into the Grid. It was a trick used by Wall Street banks and private hedge fund investment firms to avoid paying taxes. Basket trading was complicated and highly technical, which is why it had gone undetected for so long. It was the accounting tax fraud scheme that Upton had tried to shut down.

As far as Brooks could make out, basket trading was an elaborate method by which banks and hedge funds conspired to hide profits from the government: A hedge fund would put its money in a bank. The bank, in turn, would open an investment account with the same hedge fund for exactly the same amount of money.

While it looked like the hedge fund was trading the bank's funds, in reality it was trading its own money. That was step one.

The next step involved time. Each account would remain open at least a year. For tax purposes, that meant they were considered long-term investments. Inside the accounts, however, the hedge fund was executing millions of trades, most of them a few seconds long.

In the cases Upton's subcommittee had found, the largest perpetrator of this hedge fund tax fraud scheme was named Valerian Investments. Its subsidiary was called Amadeus. And it was big. In one example, Valerian made twenty-nine million trades in a single year, the average trade, three seconds, long enough to enjoy a small uptick in a stock price. Then the stocks were sold back, as Valerian's computers took advantage of the speedier trading software it had designed. The trades themselves were legal. But loaning money to a bank—pretending the money was the bank's and the hedge fund was simply investing it—was illegal. It was tax evasion. If Valerian had admitted that it had been trading in its own funds, it would have had to pay much higher taxes.

Over the course of four years, Valerian had made thirty-six billion dollars in profits with basket trades involving a single bank, Ralston Bancorp. By claiming the money belonged to Ralston, rather than to Valerian investments, and claiming that the money was held for more than twelve months rather than just a few seconds, Valerian had evaded some $7.1 billion in taxes.

When it was done investigating, Upton's subcommittee declared the scheme the single-largest tax dodge ever uncovered by the United States Senate. The panel had gone so far as to list various government programs that Valerian's seven billion dollars in taxes could have paid for. Instead, Americans had had to cover those costs themselves with their personal income taxes.

Yet almost no one had ever heard about it. In the wash of news and acrimony in Washington, the subcommittee report had not attracted much attention. A press conference and a tiny story inside the *Wall Street Journal*. An AP wire story in the Tucson and Phoenix papers.

And even though it was the largest and most profitable private equity investment fund in the country, the name Valerian Investments was largely anonymous. Valerian dealt exclusively in institutional investment funds that exceeded one hundred million dollars in assets. It didn't advertise on television. Most Americans had never heard of it.

Two other hedge funds and two other banks had engaged in basket trading schemes as well, according to Upton's subcommittee report, but on a smaller scale and for not as long. They also had stopped, Brooks found, after being caught by Upton's Senate subcommittee. And they'd settled with the IRS.

But not Valerian. It had persisted in using basket trading. And sued the IRS to fight the tax finding. The case was taking years to wend its way through the courts.

In short, Valerian had a very large bone to pick with Wendy Upton.

That was the first item Brooks had identified. The second was the key link.

Valerian's subsidiary hedge fund company, the Amadeus Corporation, had hired Vigilas to do investigative work in another dispute, this one with the California state tax authority. It was a possibly meaningless link, perhaps no more than an innocent coincidence. But maybe it was more: for it connected the hedge fund Valerian, a powerful force with a grudge against Upton, to Vigilas, which was a subsidiary of Gray Circle, the group that seemed to be hunting Upton's background and apparently setting her up in a honey trap.

Brooks would never have known if she hadn't remembered the reference to Amadeus in the Grid. And if she hadn't thought to look among the hundreds of tax subcommittee reports and hearings about basket trading.

Now Brooks just had one more thing to check. It took only a moment.

When she was done, she leaned back in her chair and rubbed her eyes.

Valerian Investments was the most profitable hedge fund in the United States. And it was owned by a man whose name Brooks had seen on Rena's whiteboard:

Wilson Gerard.

Though the exact amount had never been pinned down, according to what Brooks had found so far Gerard was believed to be the single-biggest financial donor to GOP candidate Jeff Scott.

Ellen Wiley wasn't in the conference room any longer. She'd gone down to her office to take a phone call. Brooks grabbed her laptop and headed to Wiley's office, out of breath from running the stairs when she arrived.

"Ellen," she gasped, trying to get the words out, "I think I've found our blackmailer."

THIRTY-NINE

EASTON, MARYLAND

The text message they sent to Samantha Reese was long and complicated. After trying to understand it, Reese handed her phone to Rena.

He scanned the message quickly, continuing to focus his attention on Sara Bernier.

"Who hired Gray Circle?" he asked. He tried to hide his excitement about what the text told him. Randi might have finally broken open what they needed. She certainly had given him a lot of new information to explore. Now Rena needed to get Bernier to confirm it.

They had eaten, sitting on a deck by the creek to let Bernier relax. That would make it harder for Bernier to claim she was being forced to be here. She had sat unguarded and lingered over a leisurely lunch. She was trying to calm herself down and learn as much about them as she could. But that only served their purposes more.

Now they were back in the cabin sitting around a small table. Rena was asking questions. Reese's people were outside where Bernier wouldn't see them. The sun was beginning to set.

Bernier stared back blankly at Rena.

He rephrased the question: "Do you know the client?"

"No." She answered too quickly.

"Would you like to know the client's name?"

She paused, unsure how to answer. Rena was signaling to her that he now knew who Gray Circle's client was. That must have been in the text he had seen, Bernier reasoned. For the last two hours, it had been clear to her he didn't know.

What else did he know that he had not known before? Bernier tried to recalculate.

Rena already had. Bernier, he now recognized, had been lying for several hours—whenever she thought she could get away with it. He doubted, now, that she had any real feelings for Upton. That was always going to be part of the cover story if she were caught. He was skeptical, too, of the name she had given them for the donor who had supposedly introduced her to Upton. Gray Circle would have never given up the name of another client, especially one who helped them. That was bad for business.

Rena thought Bernier might be telling the truth about not knowing who hired Gray Circle. That would be how a spy agency would have handled it—compartmentalizing information—and Gray Circle was run by former spies. If they ran their consulting firm as they had been trained to run their intelligence operations, Bernier would know as little as possible.

"Better not to know the client's name? That how you feel?" Rena said.

Bernier hesitated, then smiled.

This time Rena knew she was lying. Her eyes gave it away. Once she had decided how to answer, she was too quick with it. He realized it was something she had done several times in the last few hours. He retraced his memory as quickly as he could, trying to recall what else she had been too quick to answer.

"Have you met him, Wilson Gerard?"

"No, of course not," she said, but her eyes gave it away again.

Rena looked as if he were disappointed.

"What else was there," he asked, "besides your honey trap and digging into Upton's background?"

She shook her head. "I don't follow."

Rena leaned toward her and his voice softened. He shook his head slowly. *I have broken you now,* his expression said. *I know when you are lying to me. This is over.* But he said nothing. Just his look, for several seconds. *I have you now. I am disappointed each time you lie.*

Then, as if he had all the answers he needed, he seemed to change the subject.

"Were there operations against other campaigns?"

"I don't know," she said, again too quickly.

After two more lies, Rena began to gather his things. "Sam can take you back now, if you want. We're done. No police. But I wouldn't tell your employer we know who the client is. They'll think, Sara, that you told us. They'll think we kept you all this time because you told us everything. Because we know everything now."

He looked at her coldly.

"Really, I don't know how much you want to tell your employer about any of what happened today. You could tell them the truth. That we got you into a car and talked to you for hours. Or you could say you lost your phone, or that it died. That you just needed a day away to yourself. Or that you were running from us. Or tell them you've developed genuine feelings for Wendy. That's what you told us. Maybe stick with that."

"What do you want?" Bernier said.

Rena looked at Reese rather than Bernier.

"Twenty-four hours. Give us that. Don't tell anyone about today until tomorrow night, and we won't tell them that you spilled your guts. Maybe you'll never have to tell them anything. You guys can stay here, or head the rest of the way to the ocean in Bethany and spend the night. Or go back. It's your call. I've got a car coming to take me back to the city. But if you give us twenty-four hours, none of this ever happened. And you're off the hook."

Then Rena left the house with Bernier inside.

Reese came outside with him. "So we're kidnappers now?" she said.

He had a glint in his eye. "No, we were just 'proactive,' 'engaging in out-of-the-box thinking,' and 'showing a can-do attitude,'" he said. He was quoting the Gray Circle website.

"Don't get me arrested or sued, Peter," Reese warned him.

"I don't think we have to worry about that."

Then he got into the passenger seat of the second black Lincoln sedan that had been following them all day and had been waiting down the road for the last few hours out of sight, and headed back to the city.

FORTY

AUSTIN, TEXAS

The door to the suite on the top floor of the W Hotel in Austin, Texas, swung open, and four people who seemed in the middle of more than one conversation burst in.

A young man carrying two suitcases entered first. He wandered through the large living room and into the bedroom behind it. Inside one of the closets he found the folding luggage rack and placed it where David Traynor would prefer it, at the bottom of the left side of the bed. He placed one of the suitcases on the rack, opened it, and began taking things out. He removed a pair of slippers and found the toiletries and placed them in the bathroom. He pulled out two suits and dress shirts and hung them in the closet. He found a pair of socks and underwear for tomorrow and placed them in the top drawer of the dresser.

The second person entering the suite, a woman in her thirties carrying an iPad as though it were a clipboard, was in the living room talking to the young man through the open door, complaining about something on the schedule tomorrow.

Two older men were already in the hotel suite sitting on a sofa. They appeared to be half listening to her and half finishing a conversation of their own.

Now a man in a suit with a conspicuous earpiece entered the suite, glanced around, and stepped aside for the candidate, Senator David Traynor, to follow. Traynor, the junior senator from Colorado, was on the phone. Once in the room he hung up.

"All set," said the young man who'd been arranging Traynor's room. He appeared to be about twenty-two. His name was Steve Lepler, and he was Traynor's "body man," the person who stayed with the candidate all day, carried his coat, and made sure the candidate had whatever he needed.

"Thanks, Steve," Traynor said, and the boy wheeled his own suitcase out of the suite.

"David, we have to resolve something for tomorrow," Lauren Parker, the woman with the iPad clipboard, announced. "At eleven tomorrow morning, after the speech on entitlements here at the hotel, we come back to the suite and you have double-booked time, a meeting with donors and an interview with the *Texas Tribune*."

Traynor hadn't had time to focus on the schedule during the flight from Dallas, where they had campaigned this afternoon, and Lauren Parker hadn't been able to ride in the Escalade with Traynor into town just now because David had wanted to have private time with the mayor of Austin, who'd met him at the airport. The mayor wanted to talk about a local issue he thought Traynor should reference at the speech tonight in Austin.

"What?" Traynor said abruptly to Lauren Parker.

"Which do you want to do at eleven tomorrow? Interview with the *Texas Tribune* or meet with two donors, Helen Gilley and Sam Ford? They are double-booked."

"Make them both happen," Traynor said.

"How?"

Traynor sighed. "The interview first, but we'll give the reporter just fifteen minutes even though we tell him thirty. Ask the donors if they mind coming into the room with a reporter there. If they're okay with it, have them come in. We'll tell the reporter it was a mix-up, an overlap in the schedule we couldn't avoid. The reporter will think she's getting some behind-the-scenes color, something special. And then she won't mind when we shoo her out."

Lauren tapped this into her iPad.

"Okay?" Traynor said.

"Great," the scheduler said. She hesitated. She was unsure whether she should leave now. She wanted so much to help.

"Have a good night, Lauren."

She took an awkward step toward the door, a hint of uncertainty mixed with disappointment in her eyes. Then she turned, gave a final glance back, offered a kindly "good night," and left the suite.

TRAYNOR LOOKED AT THE MEN on the sofa and rolled his eyes.

"Well?" Traynor said impatiently.

The men looked back, uncertain what he meant. They were Sterling Moss, the chief strategist of the David Traynor for President campaign, and Quentin Phelps, the campaign manager, who coordinated the operations, paid the bills, did the hiring, made sure things happened on time.

"What about goddamn Wendy Upton?" Traynor said, raising his voice, as if saying it louder would clarify the question for his strategic consultant. "Is she going to say yes or what? Can you get me a fucking answer finally?"

Traynor liked Sterling Moss, but it annoyed him that political consultants were so expensive. They seemed to think they were Jedi masters, not hired hands, and they cost as much as hiring Kim Kardashian to come to your kid's bar mitzvah.

Moss offered Traynor a half smile back. The Colorado billionaire entrepreneur senator wasn't as wild as he tried to appear, Moss knew, but Traynor did try to provoke people to get things done.

As a young man, Sterling Moss had worked for Jesse Jackson's chaotic insurgent campaign for president in 1988. "I'm a tree shaker, not a jelly maker," Jesse used to announce to delighted crowds—meaning he saw himself as someone who shook the tree to loosen the fruit, but he was not the man who climbed the tree, picked the fruit, and turned it into jelly. It was Jackson's way of explaining, or perhaps excusing, the bedlam surrounding the whole crazy, impromptu caravan. It was also proof, however, that Jackson's was a "message campaign" and that Jesse, the man atop it, was incapable of managing the government.

David Traynor was more than a tree shaker. He was a self-made billionaire, founder of five different successful companies, still a majority shareholder in three, an NBA team owner, a U.S. senator—and now, after three years in politics, a serious contender for the Democratic Party nomination for president. A tree shaker? He was buying the freaking orchards, planting the trees, picking the fruit, taking it to market in his own trucks, and he owned the stores where it was sold.

"It's a big decision, David—to cross party lines," Moss said. "You sort of sign your own death warrant. She may never go higher in politics. If you win, she has to leave the Senate. And if she says yes, David, and you lose, she may be done. She might never get elected to anything again. She might lose her own Senate seat in the next election. In effect she'd be taking one for the country. Maybe it doesn't work out and she's history."

Traynor raised his eyebrows in a way that suggested Moss had just stated the obvious. "Yeah, that's the fucking point!" He was almost yelling. And he seemed to be enjoying himself. "You get to be at the center where history is made. And I'm looking for her to be a genuine partner here. If I win, she'd have a real portfolio. Did that get communicated?"

Moss was nodding and for good measure added a "Yes."

"Good," Trayner said even louder. "And who knows, I might decide the job stinks and just move back to Colorado and let her have it. Or maybe I'll keel over from boredom."

"That's not funny, David."

"Who's joking? Politics is fun until it's not. Those are the cold calculations she has to make. Or she should be making. I sure as hell would be making them."

Moss said nothing.

The third man in the room, Phelps, the campaign manager, watched the two men joust and remained silent. His job was to make the trains run on time. He would not get into this unless asked.

"And you don't know what's holding her up, do you?" Traynor asked.

The look on Moss's face hinted that he did not. "Gil Sedaka, Wendy's chief of staff, asked if they could have another day. And he mentioned, of course, that you and she will need to talk to face-to-face, if it gets that far."

So the candidate and his potential nominee would need to meet, just the two of them, before entering into such a peculiar union. There would be questions. And a selling job. And promises, for what they were worth.

"No shit!" Traynor said, but he was smiling when he said it. "Fair enough. But I need to know she's a yes before I get in a room with her—even if I decide at the last minute *not* to offer it to her."

"Of course," Moss said, knowing he would now have to lie to Upton's people. Wendy would never agree to the job before sitting down with Traynor first.

"So what's the holdup, Stir? You think she's playing me? You think there's anything to these rumors? That she's on the GOP short list, too?"

"I'm still checking that," Moss said.

He'd picked up that rumor only yesterday. Moss's sources on the hard right of the GOP were pretty poor now. There was a time, not so long ago, when a single phone call would have gotten him anything he needed to know from the GOP at this early stage in the race. Republican consultants he knew who would share information as Moss would with them, as a matter of professional courtesy. Not anymore. The hard right of the GOP barely spoke to the middle of its own party—let alone a Democrat.

"I don't think Wendy would play that game, playing your offer against another," Moss said. "That's not her." Moss had begun to like Upton the more they vetted her.

Traynor gave Moss a skeptical look. "Falling in love again, Marlene?" It was a line Traynor used a lot, mocking the old Marlene Dietrich song.

"Yes, David." Moss countered. "We're all falling in love with her. That's why you're considering her."

"Fuck that!" Traynor said, trying to sound outraged at the thought that he would become emotionally attached. "I'm only interested if she can help me win. A pure, cold, cynical calculation. Only kind I make."

Moss smiled. He'd signed on with Traynor reluctantly at first, but he had come to think there was something extraordinary about the man. "I'm beginning to worry you're not as good a liar as I thought you were," Moss said.

"Then we're both screwed," Traynor said. "Call her again, Stir. I mean tonight, and put some fucking heat into it. I want an answer by tomorrow morning. Find out what the dithering's all about. I heard she's hired Rena and Brooks to do a quick scrub on her. Which is a good sign, unless they found something."

Traynor had loosened his tie and kicked off his shoes and was settling into an armchair.

"I need to know by tomorrow if she's in," he said. "So time's up. And if she is, I want to meet with her on Sunday. That is, unless our scrub comes up with some red flag. And if she dithers longer, we pull the plug. Make sure she fucking knows that."

Moss nodded. They had done an initial scrub of Upton themselves, of course, and it had come up clean, but Traynor had insisted they keep digging. There really is no end to this business. You dig, and if you find nothing, you dig more. Traynor had his own computer digger, a man named Jimmy Collins, on it. Jimmy could lift just about any snotty email you ever sent or any embarrassing website you ever visited. Jimmy Collins was some serious shit, and he and Traynor had done a lot of business together, just the two of them, that no one knew about. He and Jimmy Collins liked to tell each other they might have to share a cell someday, but that was bullshit. Jimmy would take the rap. Any rap.

"I don't want Little Miss Virtue to turn out to be a closeted weirdo," Traynor said. "In this campaign, I play the weirdo. She provides the virtue. Got that?"

Moss was making a gesture with his fingers as if he were trying to remember who was the virtuous one and who was the weirdo.

"Now get the hell out of here, both of you. I want to call my wife, and not have you two guys discover that she should be president instead of me."

Moss tried for a look that said he already knew that.

DAY SIX

SATURDAY

FEBRUARY 29

FORTY-ONE

WASHINGTON, D.C.

Rena got back to Washington around 10 P.M. At the office he found everyone still working.

They spent the rest of the night learning everything they could about the man behind Valerian Investments, Wilson Gerard, the man they now believed wanted to destroy Wendy Upton.

Just after sunrise, too exhausted for more, everyone but Walt Smolonsky, still in Tucson, wandered to Bluestone Lane, a favorite West End breakfast place, all glass and natural light.

Sitting at small tables pushed together, Randi Brooks read from the Grid on her laptop, telling the story of shadowy financier Wilson Gerard.

"The most powerful person in America no one has ever heard of," she began. She was summarizing in a single narrative what they all researched overnight in separate parts. "By return on investment, he is the most successful hedge fund investor and venture capitalist in the United States. Maybe the world."

Gerard, now fifty-nine, had grown up a bright square peg in the round hole of a struggling southern Illinois agricultural family, she explained. He was shy and intense, gifted at math and computers, and interested in philosophy. His parents worried about his making friends and having a normal life. They were relieved when he discovered competitive chess and later debate team.

Then came an event that seemed even now to drive Gerard.

His father, Paul, owned an agricultural company, Gerard Farm Services, which sold seed, feed, and farm equipment. While Wilson was in high school, Gerard Farm Services began to struggle. Paul Gerard fell behind on his debts, especially his taxes. Three months after seeing his son off to Stanford University on full scholarship, Paul Gerard walked down to the root cellar of their home, rigged a shotgun with a makeshift pulley, put the barrel in his mouth, and pulled the trigger.

"In this one interview I found," Ang Liu added when Brooks got to this part, "Gerard described himself as being devastated by his father's suicide and wondered if his mother would survive. But he said he almost never went back to Illinois to see her again. He was too swept up, he said, by the new world of computing opening up to him. This was Stanford in the early 1980s."

Rena imagined a socially awkward boy, distant from his mother, confused by his father's suicide, angered by the impact of government taxes and banks, finding his tribe at the dawn of the digital age in California, and throwing himself into it.

"He stayed at Stanford for the next twelve years," Brooks said, "getting his bachelor's degree, Ph.D., and then an M.B.A. The Valley was just beginning to explode. He was a little younger than Bill Gates and Steve Jobs, four years—not quite part of the generation of technology entrepreneurs who dropped out of college to begin to commercialize personal computing and the Internet."

"By his own accounting—at least back when he was still open about it," added Liu, "he was more driven by money than Jobs and Gates were. He didn't want to be a financial failure like his father. And he was interested in how tech would change the world more than he was in the tech itself."

Liu was beginning to open up more to the team and assert herself, Rena thought. He was pleased, and he knew Brooks was as well.

Gerard's first great business vision, Brooks explained, was to create computer algorithms that would eliminate human emotion in investing.

"He was still finishing his Ph.D. He studied what happened in the first few moments of trading, when a stock began to move up or down. He saw discernible patterns in how stocks behaved in those first seconds, patterns he believed would become even more prevalent as more trading was computerized. He believed you could make reliable profits in those initial seconds if you executed rapid trades in and out of a stock. He called these microtransactions."

"I don't follow," said Jonathan Robinson, who was a political guy, not a lawyer or a computer wizard.

"If you executed such microtransactions often enough, in enough different stocks each day, you could make money without ever having to master the mysteries of any one company or any industry," Brooks said. "Gerard thought most brokerage firms were bullshitting when they said their brokers understood a given industry or stock. But algorithms could predict the first few seconds of a stock if the initial trade was up or down—whatever the industry. And the risk of any one position in microtrading was so small—since you held that stock for such a short amount of time—it didn't matter if occasionally you were wrong."

No one at the Wall Street firm where he worked was interested in his algorithm, Brooks said. His philosophy repudiated everything the brokerage firm stood for—the myth that it was their brokers' expertise that mattered.

Gerard soon left, taking with him three large clients who were intrigued by his idea, and founded Valerian Investments. It had no retail customers, a handful of brokers, and limited itself to accounts worth ten million dollars or more.

"In ten years, between 1995 and 2005, Valerian came out of nowhere to become the most successful investment company in the United States as measured by return on its investments," Brooks said. "By 2000, one hundred percent of its trading was algorithmic, more than half of that in these microtransactions, which lasted only a few seconds." She scanned the Grid a bit more. "Christ on a bike. By 2016, Valerian was the largest investment firm in America measured by assets under control, and the most profitable by gross income. And I'd never heard of the fucking company until yesterday."

"Because it has no retail clients," said Ellen Wiley, "no retail offices, and doesn't advertise."

"Then he started using profits from the Valerian hedge fund to become a venture capitalist investing in start-ups," Brooks said. "That's when he got really rich. He named his venture capital firm GFS, in honor of his father's failed agricultural supply company. Their first stake was in a something called E-Pay, which was trying to make Internet purchases easier."

"He'd become a radical libertarian by then," Wiley added, recalling this part, which she had researched. "He was suspicious of government and wanted to establish a virtual currency that was untraceable by taxing authorities—a precurser to Bitcoin. But E-Pay was gaining momentum in late 2001, just when al-Qaeda attacked the United States. The notion of an e-commerce currency largely untraceable by government seemed a way to finance terrorism. His partners worried the government would shut them down. So they made E-Pay into a more conventional way of paying online—basically just a secure method linking retailers with customers' bank accounts."

"When E-Pay was bought by the second-largest Web retailer in 2004, Gerard went from being a multimillionaire to a billionaire," Brooks said. "And now he had two major businesses—an algorithmic microtrading firm on Wall Street and an online payment service. But his third investment would be his most successful."

A year after launching E-Pay, Gerard became the first outside investor in Y'all Post, the social media platform company that started on college campuses and was now the third-biggest company in the world. In exchange for a half million dollars, Gerard got a 5 percent stake. "When Y'all Post went public in 2007, Gerard's investment was valued at four billion dollars, half of which he cashed out on the first day."

GFS since then had invested in a number of start-ups, some of them increasingly exotic. Two were dedicated to slowing the aging process, one of them based on changing people's DNA, another on the idea people could live decades longer by ingesting a derivative of their own urine.

Gerard was now worth fifty billion dollars and spent a good deal of his time on his biggest new investment, Brooks explained, something called Frontir Corp.

"I researched this," said Lupsa. "It sounds a little like *1984*."

"You tell it, then," Brooks said, pushing the laptop to him. "I'm not sure I follow it."

"Basically, it matches people's online personal data with government information about them—along with data about their location and behavior."

"What the fuck?" said Robinson. "That's Big Brother, from the big antigovernment libertarian!"

"Pretty much. And Frontir has been winning contracts from government agencies and police forces to predict who might commit crimes or become terrorists."

"This is scary," Robinson said.

"And largely unknown. Still private. But growing rapidly. Some people think it could be more profitable than his investment firm."

"The more I learn about what is going on out there, the worse it is," Robinson said. "And *we're* the swamp? No, we're the dupes."

FORTY-TWO

"What about his politics?" asked Rena. He hadn't spoken until now.

"In his early days, he was something of a public philosopher on technology and society, writing long essays in obscure but respected libertarian-leaning blogs." It was Brooks answering, but Ang Liu was nodding her head. "He gave long interviews and considered writing a book," Brooks went on. "About ten years ago he became suddenly very secretive, perhaps to the point of paranoia."

"Around the time he got active trying to reshape American politics," Ellen Wiley added from behind a mug of green tea.

"What were those early ideas?" Rena asked.

"I'd say radically libertarian. With some nuance," said Brooks.

Rena said, "What's that mean?"

"When he got to college, he believed deeply in the idea of the individual as supreme, strongly influenced by the writer Ayn Rand. He has a first edition of *Atlas Shrugged* in a display case in his living room."

Robinson was rolling his eyes. "Great, a fascist with a superman complex."

Wiley was holding her hands out so Brooks might pass the laptop over. "This was the part I was researching." Taking the computer, she began to summarize. "His ideas shifted some. In college, he was deeply influenced by a philosophy professor named Raoul Picard, who developed a theory he called Mass Social Influence. Picard's theory is that people are deeply socialized by group pressures. This explains things like fashion trends, changes in hairstyles, why we buy cars that all look alike—most marketing and the formation of markets and consumer psychology. It was this realization of the power of mass social influence, Wilson Gerard wrote before he became so reclusive, that made him believe social media platforms like Y'all Post, where people want to "be connected," had a big future in the market. Unlike his fellow Y'all Post board members, Gerard was not idealistic about what this would bring about in the world. He thought the social benefit of Y'all Post would be trivial. He just thought it would be a huge success financially and thus a major platform for collecting data and selling advertising."

The food had come now, and they were making their way through bacon and eggs, pancakes and waffles. Rena, always careful, was eating oatmeal. Wiley tried to decipher Gerard's political philosophy.

"After he stopped writing about his ideas, he became harder to track. But he let his hair down a bit in 2010, in one last essay. He talked about the two great dialectics in Western society. One is a tension between freedom and collectivism. He sees this playing out as a struggle between technology on one side and the political restrictions in the form of government regulations on the other. Society wants to control what progress technology can make. So we have speed limits and financial regulations and the like."

The group was quiet.

"The second great tension he sees is between the individual and the mass. Most great things happen, Gerard believes, when individuals are driven to change the world through ideas, visions, and technology, and are left alone. At the same time, people, by their nature, want to conform, want to be part of society, of groups, want the same cars their friends have and granite countertops and other things that

Gerard says have no real meaning. But Gerard recognizes the power of this socialization. It's what powers markets and the economy."

"I still don't understand his politics," Robinson said.

"There isn't a lot about politics per se, at least not on the record," said Wiley. "We really had to stitch this together from fragments. But the fragments form a pattern." She took a small bite of scrambled egg and swallowed before going on. "He told one interviewer, for a fairly obscure publication called *Libertarian Review,* that he thinks society is upside down."

"How?" asked Rena.

"Government helps weak people get strong and makes strong people weaker by taking their money away and inhibiting their creativity. He said he understood why that occurred. He attributed it to mass psychology and socialization—one of the great forces in society. But he thinks that mass psychology inhibits society by inhibiting creativity. That's why he thinks society is upside down."

"What?" said Robinson. "I don't think I follow this."

"An enlightened society would recognize it was better to unleash the creativity of the few for the betterment of the many. Self-interest properly understood would recognize the benefit of what Gerard called 'unfettered capitalism.' He called his own philosophy 'economic libertarianism.'"

"Simply put," Wiley said, "it means leave the rich alone so they can be entrepreneurs. Eventually the rest of us will benefit. Not limited government. Almost no government at all. Basically, limit government to public safety."

Wiley handed the laptop back to Brooks. "He was extremely vocal when he was young," she said. "Then he became enraged that people were misunderstanding him and mocking him."

Brooks scanned further: "After 2005, he no longer gave interviews or speeches or wrote anything. There are mostly bits in articles quoting people who know him or worked with him. One longtime colleague said Gerard argued that blacks in America were better off before the civil rights bill in the 1960s, which created a culture of dependence among African Americans and led to drugs and urban ghettos."

"Really?" said Jobe.

"Although he has never said so publicly, a former employee claims that Gerard feels the drug problems in America can be attributed to the civil rights movement."

Hallie Jobe closed her eyes and took in a deep breath.

"He has also reportedly told friends he thinks the problem of racism in America is exaggerated, that to say we are a racist country is an example of mass thinking, something fashionable, and that you would be shunned if you argued with it."

That was greeted by silence.

"He thinks climate change is probably real but overblown by mass psychology and that we haven't adequately studied what the impact will be. He follows a biochemist in Oregon who argues that if climate change is real, the effect might be good. This guy thinks Americans will enjoy an earth with more plant and animal life than before, and that in any case it would be more efficient and effective if the government did nothing and markets were free to solve the problems of a warming climate on their own."

"This is the politics of crazy," Lupsa said.

"When did he start becoming a political power broker?" Rena asked.

Brooks scanned the Grid timeline. She said:

"Looks like he first got involved in politics around 2010. The first round of money was largely wasted. He did conventional things, like investing in other people's PACs and super PACs. He backed libertarian candidates who all lost."

Brooks maneuvered the trackpad. "But by 2014 and beyond, his involvement got much bigger and more creative. He started a data analysis company called Millennial Insights. He became close with one of the most aggressive far-right-wing political activists, a woman named Rebecca Schultz, who was advising campaigns, running a PAC, and making attack documentaries about Democrats and Republicans she didn't like. Gerard underwrote her. Around the same time, his contributions to conventional PACs ended. Instead, he started giving to donor-advised funds, where most of his money was anonymous. No one knows how much he has actually spent in the last six years."

Gerard was hardly the only billionaire donor in the country trying to hide how much he was really spending to handpick judges and governors and to change laws.

Rena recalled Robinson's slides, which showed the twenty billionaires who had given at least twenty million dollars each, the number of $1.7 billion in dark money in the last election.

Brooks, her pancakes half eaten, pushed her plate away.

"In some ways Gerard is unique. He was interested in ideas first, in philosophy and debate. In college he talked about writing books, making his views and his philosophy known, becoming the next William F. Buckley, shaping ideas, pushing his notions about so-called economic libertarianism. He wanted to explore the dialectic between socialization, marketing, and conformity versus the freedom of independent thought. But he wanted to be rich even more. He thought that was how you changed things."

"So why has he gone so quiet?"

"Hard to say," said Brooks. "But look at the timing. In 2010 you have the Supreme Court decision in *Citizens United,* ruling that money is speech and removing the limits on what an individual can give to a PAC. A year later, the IRS starts to go after Valerian. And it finds a champion in 2014 in Wendy Upton, who leads the charge, arguing that Valerian is a tax cheat. And not just any tax cheat. The biggest tax cheat in history. If Valerian has to pay all the taxes that Wendy Upton says it should, plus penalties and whatever they've racked up since from more basket trading, it's probably ten billion dollars. It would be the biggest tax case ever. And Lord only knows what it would cost Gerard personally."

Rena saw Maureen Conner, who had stayed back to research something, entering the restaurant now, looking for them, her expression urgent.

She sat down with a glance at Brooks's pancakes. "Found it," she said.

Brooks pushed the food toward her friend. "Found what?"

"Proof that Gerard's PAC hired Gray Circle and what he hired them for."

It was the missing piece. They knew that Gerard's company had once hired Gray Circle in another matter. But they didn't have proof connecting it to a campaign yet. Apparently, Conner had now found it.

"How?" Hallie Jobe asked.

"Randi's idea," she said. "Different states have different reporting requirements about campaign contributions. Michigan's are the strictest. In federal elections, a campaign can just say it paid money to such and such and leave it at that. This much to a polling firm. This much to a law firm. So campaigns hide what they are really doing by just giving the money to law firms. But the law firms never disclose if they paid any of that money out to other subcontractors." They all knew that was how most oppo research was paid for. "But in Michigan, it's tighter," Conner said. "You're required to list what was paid downstream to subcontractors, and to name them. You're not supposed to hide what you're doing."

"And?" Brooks asked.

"And it's there. Gerard's super PAC, Freedom for America, paid the law firm Holstein Meyers. And Holstein listed that it paid Gray Circle."

Randi Brooks closed her eyes and then covered them with her hands. She was exhausted. And offended. What Gerard was trying to do to Upton struck Brooks differently and more personally than others here. Rena saw it, if no one else. The reason was because of Randi Brooks's own life. In some ways, his partner's private life was much closer to Wendy Upton's than she ever let on. When she opened her eyes again, she looked at Rena with a sense of real anger.

Rena smiled at his partner. "Randi," he said, "I know how to end this."

* * *

They were in a dark panel van with painters' logos, parked outside the breakfast joint. As the group inside the restaurant began to move, the men in the van made a phone call.

"They look like they are getting ready to break up," the one in the passenger seat said into the phone.

"How much you get?"

"Not much. What do you want us to do? If they split up, there aren't enough of us."

"Follow Rena. And don't lose him again like you did yesterday."

FORTY-THREE

Rena wanted to see Wendy Upton first. She knew nothing yet about any of this—Sara Bernier, Gray Circle, or Gerard. It would be a lot to process.

He went home briefly to sleep, exhausted from his interrogation of Bernier and the all-night scrub of Wilson Gerard.

Then he called Upton and told her they had found something that would be difficult to hear, but he needed to see her immediately.

They met at her rented town house on the Hill. They sat at a small breakfast table in her kitchen. Her roommates, two other senators, were out of town. As Upton listened, Rena explained that the woman she had been quietly seeing for the last two weeks, Sara Bernier, was a paid operative hired by the billionaire Wilson Gerard to entrap her in a sexual scandal.

Upton closed her eyes and bowed her head. She kept her face lowered a long time.

When she raised it again, her eyes were red, but there were no tears, not as there had been when he had talked to her about her sister. She put her palms up to her eyes, as if to block any tears that might be forming, and when she moved them away, Rena sensed she had wiped whatever feelings she allowed herself to feel for Sara Bernier away as well.

She looked at Rena and smiled, almost apologetically. Then shook her head. "So stupid," she said.

Then, softly, she placed one small hand on the small table, as if she were feeling to see if it were real, if the physical world were still real, and said, "This all has to stop."

"That's what I have in mind," Rena said.

"How?"

He didn't tell her everything. He admitted hiring a surveillance team to watch her for three days and explained that this was how they'd caught Bernier.

But he didn't tell her he'd all but kidnapped Bernier yesterday. And he wasn't going to tell her what he had in mind now.

"The less you the know, the better," he said.

Upton held Rena's gaze in her own, her pale intelligent eyes searching his dark melancholy ones. She seemed to be weighing everything that had occurred over the last few days: She had been seduced by Sara Bernier; threatened to stay out of the race; surveilled by Rena's people, who in turn had discovered that Bernier had set her up. They'd discovered the connection to an ex-spy group called Gray Circle and found the link between Gray Circle and Wilson Gerard, who had hired those ex-spies as revenge against Upton, probably for her catching him cheating on his taxes.

Rena wondered at the depth of Upton's humiliation, the proud, strong, good girl, this fearless woman, made such a fool of by a shady group of former foreign spies using sex to blackmail her. Her eyes never moved from his.

"You can't do anything I would be ashamed of. Or that's illegal," she said.

Rena said nothing.

Then a smile appeared on her face, meek at first, then growing until it became thoughtful. She said, "Lew Burke said I should trust you."

Rena thought of his friend Burke, of the trouble he had seen in the man's eyes, and said, "Then you should."

ON THE STOOP OUTSIDE, Rena glanced back through the glass in the front door. Wendy Upton was still sitting at the small breakfast table. Rena could see her body shuddering, hands over her face, her head bobbing up and down. She was alone, and now the tears flowed freely. Tears for how many years and how many people, he wasn't sure.

He had come to admire her, for her integrity, her courage, her preparation. Almost everyone who met her in Washington was struck by those things. She was unlike almost anyone he knew in political life, certainly in the city. And he thought, as he turned away, about what she had forfeited for that.

* * *

As Rena headed down the block toward his old Camaro, the dark panel van turned on its motor. "Not too close," the man in the passenger seat said. "Give him a block or two."

"Not my first fucking rodeo, Dick," said the driver.

"Then start showing it."

Before the van pulled out, however, two surveillance teams, both working for Samantha Reese, took photographs of the vehicle, front and back. The first team, working from a car a half block behind and on the other side of the street, took close-ups of the van's plates, which would be traced easily enough.

The second photographer was a woman jogging down the street coming toward the van. She used a camera hidden in her headband

and made sure, from looking at her phone as she went by, that the faces of the men in the van were recognizable in the shots.

As Rena got into his car, Samantha Reese texted.

"Got 'em."

Rena wasn't fond of texting—especially not emoji, which he considered a fad. Instead, he typed two words: "Thumbs-up."

FORTY-FOUR

Rena had to persuade Brooks they could trust Bill McGrath.

When they told the political consultant everything, he winced as if what he had heard caused him physical pain.

He looked away from his visitors, out the window, toward the Watergate and the Kennedy Center for the Performing Arts. Behind them, unseen from here, were the glass-roofed United States Institute of Peace and the Lincoln Memorial. Rena considered both buildings ironic. The peace institute was built while the country waged the forever war on terrorism. The memorial was built to honor the first president killed by a domestic terrorist. How far had the nation come in 155 years?

"I hate this," McGrath said, turning back from the windows to look at them. "These billionaires who want to reshape the country to their own distorted vision. They think their money conveys special rights and knowledge, which they exercise in secret, the same way they operate their businesses. That is feudalism, not democracy, and it'll ruin us."

It was 10 A.M. on the sixth day.

Before joining Rena here, Brooks had gone back to the office after breakfast to research the law. She wanted to determine whether Gerard and his companies had committed a crime—and perhaps whether Rena, in his interrogation of Bernier, might have as well. "They aren't going to sue us, not for a hundred years," Rena said. "She won't even tell anyone it happened." Brooks wasn't so confident.

When Rena suggested they needed McGrath or some other GOP insider to take the next step to stop Wilson Gerard, Brooks had worried there was too much risk. The political operative, she thought, might not want to offend the rising star in his own party and might tip off Scott or Gerard. Rena argued they couldn't do what they needed without someone's help.

"And didn't we hire him already for a dollar? So's he morally obligated? Or do you have a better plan?"

"I don't have a better plan."

So they were here, and they had just told McGrath what they'd learned, more of it than Rena had told Upton. That's when McGrath had turned and looked out the window and said he hated what big money was doing to politics, as if he and his group of professional consultants hadn't in an earlier time taken power from the parties. The smoke-filled room had its sins and its virtues. Each effort to reform politics brought new forms of abuse. Corruption was like crime, not plumbing. You had to police it. It was never fixed.

"Why did you tell me this?" McGrath asked.

"We need you to make a phone call," Brooks said. "I'll tell you what to say."

Rena got up from his chair in front of McGrath's desk. "And I have an errand to run. More of a trip, really. Randi will fill you in."

McGrath looked suspicious. "What the hell are you two playing at?"

"You will love it, Bill," Rena said, but as he left, Rena smiled in a way McGrath thought a little sad.

BROOKS AND MCGRATH SAT in chairs facing the whiteboard where five days ago he'd showed them his vision of the Republican electorate. A speakerphone sat on a small table between them. McGrath dialed the number.

"Jackie, it's Bill McGrath."

Jackie was Jack Garner, the campaign manager for Jeff Scott.

A garrulous, coffee-and-campaign-amped voice said, "Bill, what's going on, man!"

"You alone, Jack?"

"Never. Too busy, man, trying to win the presidency. Beatin' alligators off with a stick. Fightin' the lyin' media. You know."

Garner was from the Midwest, but he'd picked up a faint southern bend in his speech somewhere along the years he spent learning politics from South Carolina hard boys.

"You need to be alone, Jack. We need to have this conversation in private."

"The fuck, Bill? You got me on speaker?"

"I have Randi Brooks with me. You need to go somewhere private."

There was a pause as Garner contemplated the implications of McGrath, the old Republican political guru, sitting with Randi Brooks, the staunch liberal known as one of the most lethal political investigators in the country. "I'll call you back in three minutes," Garner said. The southern accent was gone.

McGrath drummed his fingers on the table while they waited.

What was about to occur was one of those never-to-be-told-about exchanges that political people like McGrath lived for—part of the adrenalized behind-the-scenes maneuvering that might change history and that historians almost never heard about. McGrath was one of those people who operated in power's shadows, a consultant who did not carry an official title, who never wanted to be an aide or a staffer, and whose stories were rarely told.

It took Jack Garner less than three minutes to call back.

"So what is the big fucking mystery?"

"I don't know if you were a party to what I am about to tell you, Jack," McGrath began. "I don't really care. It doesn't matter. It's your guy, and it all sticks to him, whether he knew about it or not. Unless you end it today."

"What in the name of God are you talking about, Bill?"

"Randi Brooks is going to explain it, Jack. But I think for your sake, and Jeff Scott's, you better listen."

She walked through just part of it at first—from the moment Wendy Upton got the threat to stay out of the race to her and Rena finding the threat against Upton and who was behind it. But she stopped short of telling Garner what they had found. She and McGrath wanted to see how Garner reacted to this much first, before they made their offer.

Garner just listened, collecting as much intelligence as possible without offering any back.

"You want to know what we found?"

"No, I want to keep dicking around. Go ahead, Randi. Finish it."

Brooks told him the rest, about the conspiracy, the hiring of a shadowy firm of French and Israeli ex-spies, the use of the honey trap, and that they had traced it all back to Scott's behind-the-scenes benefactor, Wilson Gerard. In Brooks's account, there was no doubt about any of it. She didn't tell him they had grabbed Bernier and confirmed most of it from her.

Garner was quiet.

And McGrath added: "It all comes back on you, Jack. You and your man, Scott. Because it was Gerard."

"I don't know what the hell you're talking about," Garner said.

"Then call Rebecca Schultz," McGrath said. Rebecca Schultz was Gerard's political adviser and ran the dark money super PAC supporting Scott. "And if you really don't know anything about it, just pass along our offer."

"What offer?"

"This one," McGrath said, and he stopped so Brooks could explain it.

She said: "Jack, you desist with the Gitmo letter. And everything else. Everything collected by Gray Circle. And we won't reveal that your side hired foreign nationals to influence an election, which, by the way, Jack, is illegal. We also won't reveal that you tried to set up Upton in a sex scandal, which is also illegal. That information will pretty much destroy your guy."

Garner was silent a long time, and it was heavy silence, and it made Brooks happy.

"Let me make a phone call," Garner said at last. "But I'm not admitting that I know anything about what you claim happened. I'm just going to find out a couple things."

Brooks looked at McGrath, who was having trouble sitting still, and said into the phone, "Don't take too much time, Jack. I'm not sure how long we can hold Senator Upton back from going to war. But I doubt you have the rest of the day."

FORTY-FIVE

David Traynor's midnight-blue Gulfstream 650 was waiting for Rena at the private aviation terminal at Reagan National.

Rena had called Traynor that morning and asked the billionaire candidate to loan him the plane. "We're trying to clear the way for Wendy Upton to consider your offer," Rena had said. "To do that, I need an airplane for the day."

"You wouldn't work for me, but you'll work for her?" Traynor said.

A year earlier, Traynor had asked Rena and Brooks to scrub his history so that the Democrat might know what would come at him in this campaign. Rena had declined.

"I just wanted to know what it was like to fly on one of these Gulfstreams," Rena answered. "I heard yours was really nice. So can I borrow it?"

He heard Traynor laugh. "Hell, I can't use it to campaign. The damn thing isn't big enough. I have to charter—goddamn press in the back, same speech four times a day, everyone pecking at you, trying to pick fights. What a way to choose the leader of the free world. I envy you flying alone today."

"Thank you," Rena said.

THE FLIGHT TO EAST HAMPTON took forty minutes. The seven-mile drive from there to Wilson Gerard's estate in Sag Harbor took another fifteen. Rena had called Rebecca Schultz, Gerard's political adviser, and said she should meet him at the billionaire's home in two hours. She hadn't fully agreed until Jack Garner of the Scott campaign called her, too, telling her to hear Rena out. That was part of the deal that McGrath and Brooks had made with the Scott campaign.

"Simple flanking tactics," Rena had told Brooks. "Learned the first month at West Point. Distract them from the front by attacking them from the side."

Confronting Gerard at his home was attacking his front. Putting pressure on Jeff Scott through his campaign manager was his flank.

When he had called Schultz this morning, she had protested and demanded answers. Rena had said she would get them all later that day. If she met him at Gerard's.

If she refused, his next call would be to the FBI, and he was confident, given his contacts in the Nash administration, that Gerard could expect to be contacted by special agents that afternoon. Schultz claimed she had no idea what Rena was implying. "Then meet me in a couple hours at your boss's place."

The house was hidden down a long, forested road behind a stone wall with electrification lining the top. Rena had no love for the Hamptons, but Sag Harbor, the older part at least, was different, less a beach town and more a bay community, and the narcissistic excess that had consumed Southampton, Bridgehampton, and East Hampton had not set in in quite the same way. But great wealth still made Rena edgy.

Rebecca Schultz had messaged Rena he'd be admitted at the gate. She met him in the circular gravel drive.

Wilson Gerard was an eager-to-learn student of many things, among them ornithology. Each of his homes—this one on Long Island, the apartment in Manhattan, the estate in Portola Valley in the hills above Silicon Valley—was named for a different bird. The Long Island estate was called Red Tail, for the hawks that thrived in the marshes lining Long Island Sound.

The house was circular and massive, a showplace, fifteen thousand square feet, according to Wiley's quickly assembled file, which Rena had read on the plane. It was backed by marshland, which offered seclusion before you reached the private dock, located between two bays, Little Peconic and Gardiners.

"Explain yourself to me, Mr. Rena," Schultz demanded when they met in the driveway.

Rena and Rebecca Schultz had met only once or twice, but Rena had heard the political strategist had grown haughty over the years as she had become more affluent and powerful. With each new expensive suit, she also had become progressively more blond. Schultz had started as a congressional aide a couple of decades ago and then moved into campaign work, raising money for Republican PACs and later running them. She was a master of attack politics, and her "third-party" ads and documentaries were famous for turning rumors into dark conspiracies so sinister, audiences assumed something terrible must be going on, even if the stories were only half true.

She called her methods "spectrum messaging." The concept was one Rena despised: if you argue the worst case, even if you are stretching well beyond what happened, audiences would assume the truth was somewhere on the spectrum of what you had alleged and was pretty bad.

"Is he inside?" Rena said.

"First you tell me what you're up to."

She tried to sound puffed up, as if she were holding better cards than she was.

"I did. On the phone. This is your chance not to be arrested."

She shifted her weight and her red-soled Louboutin heels

settled in the gravel of the driveway. "If you want to go inside, you talk to me first, Mr. Rena."

Rena assumed Garner had already told Schultz as much as she needed to know for now.

Plus, he didn't like her.

Or what she represented in politics.

"No," he said, and he headed toward Gerard's front door.

She didn't stop him. Frankly, she couldn't have run fast enough in those heels to catch him.

"I can ruin you," she called to Rena's back.

He stopped and turned partway to look back at her.

"Then do it. But don't make threats and act like a bully. It's a sign of weakness."

He didn't quite catch the curse she hurled back, but it sounded pretty nasty.

The door was unlocked, as Rena had guessed it would be, and he walked in. A butler scuttled toward him. Schultz was running through the gravel to catch up.

"It's okay, Glenn," she told the man.

Who had butlers in the twenty-first century, was all Rena could think. This really was another world.

"Where is Wilson?" Schultz asked the butler.

"In the study."

And who the hell had butlers who said the master was waiting for them in the study? It was like a rich man's fantasy of an old movie. The butler tried to lead Rena into the room. Rena stepped in front of him and said, "I'll announce myself." He had seen a few old movies, too.

FORTY-SIX

Gerard stood at an ornately carved desk.

Rena, whose father was an Italian stone artisan, registered it in his mind without thinking. Walnut. Hand carved. From the Renaissance. The cost would be hard to imagine.

On the walls, Monet, Picasso, van Gogh. And others Rena couldn't identify. A room arranged to show not just affluence but unimaginable wealth. Art as power, as ego, as a shrine to self—art distorted.

Rena moved toward Gerard. The man was pale, and his hair had lost much of its color and was thinned to the point that you could see through to the scalp. His eyes were gray and he wore an expensive suit that hid a slight bulge.

"I'm sorry, sir. He ran ahead of me," the butler said. Schultz was in the room now.

"It's fine," Gerard said.

His gray eyes were lively, the former chess prodigy assessing his opponent, calculating the moves ahead.

"Let's sit. We should be civilized," Gerard said.

He pointed to a sofa and chairs by a window overlooking a rugged spit of land that spread out to the bay. Rena waited for Gerard to move first, then Schultz, and then he followed. When they were seated, Gerard began.

"What is it you think you know, young man?"

Jack Garner had called ahead, warning Gerard and Shultz that Rena knew things and was coming. So Gerard's question was meant to pin down how much of what Rena was about tell them he actually knew and how much he was guessing.

"We know you threatened Wendy Upton to stay out of the race. We also know you hired Gray Circle to investigate her and to send an operative to get to know her and put her in a position that could be considered compromising."

Schultz and Gerard were silent.

"The woman, Sara Bernier, is also a French national. She's with my people at the moment, who are getting all the details she can provide. The hiring of foreign nationals to influence an election is a violation of federal law. Gray Circle has only a few American employees, and Bernier was supervised by another French national, François Gui, which makes the violation more clear cut."

Rebecca Schultz wanted to say something, but Gerard touched her arm.

"But that's not really the issue, is it?" Rena continued. "Along with the threat you made six days ago, you've engaged in a conspiracy to commit blackmail, which is a crime under statutory law in the District of Columbia. We have enough in hand to get an arrest warrant for both of you. I don't know if you recall, but my partner and I have worked fairly closely with the attorney general of the United States and the White House counsel over the past couple of years."

"You're bluffing," Schultz said. "You might prompt an inquiry with all this. But we deny everything you're alleging. I've never hired any organization called Gray Circle. Nor has Mr. Gerard."

Gerard watched.

"No, Holstein Meyers signed the contract with Gray Circle," Rena said, referring to the law firm Gerard and Schultz used for most of their PAC's legal work. "But they'll own up. Attorneys are forbidden under bar rules from engaging in illegal activities. There will be efforts to disbar them. To save their law licenses, they'll be obligated to reveal who the client was. Your identity won't be covered by attorney-client privilege. They'll admit their guilt, blame you, and apologize. You're not protected here."

Rena paused.

"We've also got Gray Circle for eavesdropping on my house and my employees, and stalking me. We even have photos of Gray Circle's thugs in the act."

This, Rena knew, would be a surprise. They hadn't shared that fact with Jack Garner, Scott's campaign man. They were holding it in case Garner didn't budge. But the prospect of Jeff Scott being connected to setting up Wendy Upton in a honey trap and using it to keep her out of the race had seemed persuasive enough to Garner. The campaign man's job was to protect his candidate, Scott, not some campaign contributor, Gerard.

Gerard spoke. "I'm not admitting knowledge of any of these alleged activities, if they did occur or not. But I'm sure everything Ms. Schultz has done has complied with the law. I insist on that in all my companies and charitable work at all times."

Rena leaned forward and his voice became low, just above a whisper. "What is it that frightens you, Mr. Gerard? Immigrants? Whites becoming a minority in the United States? The Civil Rights Act? Was it Brown vs. Board of Education? Or is it just people of color in general? Where was it exactly you think the country began to go off course?"

Gerard didn't answer.

"Or is race just a cynical card you play to scare people? Because you think if you have more money, you should have more say."

"That is the natural way, isn't it?"

"It's just the old way."

Gerard smiled as if Rena were naïve.

Rebecca Schultz said: "What are you asking for?"

"Me?" said Rena, straightening in his chair. "If it were me, I'd have both of you walking out of here in handcuffs. The more public, the better. I'd put this all in the hands of the Justice Department. And give it to the press."

He turned to Gerard. "Because, you see, I want you out of politics. Your money and your ideas, which are insane. Without your money, your ideas would be laughed at."

Wilson's eyes flared.

"We deny everything," Schultz said. "These are lies. You are lying."

Gerard held up a hand again. "Please, Rebecca."

To Rena he said: "But that's not what you're asking for."

Rena smiled. "Yes, lucky for you. I'm not calling the shots."

"Then why are you here?"

"To tell you what we've learned. And tell you what's going to happen."

"And what's that?"

"Senator Upton and Governor Scott's people have been in contact, and I believe they've agreed on one thing. Nothing collected by Gray Circle, or other agents working for you, should ever see the light of day. I think Governor Scott is now persuaded that any connection between his campaign and your PAC and its consulting firm Gray Circle will destroy his candidacy."

A smile almost crept onto Gerard's face. "You are blackmailing me to keep silent."

Rena smiled back. "No, you misunderstand me, Mr. Gerard. If it were me, I'd have you prosecuted. Doing a perp walk, handcuffs in front, face uncovered. With TV cameras in your front yard. But I am not going to get my way. I just flew up here to tell you we'd caught you. That's what I do. I find out things. And then tell the people what we found." He paused for a breath. "So I'm not demanding anything. It's the political people you're in bed with who need your silence."

He waited to see if Gerard understood.

"You see, Mr. Gerard, there are still lines you can't cross. Ideas that are too extreme. We caught you and now you're toxic. You've become one of those people no one wants to be next to. And your money can't change that."

Gerard stared back.

"What is it that really bothers you?" Rena added, just because he didn't like Gerard. "Or is this just anger over your father?"

Gerard's eyes widened, finally, in genuine anger.

"You're not very good at this," Rena said.

Gerard hesitated only for a moment and then said ominously: "We're still learning. We'll get better."

Rena rose.

So did Gerard.

"May I walk you out, Mr. Rena?"

"No, you may not."

FORTY-SEVEN

Randi Brooks had kept digging.

While Rena was in New York, something had been gnawing at her: Rena's suggestion that the attacks at the different campaign rallies might be connected to one another. Was it possible those incidents, which had gotten increasingly violent, might be parts of some orchestrated plan?

The violence over the last week had hurt Bakke, Pena, Fulwood, and Traynor because the people arrested had claimed to be supporters of their campaigns. Each incident was said to be revenge for an earlier attack on their candidate.

The only campaign that seemed ready for the violence was Jeff Scott's. His security personnel had caught the perpetrators before they could disrupt his rally.

A narrative had swelled in fringe media all week and was spilling into social: that the people supporting Bakke, Pena, Fulwood, and even Traynor were dangerous and crazy. And only Jeff Scott could handle them.

Rena had said the police weren't looking for any connection between these people or these incidents. Randi Brooks wondered not only whether there might be one. She wondered now if the connection might be Rebecca Shultz and Wilson Gerard.

In the footnotes of the Michigan campaign finance disclosure records, Maureen Conner had found confirmation that Wilson Gerard's PAC had hired Gray Circle. What else might they find in the Michigan financial disclosure records, the strictest in the country?

There were three different PACs to which Gerard gave dark money that they knew about. All three used Holstein Meyers for their legal work. That was how Conner had found payments to Gray Circle from Gerard's PAC in the first place.

Brooks checked Jeff Scott's last run for governor and filings for his current run for president to see what else might be there. She checked other races where Gerard's PAC had made contributions.

She double-checked. And cross-checked. Every campaign she could think of. And then.

In a filing for a Michigan Senate race not involving Scott, Brooks found something. One of the Gerard/Shultz PACs had paid money to Holstein Meyers, which in turn had hired a campaign events consulting firm. In a list of people associated with that firm Brooks saw a name she recognized: Joseph E. Filipaldi.

That was the name of the man arrested in the first fight, at the Maria Pena rally, wearing a Bakke for President T-shirt.

She carried her laptop into Ellen Wiley's office. "Might have found something interesting," she said.

She put her laptop down on Wiley's desk and stood over her shoulder so she could show her. She explained what she had been doing.

"So you remember that in Michigan they ask for a lot more detail on campaign finance records than elsewhere. People have to list not just who the campaign paid, but who the subcontractors were."

"Right," Wiley said. "So?"

"So look here, under the name Campaign Events LLC, here."

"Who or what is Campaign Events LLC?" Wiley asked.

"I don't know yet. But remember the name Joseph E. Filipaldi?"

"Not really."

"I remember him," said a voice in the doorway. It was Rena's. He had just arrived back from his visit to Sag Harbor and his confrontation with Gerard.

"Who is Joe Filipaldi?" asked Wiley.

"Joe Filipaldi was the guy arrested in the altercation at the Maria Pena rally this week. Wearing a Bakke for President T-shirt," Brooks answered. "The day before the second fight, at the Omar Fulwood rally."

"You don't say?" Wiley said. "So Rebecca Shultz had done business in the past with someone who is disrupting presidential campaign rallies now?"

"What do you think the odds are that's a coincidence?" asked Brooks.

Rena came over to Wiley's desk to see for himself. Brooks began to form a plan.

"Ellen," she said, "you and Arvid find everything you can about Joseph Filipaldi and this firm Campaign Events LLC. Everything you can."

It took a few hours to get a sense of it. And they would fill in more in the next few days. But the basics were clear enough. Campaign Events LLC was a firm that specialized in organizing counterprotests and other disruptive political activities. If someone wanted to infiltrate an opposing political organization, or disrupt a protest or stage a counterprotest, Campaign Events LLC would oblige. Joe Filipaldi was an officer of the company. But he appeared to be an even more aggressive character. You could hire him separately, along with another LLC he was associated with, if you wanted a counterprotest to get a little more violent.

Wiley and Brooks hadn't connected everyone arrested at the rallies yet to Filipaldi or the dirty tricks firm. Brooks had no doubt that in time they would find more connections. But they had what they needed most—the fact that Rebecca Schultz had hired Filipaldi, at least in the past. And within a few hours they had found she had done so in more than one campaign.

So the TV correspondent Matt Alabama's suspicions, Rena thought, had been right. The campaign rally riots were engineered. And now they knew Rebecca Schultz and Wilson Gerard had probably done the engineering.

Money corrupts, Rena thought. It was just that simple. He felt that corruption in every inch of Gerard's home, in the private marshland to the bay, the Renaissance desk, the paintings on the walls. He saw it in the look in the man's gray eyes when Rena had challenged him. When was the last time Gerard had been defied?

A soldier, Rena had been trained in the discipline of commitment to something higher than self. In Gerard's eyes, Rena had seen something he didn't recognize at first. Self-regard in its purest, most naked form.

Wealth would always be power. But it had become something bigger, twisted, and even dangerous, which we hadn't fully recognized while we were busy extolling the virtues of the new economy and the prosperity we worried the country was losing. We were enabling the wealthiest, hoping they would save us and lead us to a new world we didn't understand. And now those same billionaires, left and right, were financing a new populism in both parties to protect themselves against the backlash that was certain to come because they could not save us. The irony was comic.

AFTER

SUNDAY

MARCH 8

FORTY-EIGHT

Peter Rena sat on the patio of Senator Llewellyn Burke's house overlooking the Potomac River at the Chain Bridge.

Burke's wife, Evangeline, was in the kitchen making salad and talking to Randi Brooks.

Another week had passed. It was now something once called the weekend.

And Rena was still trying to process everything that had transpired in the days since. Three days after he had seen Wilson Gerard, Jeff Scott had all but swept the first Super Tuesday primaries, winning seven states, including California and Texas. Dick Bakke had taken only two.

The allegations against Wendy Upton had never come to light.

The day after those primaries, Upton and her chief of staff, Gil Sedaka, had met with Richard Bakke and his strategist Bobby Means in a secret meeting in D.C. "You waited too long," Bakke told them. "But I couldn't have offered it to you anyway. I need to move right, not left. And you would have been miserable." In his recounting of the meeting, Sedaka told Rena and Brooks that Bakke looked haggard and had lost his voice.

Wendy Upton had wished Bakke well. And, at least in Sedaka's telling, Bobby Means, his eyes briefly clinging to the chief of staff's, appeared to be disappointed.

Did Jeff Scott have a role in hiring Gray Circle and trying to smear Upton? Rena didn't know for sure, but he doubted it. Jack Garner, Scott's campaign manager, swore to Brooks he did not. The scheme to hire Gray Circle to entrap Upton in a sexual encounter posed too many risks for Scott's candidacy, Garner argued. And Brooks believed him. Scott and Garner, she said, were too canny to have condoned it. Rena wasn't sure. But he would never be able to find out without revealing Upton's secrets. And they were not his secrets to tell.

Two days after meeting with Bakke, Upton ran into Scott in a private aviation terminal in St. Louis. The governor was gracious, smiling, and triumphant. He could afford to be. In a few days, six more primaries would be held, and Scott's nomination appeared all but inevitable.

THIS MORNING, however, something else had occurred. Wendy Upton had agreed to join David Traynor as his running mate, creating the first cross-party ticket since 1864.

Burke had an iPad streaming television news on the patio and the story was playing continuously.

"With this partnership, we are taking a first step, but a real one, to realign our country, fix our politics, and find a common ground our nation seems to have lost," Traynor said in the clip replaying over and over. Traynor was standing in front of Red Rocks, the picturesque venue so popular with Colorado politicians.

Standing next to Traynor, Wendy Upton struck a more confessional tone. "I did not come lightly to this. You will hear, in the next few days, cynics scoff that a Republican has crossed the aisle to join a Democrat. They'll call it crass ambition. Some will call it political suicide." Traynor was grinning as he listened to Upton.

"And this *is* risky," she admitted. "I made friends angry with me this morning. But many more have told me our country is in trouble and we need to lock arms in common cause and put our smaller differences aside. That was how our country was born. It is also how, at moments of crisis in our history, it has been renewed."

Conservatives were calling the move desperate and naïve. "It has the whiff of unreality and wishful thinking," the editor of *The Week Ahead* had written in a blog post.

"Vice presidential picks rarely help," the editor of *The National Perspective* had written. "Does Traynor's stunt with Upton suggest a new way in politics—or that he has no principles? Or maybe she is not really a conservative."

The first noises from the left sounded similar. "Traynor's electric slide toward the vague middle is a move progressives should reject, an echo of another time, in the end a cynical gesture," *The Next Wave* had already editorialized.

There were a few sounds of praise, mostly from what remained of media that tried to be nonideological. "This might just change the paradigm, if Democrats respond well. If Traynor survives the primaries—and it remains to be seen if this gambit helps or hurts in his battle against Maria Pena—the early calculation has to be that this gives the ticket an enormous advantage in the general election," Stanley Turn had written in the *New York Times*.

On the new *Matt Alabama's* program—his network had given him an interview and public affairs show on its new digital streaming channel—Rena's friend used the last eight minutes of today's show to talk about what he had seen on the campaign trail and how this ticket could be a small step in the right direction. The video of Alabama's editorial was getting traction on social media.

Upton's candor had helped, the acknowledgment that her decision risked making her "a political orphan." Analysts seemed to like the sacrificial tone. Her career had been in ascendance. She didn't need to take this risk.

"Many in my own party will never look at me the same," she'd said. "Democrats may never fully trust me—unless I become one of them. But I am not leaving my party. My conservatism is a matter of principle, bred into my bones. I am making this alliance because I sense in Senator Traynor's candidacy a third way. And something in our country needs to change."

The rhetoric was uncharacteristically lofty for Upton, Rena thought. But perhaps, given all that had happened, that was to be expected.

He especially had liked the fact that standing next to Upton was her sister, Emily. There was something about that image, the two of them together against that large stage, two sisters against the world, that Rena found moving. It wouldn't mean much to most people. It was just something Upton had said she wanted. Brooks had loved it, too. Rena thought perhaps she had even suggested it.

Llewellyn Burke seemed pleased as well, Rena thought, though his mentor never confided how he felt, and Rena wouldn't ask. He imagined Burke had his doubts about David Traynor. But Rena thought that much of the maverick Democrat's message—about taking on entitlements, confronting climate change, and reforming government—aligned with the "compassionate conservativism" Burke believed in.

Whatever Burke's private thoughts, the risk Upton had taken this morning changed things. People like Burke, if they had the courage to do so, had another place to stand now. Burke could endorse Upton and Traynor, and repudiate things in his own party Rena knew he disapproved of. But Rena honestly didn't know whether that would happen. To go with Upton, people either had to take a stand on principle—which was rare in politics—or they had to gamble that enough Americans wanted to recenter and recalibrate where the country was heading. Upton was trying to change the dynamic. Now they would see if anyone else would join her.

HE HEARD A YELL from the kitchen.

"What the . . . Lew!"

Evangeline Burke came outside quickly.

She was holding her phone. She held it out for Burke to read. The news alert read *FBI arrests GOP strategist Rebecca Schultz and conservative funder Wilson Gerard.* There was a picture of Gerard in handcuffs walking out of his Long Island estate.

A billionaire in a perp walk.

This would be the story everyone would see. Worldwide.

"Did you know?" Evangeline asked Rena.

But the operative just looked back at her in silence, his endlessly dark eyes confirming nothing.

Rena and Brooks had debated it all week. Peter had argued their discovery that Gerard had paid men to disrupt the campaign rallies of rivals in both parties was separate from the deal they'd made with the financier to keep silent to protect Upton. Brooks had finally agreed, and they had called the attorney general, Charles Penopopoulis.

President James Nash had been particularly incensed. "The integrity of our elections matters. If the government does not intervene and hard, we are culpable, too."

The director of the FBI was also persuaded. "Make a goddamn statement," he'd instructed his agents. "Arrest the SOB. Walk him out, cuffs in front where the fucking cameras can see them. Then arraign him. He's got all the money in the world to fight it. But that goddamn picture will live forever."

It was part of a new ruthlessness in Rena that Brooks noticed—and worried about.

Llewellyn Burke was looking at his wife.

"Did you know?" she asked him. He shook his head. "Absolutely not," he answered. "But I know how persuasive Peter can be when he puts his mind to it." Evangeline thought she detected a grin concealed on her husband's face.

Rena, however, had already wandered off. He was standing at the edge of the gorge, at the fence line overlooking the river raging below. Then he felt his phone vibrate with a text. He hesitated to break the mood, a moment of triumph, and then pulled the device from his pocket.

It was Walt Smolonsky, whom Rena had sent to Texas from Arizona to try to tie up one last loose end. Rena had wondered who had thrown the brick at Richard Bakke through the window at the restaurant in Dallas. He had a theory. Senator Bakke was already suspicious about the campaign violence, Alabama had said. Why would the first rioter have worn a Bakke T-shirt to beat up someone at a Pena rally? It felt manipulated from the beginning.

"Good guess," read Smolo's text.

Rena had been right about something: Bakke had hired someone to throw the brick at him, to make Bakke a victim before whoever was disrupting the campaign made him a villain.

Another text followed. "Can't prove it, though."

It didn't matter. Bakke was headed back to the Senate. No one cared what a losing candidate did.

Rena put the phone away and turned back to the river, staring for a long time into the gorge at the swirling violence below, the water churning as if it were trying to claw back up into the mountains where it came from, to reverse its history and return to its source, rather than tumble east, past the capital city, and vanish into the sea.

ACKNOWLEDGMENTS

The more fiction I write, the more I recognize how much "made up" stories are a shared effort. The list keeps lengthening. There are friends who help me puzzle out and fix the problems in my stories; others who sit down with me and tell me their real-life stories so I can be sure my make-believe ones are true to life; those I have never met but discovered in my research who sat down with reporters and historians and told their own stories. Then there are those who edit, design, market, social market, copy edit, and do all the rest of what must happen for a book to live in the age of ones and zeros.

To anyone whose work brushes against the public good, a plea: Please think about history. And share what you know, even if you only do so at the very end of your career or your life. That is how the rest of us will know the truth.

For this book, *Oppo,* many old friends and many new ones were essential. I had to learn about the parts of campaigns that were invisible to me as a reporter. I also had to learn how modern campaigning has changed since I was out there as a scribe and then a campaign book writer. My old friend political-consultant Jim Margolis was open about the best and worst moments in his career, which began in college. He has been at the top rank of political consulting for four decades, and only fiction could contain many of his tales, for they could never be told on the record. Joe Trippi was also generous and candid with his insights about when campaigns have gotten into trouble and the psychology of those who want to hold the nuclear football. Joe is a remarkable mix of insider cunning and outsider wonder. My friend Drew Lippman offered wonderful insight into the relationships that form between political leaders and trusted staff. Drew is a born storyteller, and he can speak with equal force and intelligence about books, films, policy, strategy, or morality. Nice trick. Jon Haber was also generous with his insights about the mysteries of the Hill and the chemistry there between aides and bosses. Mike McCurry, who has been implicated in my life for the past forty-eight years, has fine stories to tell as well. He is too loyal to tell the best of them. Nonetheless, his sense of how Washington works is impeccable. Still others sat with me and asked not to be named.

There are countless other friends and colleagues who are reflected in this book whose insights I gained from the years on campaigns—years that stretch from Jesse and Hymie Town to Gary Hart and the condo, Dukakis and the Tank, Clinton and the letter (and then another letter and another), learning from Lee Atwater, jousting with Roger Ailes, to the doleful campaign march of Robert Dole, a politician whom I like a good deal. There are too many friends and sources and rental cars and chartered flights to name or even remember. For a novelist they all became moments from which to learn.

On the political side, that list includes Michael Murphy, Frank Greer, the late Lee Atwater again, the late Michael Deaver, Mandy Grunwald, James Lake, David Gergen, Charlie Black, Ari Shapiro, the great Marlin Fitzwater, Paul Begala, David Axelrod, the late Tony Blankley, and many others. I cannot count all the people I am leaving out.

On the journalist side, the list of those I have known and spent countless hours with is even longer. I will protect the guilty. But I want to recall some late names who early in my career were generous with their time and sincere and uncynical about trying to understand the mystery of elections: David Broder, Jack Germond, R. W. "Johnny" Apple, and Jack Nelson, to name only a few. What would they think of the parade now? While they may be remembered as oligarchs, they also considered themselves guardians in the best sense of the word. And there are many current friends from whom I still learn: Dan Balz, Jules Witcover, Karen Tumulty, E. J. Dionne, Ron Brownstein, David Shribman, to name a few. My friend Bill Kovach is my model for me in many things. And when it comes to understanding politics, no matter how celebrated Jeff Greenfield becomes, he will be underrated. And Jim Wooten, again, who will see himself here I hope, again.

Janos and Rebbeca Wilder were my fact-checkers and guides about Tucson—and teachers about how to be great people.

I am very grateful to the National War College at Fort Lesley J. McNair in Washington, D.C., where I had the privilege and honor to be asked to do lectures on media to national security officers.

I also want to thank the growing community of writers I have come to know, for their support and for their superb work. Don't fear for book writing. It is, in its own right, in a golden age. To my friends around the country, new and old, who have read my books and offered their love and support.

The largest possible debt goes to my great friend John Gomperts, who reads my drafts, bad, worse, and better—and is getting very good at it.

More thanks than I can express go to Zachary Wagman at Ecco, my partner and teacher (my young Yoda), and to the whole Ecco team: Meghan Deans; Miriam Parker; Kapo Ng, who designed the cover for *Oppo;* Sonya Cheuse; Caitlin Mulrooney-Lyski and the publicity department; and, of course, Daniel Halpern—thank you, Daniel and everyone, for your faith in me.

To David Black, the man who has my back and my loyalty in return. Some bonds are deep and go beyond work. And to everyone at the David Black Agency: yowza.

Above all, to the three women who make the music of my life a quartet: my wife, Rima, and my wonderful daughters, Leah and Kira (now my marketing master as well)—the "core four."